MEMOIRS OF A GIRL WHO LOVES GOD

C. L. WELLS

WHAT READERS ARE SAYING

"This is a heartwarming story that was written from the heart. It brought real meaning to me—of some things in life—that never made sense before. It made me smile, and also brought tears to my eyes. This is a must read. I wasn't able to put it down once I started."

"A compelling story that will have readers touched and unable to put it down. I've read it more than once and each and every time it brings tears to my eyes."

"WOW! It is not an easy book to read, but it is a powerful book. Heartbreaking, heartwarming, challenging and uplifting."

First Printing, June 2015
Lillie's Flowers & Phillip Publishing

The author would like to acknowledge the work from which the author has mentioned In Darkness, a Light Still Shines and thank the author, Barry Feaker, for giving permission to do so.

"The Wind" poem copyright @2015 Ms. Judith M. Wells
and co-written with C.L. Wells.

ISBN 978-0-9964317-0-5

Copy Editor and Proofreader by Melissa Manes – scriptionis.com
Content and Structural Editor by Alex McGilvery - celticfrogediting.com/
Cover Design by Zei Llamas - zeiruch153.wix.com/zeidigital
Digital Imaging Retouching by Carey Bradshaw - carey-bradshaw.com
Title Font and Wraparound Cover by Victorine Lieske - indiebookcovers.blogspot.com
Formatting by indyscribabledesigns.com
Basement photo provided free by Shudder-Stock/Weeja's Stock

For God, because without God, nothing makes sense.

Chapter 1

As Krystal sat on the front porch steps, rapidly sketching her pain into the page, she cried. A wayward tear fell, smearing the charcoal pencil's last streak. She stopped drawing, forced to acknowledge the pain from her most recent cut. It throbbed now. She rolled her sleeve back and looked at the raised red welt and dried blood. Evidence of everything going on inside her. She adjusted her sleeve, running it across her face, drying her tears before wiping her nose.

She took a deep breath and then sighed. The ache in her chest remained.

The sun was setting, stealing her light to shine elsewhere. Bummer. Picking up her sketchpad and pencils, she went inside. An unfinished, eyeless owl waited patiently for sight on the easel in her room.

Krystal glanced into the living room as she passed through the kitchen. She could see her sister, Esme, on the floor with the baby. Esme had her back against the couch and her knees up. The baby was lying tummy down on her thighs, facing away from Esme. Superman style.

Esme lightly tapped her feet, giving the baby a bit of a bounce. With each bounce she made the yellow banana rattle rumble. The baby's feet pushed into Esme's stomach as if she thought she caused the motion herself. Under different circumstances it would've been cute, but the sight only drove Krystal's resentment deeper.

Esme looked up and their eyes met.

She'd been caught staring and turned to go.

"Krystal," Esme said her name softly.

Krystal paused, eyebrows raised. She rarely exchanged words with anyone else in her family. It had been that way for months now.

"Why do you hate her?" Esme asked.

"I don't."

"It seems like it."

"You wouldn't understand," Krystal said dismissively, sliding her hands into her back pockets.

Esme's back straightened against the couch.

"I'm eleven, you know."

Krystal rolled her eyes.

"Yeah, I know how old you are."

"You're only three years older than me. That's not very much."

"And you're only three years older than Rosie and Jaime," Krystal said pointedly, referring to the twins. Esme's posture slackened. She got the point.

Krystal sighed. Everyone probably thought she hated the baby, but she didn't. What she did hate was what the baby, Sofia, represented. She was a visible product of everything that had gone wrong. By merely existing, Sofia sealed Krystal's fate.

She turned away. The carpeted stairs carried her silently down to her bedroom door, her sanctuary and asylum all in one.

Chapter 2

Krystal's hand came down on her alarm clock like a hammer, silencing the most vexatious buzzer in the world. A peek from under her lashes told her it was 7:15 a.m. She didn't want to go to school. In fact, she loathed the existence of any institution that required her presence so early in the morning.

Maybe she'd skip today. She'd done it before, but was always bored stiff after the first couple of hours. Besides, there wasn't anywhere to go, and hovering around the house all day would require her to speak to her mother.

Not that she would go upstairs much; she had nearly everything she needed down here, including her own bathroom. An old toilet, a wobbly sink, and a showerhead that protruded from the concrete wall sat on the unfinished side of the basement. It all worked too. But, well, she would need food.

Did I eat that whole bag of Doritos? Probably.... Krystal dragged the covers over her head and dozed off again while taking a mental inventory of her stash of snacks.

Seven minutes later, her snooze alarm screamed like a banshee. Had she been a cat, she'd already be upside down with her claws stuck in the popcorn ceiling.

"Oh my gosh!" she whined as she blindly batted at the clock, trying to shut it off. Instead, she only succeeded in knocking it off the table. Annoyance lifted her from the mattress and she sat up on the edge of the bed.

The still wailing but muffled enemy had landed upside down next to the bedside table. Like a Warrior Princess, she brought her heel down and silenced it, quite possibly forever.

"Oops."

Krystal rubbed her eyes. Why did she even bother, she wondered. Almost all of her grades were crap. C's, D's, and one F littered her last report card. Heck, she wasn't even doing well in gym due to lack of participation—that was one of the C's.

It was likely she'd be repeating her freshman year. Art was the only class she had a good grade in, and that she was passing with flying colors. Because of extra credit, she actually had over a hundred percent. Too bad she couldn't share some of it with her F in Biology.

Her middle school teachers didn't have a clue about what became of her. They'd be mortified at all of the changes in her since last school year. She'd more than changed; she'd been ripped up into tiny pieces and fed through the back of a fan set on the highest speed. Not a shred of her former self was left intact.

The idea of skipping and sleeping all day sounded better and better.

Right on cue, she could hear the rest of the house coming to life above her head and any hope of extra rest was discarded. The twins didn't understand the concept of walking; instead, they clunked around like little rhinos.

Krystal's zombie-like gaze rested on the open sketchpad she'd left by the bed the night before. The girl she'd drawn still sat in the corner of the musty prison-like room. Gazing upward at the light seeping through an invisible opening in the cracked glass wall—she hoped for freedom.

"Good luck with that," Krystal told her.

She stood and grabbed the black skinny jeans that she'd thrown over the arm of the chair in the corner, and then pulled a t-shirt out of the basket by her bed. Her chucks were still by the door where she had kicked them off the night before.

Once dressed, she donned her black hoodie, zipping it all the way up. It was still chilly out, even for April.

"Now, where'd I leave my iPod?"

"There you are." It was sticking out from under the bed. She picked it up, put her earbuds in and her hood up. Hot pink bangs swooped across her forehead, a rallying cry against conformity and adaptation. The rest of her strands matched the black hair shade of her family.

Krystal smirked at the memory of her mom's reaction to her pink bangs.

She'd chopped off her locks before bleaching and coloring her bangs before starting classes at her new school. Faded pink streaks still stained the concrete floor of her bathroom. Who knew concrete could stain? Not that it mattered…it added character to the ugly little bathroom.

When she went upstairs the next morning, her mom's jaw hit the floor before she hit the roof! Screaming insults escalated instantly. Her mom's angry words rolled into her native tongue, but Krystal refused to speak Spanish to her family now. It wasn't special anymore.

Sofia added to the commotion with her crying, which quickly intensified into shrill wails. That's when her mom stopped everything. Stopped yelling, stopped fighting, and stopped trying to make Krystal be a part of their maimed family.

Following that morning, the days of cute girly blouses and headbands were over. The pink in her bangs

was the only girly thing her mom was getting. She decided
to let her outside reflect her inside.

Krystal grabbed her dark purple nail polish and threw
it in her bag. It was her favorite color. Deep and moody....
Perfect, considering the reputation of its primary creators—
red for anger and blue for sadness. The same shade of
purple now covered her bedroom walls. White Christmas
lights zigzagged across the paint, setting the perfect tone.
The effect inspired her artistic senses.

She cranked her music all the way up and headed up
the stairs to the main floor.

As she walked into the kitchen where her mom was
cleaning up after breakfast, she draped the strap of her
messenger bag over her head. Aromas from the food drew a
growl from her stomach. Josefina, her mom, made a gesture
for her to remove her earbuds. Krystal rolled her eyes and
ignored her. Josefina turned away.

Warm tortillas sat stacked in the center of the table.
She peeled one off the top and scooped some eggs out of
the skillet, rolling it into a burrito and taking a bite.

Esme sat at the kitchen table with a plate in front of
her. For a moment she looked at Krystal, then looked away.

Krystal took an apple from the crisper in the fridge
and put it in her messenger bag for later. Heading for the
door, she could see her sister Rosie making stupid faces at
the baby in the living room. Jaime sat on the sofa with a
game controller in hand, staring intently at the TV. He
leaned into every curve as his car sped around the track.

She used to have fun with her siblings, but now they
were strangers. They all cooed over the baby as if nothing
was wrong. It made no sense to Krystal. They were traitors,
mini sellouts, swayed by the Man and his friendly
demeanor and attention. Krystal grimaced.

The Man was coming in as she was going out. Krystal diverted her eyes and wondered if he noticed the pained look on her face.

All for you.

Neither spoke, as usual. He had quit trying too. Didn't take him long, either. She shoved what was left of the burrito in her mouth and headed to school, letting her long legs do double time to make up for sleeping so late.

Chapter 3

Krystal spotted her best friend as she started up the stairs to the front doors.

"Em, wait up."

Emily turned and Krystal picked up her pace a bit. She pulled her earbuds out, letting them hang down the front of her hoodie.

Krystal typically got along better with boys than she did girls, but Em was an exception. Besides, most of her other friends from before the move went to a different school, and she hadn't kept up with any of them. She had closed her Facebook account months ago, purposefully severing all connections. Embarrassed by her family and not wanting to be bothered with questions, it had been her only choice.

She and Em were an unlikely pair. Krystal wasn't looking for a friend when she met Em, but it was inevitable. They'd been partners in a science class last semester, and no matter how distant Krystal came across, Emily Sampson didn't give up. While Em was the most genuinely kind person Krystal had ever met, she was equally assertive. All of Krystal's attempts to evade conversation failed.

In class, they'd both get in trouble for talking too much, even though Em was the one rattling on and on.

One day when Mr. Hoffman got fed up, he sent them to the office. Together! The office staff was sidetracked, learning new software, and pretty much made them sit there for the rest of the hour. Em wasn't even apologetic for getting Krystal in trouble.

That day, during Em's monologue about grasshoppers and how their ears are on their bellies, Krystal caved because she couldn't keep herself from laughing, and they'd been best friends ever since.

Krystal's style was in stark contrast to Em's. Em would tell you Krystal didn't have any style. Her tall frame was always adorned in skinny jeans, hoodies, and sneakers. She wore no makeup, and her hair, cut in choppy layers, reached a few inches past her shoulders. Her plain appearance wouldn't draw any real attention if it weren't for her bangs.

Emily, on the other hand, was all girly-girl: perfect makeup, stylish outfits, and a new hairdo every other day. Today her ensemble included a soft amber-colored blouse layered over a white tee, brown leggings, and a pair of gold flats with little flowers across the toes.

Her hair fell in a million ringlets down her back. She had natural golden-brown highlights you could see when they were outside in the sun.

Krystal forgave Em's sarcasm—daily, sometimes hourly, because Em was awesome. She knew what was coming.

"Oh, is that a new black hoodie?" greeted Em in a playful but mocking singsong voice.

"Oh, is that a new joke?" Krystal mimicked before returning to her own naturally monotone hum. "Hmmm, no, I think I heard that one just yesterday. Your creativity does *not* astound me." She opened the door and they walked through it at the same time.

Em laughed. "Sorry, I'm always hoping your mourning will end soon. You'd think you were a teenage widow or something."

"Not quite, besides, the one I wore yesterday was blue." Half smiling, she rolled her eyes. "Man, did you perm your hair or did you get up at like, 3 a.m. and do all that with a curling iron?" Krystal turned Em around by the shoulders to get a good look at the back of her head.

"It's not a perm, but it's a whole crazy process." Em picked up a long curl that was hanging over her shoulder, checking it over before they started walking down the east hall. "My mom did it last night and we took out the fabric this morning. I did get up an hour early though—totally worth it. Don't you think?" Em asked, whipping her head around, causing all her curls to go airborne.

"Fabric? Never mind. Don't tell me. I don't want to know," Krystal said. "And no, not worth it. Looks great, but sleep is much too valuable to me."

With four minutes to get to their first class, they picked up their pace. Luckily, they had several classes together, though it had taken some work. Unfortunately, first hour was not one of those. They parted ways and Krystal's mood dipped a bit again.

Krystal's day was a drag, as usual. Nothing more than a series of ups and downs. Up when she had a class with Em, down otherwise. It made for a long day full of stress-induced stomachaches.

"Why do you dress like a boy?" a snobby girl called out in a high-pitched 'faux-valley girl' tone. Her gaggle of clones laughed, right on cue. Krystal's stomach knotted instantly, but she wouldn't run. It wasn't in her to run away from confrontation.

Instead, she turned around and looked 'snobby girl' in the eyes. She didn't say anything, she simply stared her down.

The girl's discomfort was visible as she shifted her weight and tried to disguise her unease by pushing her shoulders back and lifting her chin. She'd clearly thought Krystal would just keep walking, but Krystal called her bluff.

Fear flicked in the girl's eyes when Krystal took several steps toward her. The girl unconsciously took a step back. Other students gathered and murmurs rippled through the small crowd.

Krystal envisioned punching the girl in the face, even craved the satisfaction it would bring, but wouldn't strike first.

Snobby girl, clearly unnerved, sensed the threat. Maybe she thought Krystal was fresh out of juvie.

The girl turned on her heel and motioned her minions to follow. Krystal heard her say, 'I think she's a witch or something' as they turned down the north corridor.

Well, that was different. Hopefully, now, she could return to being invisible to everyone but Em again.

Finally, it was time for art class. Krystal walked in, and Mr. Z smiled and nodded. Briefly returning his smile, she walked to her work area. If she could just stay in here all day, it would be a dream.

You wouldn't know Mr. Z was an artist by looking at him. What hair he did have was gray, and he looked more like an Uncle Bob than the man who sold his pet lovers themed art over the Internet. His work wasn't cheesy; it was quite intricate and captured all of the sensitive, warm, and playful moments people cherished with their animals. Krystal wasn't sure what kind of money he made, but she'd be willing to bet he was teaching by choice and not out of need.

Mr. Z was totally supportive of her talent and she knew she was his favorite student. She knew because he always said so.

"How's my best artist today?" Mr. Z asked, stopping by Krystal's easel. Nonplussed by the side-glances the other students gave him, he clapped Krystal on the shoulder.

"Ready to work," she answered. This was how she always responded, and it was always true.

"That's what I like to hear." He moved on to another easel and she immersed herself in her work. Art was her world. Her talent was advanced far beyond any of the other students, and Mr. Z rewarded her for it. She received special assignments, and most of her lessons for technique were one on one. Currently, she had two assignments. One was to create a story-telling piece, which was what she was currently working on, and the other was her wildlife project.

After school, Krystal walked down the steps to the sidewalk. The moment her foot slid off the last step, she was suddenly pulled backwards with force. Automatically putting her right foot back to steady herself, she collided with another body, knocking the wind out of them both.

Heat gurgled in her belly, and she whipped around, furious, with fists clenched. Em stood there, eyes lit in amusement, trying to not bust a gut laughing. Em had snatched her hood and yanked her straight back.

Krystal pulled her earbuds out. "Are you trying to kill me or something?" she said, with her hand on her hip and her chin jutted out.

"Well, K…." Yes, they were Em and K. The nicknames started and then stuck after a *Men In Black* movie night. "I called your name, like, twenty times and you kept going. And I actually waited for you to get off the stairs, so the answer is no. I wasn't trying to kill you. But I didn't quite expect it to go that way either." Em threw her head back and laughed. "That was so funny! Oh, and the look on your face. Priceless!" Em sang. Literally sang. She was in choir and had the best set of pipes in the entire school.

"You know, you aren't going to be able to hear a thing when you get old."

Em cupped her hand around her ear and scrunched her face up in her best impression of an old lady, and said, "What'd ya say, young'n'?"

Krystal rolled her eyes and laughed. "Great. You nearly killed me to act like my mother…or grandmother? You wouldn't be laughing if I'd swung before I saw you. You'd be asleep on the ground right now."

Em roared with laughter. With tears rolling down her face, she looked at Krystal. "I'm sorry, but that was hilarious. I am glad you didn't clock me when you turned around though. You know you would've felt bad if you'd hurt me." Em snorted.

"I'm glad you're so easily amused," Krystal said, pressing her lips together, unwilling to give Em the satisfaction of seeing her laugh at herself.

Taking a deep breath, Em finally answered Krystal's question. "But, no, I have another reason for nearly killing you. What are you getting ready to do?"

"Go home."

Em knew what that meant. Krystal would spend the evening alone, in her room, like she did most every night.

"Well, my family and I are going to volunteer at the food kitchen tonight. It's something new we're doing. You know, serving our community and all. Wanna come?" Em cocked an eyebrow and looked at her expectantly.

"That's not my thing, Em. I think I'll pass."

Em's shoulders drooped, but she shifted her weight to her other leg and took a deep breath. Krystal knew Em was preparing to "reason" with her.

"You barely talk to anyone in your house right now. We'll be done by seven, and we can probably work somewhere in the back so you won't have to be social. C'mon, I don't want to go with just my parents and little brother."

"Uh…." The idea didn't sound too bad, and Em knew her well enough to know that she did feel like a stranger at home. She only used the word 'home' for lack of a better substitution. She could say 'place of dwelling,' but that'd take too much energy. Krystal wasn't the type to make conversation with complete strangers, but it was better than the alternative. "Okay. I guess."

Em smiled like a champion and then cocked her head to the right, reminding Krystal of a parrot.

"I'm guessing you don't want to use my phone to call your mom?"

"No."

"Ooookay then. I think you should, but you won't, so let's go. My mom and dad will be here any minute. They had to pick up Zach from school first, then we need to get there quickly to do a tour."

Chapter 4

Krystal second-guessed her decision as they pulled up. The shelter sat at the furthest end of Kansas Avenue. They were stopped by a train a block and a half from the shelter. Mike, Em's dad, said there was a way to go around the tracks and get there, but he didn't know how.

She'd never been to a homeless shelter before, and had no idea what to say to people half the time in normal circumstances. What did you say to people who didn't have a home? *Would there be lots of drunks carrying around bottles of vodka in brown paper bags? Was this even safe?*

Two buildings stood on either side of Kansas Avenue, which was a narrow street at this end. Two big trucks couldn't pass each other. The similar structures were the color of eggshells. They had a matching, bold blue stripe around the entire buildings, with matching trim over the awnings and doors.

The building on the south side of the street had a sign that read: TOPEKA RESCUE MISSION. On top of the building stood a big cross, which read 'Jesus Saves.' Jesus ran vertically in the cross section with the middle S being shared for the word saves. In the top part of the cross there was another smaller cross.

Krystal stepped out of the car and looked around. People were all over. Some were walking toward the shelter from the intersection of Norris Street and North Kansas Avenue. Surprisingly, she saw entire families, a few moms pushing strollers, and individuals making their way alone. Others were leaning against the building talking, smoking, or hanging out. Whatever she'd been expecting, this wasn't it.

Halfway down the block, she could see an old man with a dog making his way down Kansas Avenue. At first, she thought the animal was a guide dog because of the special harness, which read SERVICE ANIMAL, but the man didn't appear to be blind. Though he walked with a hitch in his gait and bent slightly forward, he didn't seem to need any cues from his companion.

Em's mom rang the doorbell of the designated employee slash volunteer door. A tall man who reminded Krystal of Santa, with bright, happy eyes, opened the door for them. He had white hair, a mustache, and a beard. His eyebrows were long and bushy, pointing in various directions, making him look a bit comical. He was wearing a white t-shirt, covered by a long, red apron, black pants and work boots. Krystal snorted quietly at the irony.

"Ah, new faces," Santa said. "My name is Nick and I'll show you where to get signed in." Krystal almost laughed out loud. Ha! St. Nick—seriously? Should she look for Rudolph, since she was probably going to be one of his elves? Immediately after the thought crossed her mind, he winked at her.

He knows I'm on to him! Krystal looked away and stopped herself from rolling her eyes. She couldn't help but smile a bit. He was so…well…jolly!

"Dinnertime starts at five and ends at six-thirty," Nick said. "So, we haven't much time. I'll try to keep it short. That's quite a task for me, however. Normally we'd start the tour at the Distribution Center, which is a couple blocks away, but we'll forgo that part and do it another time."

"Tours usually happen days before volunteers even begin; however, we've lost several volunteers recently. One moved out of state. Another of our ladies took ill."

They all followed as he took them down a short hallway that smelled of pine.

"Watch your step," Nick cautioned. "The floors were waxed today."

Ribbon photo boards hung on either side of the hallway, overflowing with pictures. Krystal spotted Nick in one of the photos as she passed. He had his arm around a tiny but sturdy-looking elderly lady and was grinning broadly. The lady was holding a sheet cake with Nick's name spread across the center and tons of candles around it.

Krystal wanted to stop and look at all the photos, but Em tugged her along.

"Mama Maggie. She's volunteered here for fifteen years, starting when she was seventy." Krystal and Em's eyebrows shot up as they looked at each other. The math was easy, Mama Maggie had still been volunteering at eighty-five years of age.

"But," Nick continued, "her health is giving her some trouble so she had to take a break. She might be back, hopefully. We had a few kids go off to college so when your applications came through, it was right on time. God has a way of working those things out for us here at TRM. It's great you are doing it as a family, and Krystal, I'm glad you came along," he said, and winked again.

Krystal smiled at Nick; she liked him. She wasn't sure why. There was just something about him.

The short tour was packed with information.

"Some are astounded when they hear about how great the need is in our city. Last year, before the sequester, we served about 180 people at every meal. After the sequester, the number scaled to 400! We were scrambling to keep up. But, as always, God provided."

"What's a sequester?" Zach asked.

"Good question, young man," Nick said, placing a hand on Zach's shoulder. "The government gives money to programs that help people in their community. Last year, many of those programs didn't get the same amount of money as the previous years. It was drastically less, which meant they couldn't help as many people."

"So the shelter's funds were cut too?" Mike asked.

"No, our shelter doesn't utilize government funding. We wouldn't be able to tell people about God if we did, but the impact on the other organizations hurt so much, more people came to us for help."

"That's brave," Sharon said.

"Do you ever not have what you need?" Em asked.

"In the beginning, it seemed we always needed more than what we had," Nick answered. "But now, all these years later, we're blessed beyond measure. We've expanded a few times and still have more expanding to do."

"What if the people who come to you for help don't want to talk about God?" Krystal blurted out before even she realized she was going to speak. Everyone looked at her, and she wished for a cloak of invisibility. But Nick didn't seem offended in the least. Instead, he smiled.

"Sometimes people don't want to hear about God at all. We operate on the basis of showing Christ to others by assisting them in whatever their needs might be. The keyword there is 'showing.' We're not here to shove God down people's throats," he said, "but to show them God's love and leave the door open when they're ready to talk. We meet people wherever they are in life. Just as they are."

Nick's passion for God confused Krystal. He saw homeless and hurting people every day, but still thought God loved everyone. She seriously doubted that. If God loved her and her family, they'd all still be together, and there wouldn't be any need for shelters because everyone would have homes and food.

Nick showed them the area where the men stayed. There were five rooms with ten bunk beds each.

"Every single bed has been occupied for the last three days so we pulled folding cots into the lobby for the others to sleep on," he said. "Last night, every single cot was taken. We prayed no one else would come and thankfully, no one did. That's the third time we've run out of beds in the last six months."

Men of all ages were walking around, going to and fro. As she peeked through the open chapel door, she saw some on their knees praying. Others, she saw in the sitting room watching TV or reading, a few talking on cell phones. Had she seen many of these men anywhere else, she would've never guessed they were homeless. Most of them were clean and shaven, dressed like any other normal person you might see at the grocery store.

One guy, who obviously suffered from…something, was walking around arguing with…someone, whom no one else could see.

"I told you not to speak to me that way! You're not my boss!" he yelled suddenly.

Unalarmed, one of the men behind the desk looked up from his magazine. "Larry. Calm down, please."

Larry looked at him and Krystal could see him 'return.' His eyes cleared and sharpened.

"Sorry, Nate," he said in a very ordinary manner, as if warned his music was too loud.

"He hears voices," Nick said in a matter-of-fact tone. "Head on is the only way to deal with it. There's no reason to be secretive or make them feel ashamed for what challenges them in their life. We want to help them cope and overcome."

"Bravo," Sharon said. Mike nodded in agreement.

Krystal and Em wandered over to the window. Looking out, Krystal could see a playground in the distance.

"Your parents do this type of work, don't they?" Krystal asked as she turned around and leaned against the windowsill. "I mean, you said they have degrees in psychology, right?"

"Yeah, but they don't *really* do this type of work," Em said, gesturing toward the general area before pushing a strand of curls behind her ear. "Mom is a counselor at church and Dad works for a youth-at-risk program."

"Like for kids in jail?"

"No, I mean, some of them have been in juvenile detention, and then they stay at a group home for a while. For others, it's a chance for them to get help before they end up in a more restricted environment."

"Sounds sad."

"It is," she agreed. "There are lots of days he comes home with a broken heart."

Krystal wondered why Mike would want to come here after dealing with his job every day. *Maybe he's a glutton for pain? Hi, Pot, I'm Kettle.*

"C'mon girls." Sharon waved them over to follow.

The other building had several sections: one for single women, one for women with children, and an area for two-parent families. As they had on the men's side, the single women stayed in similar rooms. But women with children shared rooms with each other, and families got their own.

Tiny was the first word that came to Krystal's mind when Nick led them into a room two single moms might share, but that was an understatement. *Miniscule is more fitting.*

This room had two twin beds and two sets of bunk beds. A metal wardrobe sat against the wall, one little plastic two-drawer compartment was between the two twin beds, and a couple of plastic footlockers were at the end of each bunk. Six people could potentially stay in that room together. Em's family, Nick, and including herself made six. They all had to enter and exit in a single file line in order to fit.

Nick's presence alone dwarfed the room; he was such a big guy. Even as she was standing in the room, she couldn't imagine her family being stuffed into the tiny quarters.

Like the men's side, the women's side was also full. Cots filled the lobby as they had across the street.

The end of the tour brought them to the kitchen. It too was small. Only three people were there, working feverishly to prepare for dinner.

"We ask our volunteers to clean up their station, store the leftovers, and take the empty dishes to the dish area. Leslie over there will take care of all the dishes," Nick said as he pointed at the lady in the dish area in the back of the kitchen. Leslie smiled and waved. Mark will be here a bit later to clean up the floors, tables, and chairs. He works clear across town and doesn't usually get here until around six, which isn't too long before dinner ends, to help get things back in order again."

Krystal saw Leslie pull the stainless steel door down on the industrial grade dishwasher, which automatically started the cycle.

"Leslie works full-time as a dental hygienist then comes here after work several times a week to help us get through dinner. Our volunteers and their stories are as diverse as our guests. For instance, Mel here." Nick snagged Mel's apron string, successfully untying it, as he was setting a big pot of soup on the burner.

Em leaned into Krystal, elbowing her in the ribs. That was code for 'cute boy.'

"Gets me every time," Mel said. Krystal guessed Mel to be in his early twenties. He had a tattoo of a cougar on his left forearm, and another tattoo on his right arm Krystal couldn't make out.

Mel laughed at Nick, then propped his left elbow up on Nick's shoulder as if it was normal to use Nick as a resting post.

"How are you all doing?" Mel smiled and met everyone's eyes. Krystal looked down then back up again, uneasy with the direct eye contact. It didn't bother her with Nick, but Mel was younger—and a guy—and as Em had pointed out, cute. She saw Mel's ears sported 8 millimeter round black discs, and even more ink in a design behind his ear. Cool!

"Mel used to be a guest here," Nick said.

Krystal's mouth gaped open. Nick just threw everyone's business out there.

"Best thing that ever happened to me," Mel cut in with a grin. "Remind me to tell you all sometime, I love sharing my story. But for now, I better get the other pot of soup going. Holler if you need anything, I'll be bringing out replenishments throughout dinnertime." He nodded and winked before he walked away. Krystal wondered what all the winking meant. Was there some secret they all knew that no one else did?

"Just to reiterate, we are truly thankful for our volunteers. We couldn't do what we do without people like you all," Nick said in a soft tone. "You'll come to see this place is God's magic."

Hmmm, magic huh? Krystal wanted to roll her eyes but held back.

"We're happy to be of service," Mike said, shaking Nick's hand.

After meeting a few other people, Em's parents jumped on the front line, dishing up baked chicken, mashed potatoes, and green beans. The front line consisted of a short stainless steel warmer with a sneeze guard so scratched up you could barely see through it.

The entire room buzzed with noises and voices. The task of feeding the multitude, though taxing, was organized and efficient. The homeless and hungry conversed with greeters as they waited patiently for their plates.

Em's parents were especially friendly; it was easy to see where Em got her pleasant disposition. They genuinely enjoyed making conversation with those going through the line, making it seem effortless. Em's little nine-year-old brother, Zach, assisted another volunteer, who collected trays from the departing guests. Zach enjoyed the attention he was receiving from the diners. They hadn't seen anyone so young helping here before. There were variations of "Thanks, little man," and "Look at this handsome fella."

The Sampsons were the perfect family.

Em and Krystal ladled soup into cups behind all the action. Krystal had chicken and noodle. Em had chili. While the tight quarters were challenging, they found their rhythm and stayed a cup ahead of Mike and Sharon. It wasn't a difficult task with both of them serving, but oh, the heat! Between the stoves, warmers, and bodies, the heat was downright stifling.

Em glanced up at Krystal and started laughing.

"What?" Krystal asked.

"Before we leave, I'm taking a picture of us with our hairnets on," she answered.

"Okay!"

"You should take your hoodie off," Em said, looking over at her. "You've got to be sweating to death with that on in here."

"It's all good," Krystal said. She wasn't going to admit that her pits were thoroughly soaked.

Em shifted her weight and began using her bossy mom voice.

"At least roll your sleeves up. You're going to get soup on them."

"No! I said I'm good." Inwardly flinching, she knew she'd overreacted. Frustrated, she would love nothing more than to strip off her hoodie, which was now at least four times its weight because of the sweat. But that didn't have anything to do with Em. "I'm fine," she said more softly, wishing she could take back her harsh tone.

Em eyed her from under her bangs as she poured another cup of soup. Krystal turned around to see how many people were in line, and noticed the room was entirely full.

She watched the little old man at a back table against the wall tear off a piece of bread and offer it to his dog, which it took gently from his hand. Glancing around, she still didn't see anyone else with a pet.

It saddened her to see the old man. She was happy he had a companion, but hated that he had to find food in this place. He should be in a cozy home, sitting in a recliner with his dog curled up next to him. Maybe she'd paint him that way.

She turned back to the soup station, lifted the ladle, and filled another cup. More than ready to go, she looked at the line of people again, hoping it would be shorter than it was ten seconds ago.

No such luck. Worse yet, Em was still acting wounded and made it a point to not look at Krystal at all.

Suddenly, she sucked in her breath and held it when through a gap in the line, she saw a boy from her school sitting at a nearby table. Brandon, she thought, his name is Brandon, and he's in my French class. She didn't know much about him other than he was a sophomore.

What was he doing here? She wondered frantically. It was clear he was eating, but how could that be? She couldn't stop staring.

He sat hunched over, with his head slightly turned the opposite direction. Had he spotted her first, hoping to not be seen? Sitting with his left cheek propped on his fist, elbow resting on the table, he kept his eyes down as he ate. As she was about to turn away, she saw him peek over his hand in her direction and their eyes met.

Krystal's face went hot. A tingle shot up her spine and danced on her scalp.

Frozen, she gazed into her soup. Why did she stare so long? What the heck is wrong with her?

"Krystal?" Mike said.

"Sorry." She scooped a cup of soup and handed it to him.

Krystal thought she had this place figured out. But she didn't. What she thought she knew changed when someone from her school had to come into a place like this for meals. But Brandon didn't look poor or hungry. *Later, I'll think this through later.*

By six-thirty, they were done working. They poured what little remained into storage containers. They pasted a paper label on the front of each one and wrote the full date and type of soup with a permanent marker. Afterward, they returned the soup to the cooler and the last pot to the dish area.

Krystal was spraying their stations down when Em walked up from behind her.

Em threw her left arm over Krystal's shoulder and put her cheek next to Krystal's.

"Smile!" she commanded.

Krystal couldn't help but obey, she was happy Em was over her hurt feelings. It never took Em long to forgive her.

Em thumbed the shutter button on her phone and touched the pic that sat in the corner to bring it fully to the screen. The girls giggled at their image. Em's big smile looked sweet while Krystal had unconsciously raised her eyebrows and had a super cheesy grin. Some of her bangs had fallen out of the hair net and was plastered to her forehead. A pink parrot came to mind.

"Oh gosh! I'm always the awkward one," Krystal guffawed. "You're not allowed to show that to anyone."

Krystal looked up and saw Sharon and Mike motioning them over. Nick stood there with his hands on his hips. Nearly towering a full head above the rest of them, he had a bit of a belly, but he was more stocky than heavy. At least he didn't have a full Santa belly.

"So, how did it go, everyone?" Nick asked.

"Great!" Sharon said. "It's quite humbling."

Mike nodded his agreement.

"It was amazing how so many people seem to have it so hard, yet they're so kind. They kept thanking us," he said, somewhat bewildered.

"They know you could be doing other things besides filling their bellies," Nick said. "They're grateful. And you, young man! You did a fine job!" he said, looking at Zach. "They kept you on your toes, didn't they?"

"Yes sir," Zach replied politely.

Nick directed his attention to Em and Krystal.

"Well, ladies? How did you fare on the soup scoop?"

"Fine," Em replied. "We were so busy that time just flew by."

"Yeah, that's about how the meals go around here, everything really. One task to another and before you know it, it's time to help people get tucked in. Now that you've been through a shift, will you still be back every Tuesday night?"

"Most definitely," Sharon answered.

"How about you, young lady?" Nick knew Krystal wasn't on the list originally. "Will you be back next Tuesday with the Sampsons?"

Krystal's mind raced as she tried to come up with an answer. It was hot and miserable, but she knew they were doing a good thing. Something about Nick, about this place, drew her, willed her to return.

"Sure," she blurted out even though she wasn't sure at all.

"Good!" Nick said enthusiastically. He turned his eyes to Sharon and Mike. "Since she'll be volunteering with you, we'll have her fill out an information sheet and attach it to your paperwork."

Chapter 5

A comfortable silence enveloped them on the ride home. Sobered by their experience, they declined Nick's offer to grab a plate after their shift, they were all ready to go. Mike and Sharon wanted to get Zach home in time for his nine o'clock bedtime. So instead, they opted for fast food, which Krystal found weird. It just seemed wrong after working in a food kitchen all evening.

It seemed wrong to have the luxury of fast food when all she could think about was the old man and Brandon. Krystal could see Em eyeing her in her peripheral, but she turned her head to look at the passing traffic.

Mike must have been reading her thoughts. "Tonight's experience shouldn't make us ashamed for having, it should make us thankful, grateful, and more giving."

"Right," Sharon seconded, "It's about understanding how blessed we are and knowing we can do something to help others."

It was a bit overwhelming, but what they said was true; it felt good. They'd done something important tonight. They'd made a difference.

The Sampsons pulled up in front of Krystal's house a quarter after eight. After saying goodnight, she walked into the house.

Discontentment was evident as Josefina stood, glaring at Krystal. Her hands rested on the arms now crossed over her chest. A scowl covered her face.

Krystal's protective walls rose defiantly and locked in place around her. The reverent feeling she'd been carrying after a night of service evaporated.

"Where were you, Krystal?" Her mom's accent remained thick after all these years. She pronounced her name Cree-StAL. "Should I call the police next time? You just think you can do what you want all the time?"

Krystal was a bit baffled over the concern her mom was showing, even though it was coming out as anger. She had been doing what she wanted for months now. Granted, this was about as late as she ever walked in on a school night after hanging out with Em.

"I was with my friend," Krystal said, without bothering to explain where she had been. *What do you care?*

"You need to call your father. His payday is tomorrow and you need to let him know I need the money right away this week, not Sunday when you go to see him. Your Tia Maria will drive you to get the money when he is finished working tomorrow."

So there it is. She should have guessed it, even though it's early in the week. *She wasn't concerned about me not being home; she was mad I wasn't there to make the phone call right when she wanted it done!*

As much English as her mother spoke, family titles would always be in Spanish. So her Tia, meaning Aunt Maria, wasn't exempt from being dragged in with Krystal for her mom's dirty work. As smart as her aunt was, Krystal was clueless as to why she'd do her mom's bidding…sister or not!

"You've got to be kidding me. Why don't you just call yourself? You're going to have to talk to him again someday!"

"I will never speak to him again," Josefina said, walking away. "Call!"

"You can't make me do this forever and you shouldn't expect the others to either." The idea of Esme having to do this next irked her beyond words, but then again, maybe Esme would be just peachy with it all. Who knew?

"You're being ridiculous," Josefina said, as if it was the most factual thing in the world.

"You're the one who went off and got pregnant by some other guy!"

Josefina stood there like a statue, hurt flickering in her eyes, before taking a backseat to stubbornness.

Stomping over to the phone in the kitchen, Krystal punched in her dad's number; her blood was boiling so much the phone shook in her hands. In a controlled voice, she told him what her mom said about needing the money the next day.

"No," he said immediately.

Krystal blew out her breath and waited for the rest. This was obviously not going to be a one-call scenario either. She didn't care whether he handed the money over or not, but she'd be stuck relaying messages for an hour if he didn't.

Her dad could speak English, but still spoke to her in Spanish when they talked. She had quit speaking to them in Spanish when they moved into the Man's house. Her mom quit trying and now just spoke to her in English.

Even though her dad still spoke to her in Spanish, she would only answer him in English. It upset him, but Krystal was stubborn, and most of the time now, he let it go. Gradually, the habit spilled over to the other kids and they started speaking in English too. Both Josefina and Roberto gave up.

"She only wants to make an excuse to not let you come on Sunday. If she gets the money now, I don't see my kids then. Tell her she can have it on Sunday," Roberto said.

Hip against the counter, Krystal said she would and hung up the phone. She wondered what her mom would do if she just started banging her head into the cabinet doors. Would she finally understand this was pure torment for her?

In the beginning she would hold the phone in her hand and relay these messages, but that didn't work out so well. When her parents could hear each other's voices, it made them crazy. They were like two cats that hated each other. Despite the fact they were separated, just knowing the other was near caused them to arch their backs and howl in rage.

Now, ridiculously, all the hissing and spitting was kept to a minimum at the cost of one arrangement being accomplished through many phone calls. Krystal knew her father's worries about them not coming on Sunday were unfounded. Didn't he realize on Sundays while they were away, her mom and the Man got to pretend they were one little happy family and just be with the baby?

She relayed her father's message and it went just like she had known it would. Josefina assumed her 'I'm ticked off now!' stance. All her weight shifted to her left leg, and her hands went to her hips. It ended with one exaggerated head toss to get her mane out of the way before she starting speaking.

Krystal had performed this for Em a couple times. It was a great stress reliever and usually left both of them in a fit of giggles.

"Just because he plays games, he thinks I play games. Aye! Call him back, Krystal," Josefina said, her hand in the air.

Krystal had no idea what games her mother was referring to, unsure if the words were for dramatic flair or if there was something behind the accusation. All she knew was her mom had never been so unreasonable or immature in any other area of life except when it came to her dad.

"Tell him I need the money to pay for Esme's clarinet. I have to pay by Friday. Assure him I am not canceling Sunday's visit."

Thoroughly disgusted, she walked over to the phone, hit the redial button, and repeated what her mom said. Her mom stood waiting with her arms crossed over her chest. Krystal turned away. As soon as her dad said okay, she slammed the phone down, hanging up the call. No good-bye was necessary; her world had already been filled with too many of those as it was.

"Are you happy now?" She whirled around, her fists tightly balled at her sides, and her body rigid.

Her mom and dad had spent a million years together, and now they couldn't so much as have a conversation! If this is what it meant to be an adult, then screw that! But, she knew everyone didn't act as nuts as her parents.

She thought about Em's parents and knew nothing of the sort would ever happen between them. Knowing that made it worse. Why were her parents the failures?

Josefina's look softened a fraction. She directed her eyes at Krystal. "Thank you. Esme is excited about this, and I don't want her to miss out." Josefina took a deep breath. Krystal waited. She knew her mom had more to say, and she was hungry to hear something besides an apology, which was all she got in the beginning. She needed an explanation!

Just then, the baby started crying in the other room. Josefina opened her mouth to speak, but now Sofia was screaming at the top of her lungs. Whatever might have been spoken was lost in the chaotic sounds of the howling baby. With a brief apologetic look, Josefina darted off to tend to the baby.

Krystal stood there, deflated. All of the good energy from her evening at the shelter was gone and the anger her mother stirred up had departed. She was exhausted.

It dawned on her that the house was strangely quiet. Krystal walked into her mom's room. Josefina was hugging the baby to her chest and bouncing her.

"Mama is here, beautiful girl," she cooed in the baby's ear.

"Where is everyone anyway?" Krystal asked, crossing her arms over her chest and sticking her hip out.

"Eliseo took them for ice cream. You missed out."

"I didn't miss out on anything!" Krystal said through clenched teeth before walking off.

"Krystal!"

Pivoting to face her mother, she leaned forward, bared her teeth. "He is nobody."

Pounding down the stairs to her room, Krystal slammed the door. With tears streaming down her face, she paced the length of her room. She stopped in front of her dresser, glaring at the jewelry box her mom had bought her two birthdays ago. She remembered when her mom gave it to her, how special it made her feel. For my little girl who is growing up so fast, her mom had said. Filled with trinkets she never wore now, little girl things in little girl colors.

Well, I'm not a little girl anymore. She swung wide with her right hand, striking the box with her open palm. The force of the blow sent the box flying across the room and crashing to the floor, one of its doors now broken off at the hinges, lying in a twisted heap. Necklaces, bangles, and barrettes scattered across the room.

She hated this! Hated it! Hated it! Hated it! She hated her parents - hated the Man - hated that he did things with her siblings. She hated they liked to go places with him. They should hate him too!

Pacing again, she threaded her fingers through her hair, interlocking fingers. Anger, hate, hurt all pummeled her at once; she didn't think she could take it another minute. Her chest ached and her stomach hurt. Nausea caused by the heavy pressure in her head had her gasping for air. Tears crested under her eyes before spilling down her cheeks.

She put her hand on her throat; her pulse thudded in her neck. Where was the air? She started to hyperventilate. Krystal sat down on her bed and put her head between her knees, catching her breath long enough only to begin crying again. She lay on her side and buried her face in her pillow. Sobs wracked her body and she was grateful for her soundproof room.

None of the noise she made ever drew a soul down the stairs to check on her. Then again, maybe they didn't care if she was hurt. Surely, all their lives would be easier if she weren't around to complicate matters. No one would miss her until her mom needed Krystal to call her dad.

She walked over to her dresser and opened a hardback book filled with photographs of stars during the fifties and sixties. In the middle was a small piece of glass about the size of a half-dollar.

Five months ago, the Sunday after a disastrous Thanksgiving that did not include extended family because neither of her parents wanted to explain circumstances, there had been an unusually early and prominent snowfall.

Jaime had thrown a hard snowball through the top panel of the screen door at their dad's house. Glass shattered. She stooped down to help clean it up and this piece stood out. Jagged and asymmetrical, with a crack in the center, you could still see the heart shape. *It's my heart,* she had thought. She kept it. The very next day, right here in this room, she used the jagged heart. It had been her first time cutting.

Krystal shut out her thoughts. Just holding the glass heart dispensed a calming effect like a drug injected directly into her veins. Her breathing steadied and she focused.

Covered in darkness after flicking the light switch, a small lamp on her dresser was her only source of light. She took her hoodie off and laid it beside her. Slowly, she slid off her bed onto the floor and placed a dark blue towel under her arm.

Holding the glass by what would be the top of the heart, she positioned the point next to yesterday's cut. Her forearms were decorated with red, pink, and white lines in various stages of healing. The sight gave her a charge right now; later it would bring shame. But who was thinking about later?

Pushing the glass down until she saw the first bit of blood rise to the top, she maintained the pressure as she dragged the glass straight down another three inches. Clenching her teeth, she didn't groan or make any sound.

Sensation shot through her and relief was instantaneous. With her arm resting outward on her knee, she let her head fall back against the bed. Her eyes flitted closed. She welcomed the pain and rode the stream as it cascaded down her arm and was captured by deep blue. Breathing was easy again.

Chapter 6

It was 10 p.m. and Nick did his final rounds before his shift ended. Pleased with the evening and with the new dinnertime volunteers, he reached into the chapel, feeling for the switch to turn the lights off. He reached into his pocket for a Hershey's Kiss and popped it into his mouth, then wadded the foil wrapper into a tiny little ball and shoved it back in his pocket.

The Sampson family was exceptional, as was Krystal, but he wondered what her story was. He sensed she was carrying a burden and knew there was a work to be done where she was concerned, but he didn't know what yet. Hopefully, she would come back the following Tuesday. She said she would, but he wasn't convinced.

"Hey, Nick." Nick turned to see Ralph coming down the hall. "Thank you for taking care of Cathy tonight. She was doing much better after speaking with you. Man, she is going through a lot!"

"It was my pleasure, Ralphy. Cathy's going to be okay; she is one tough lady."

"That she is."

"She gave me a bunch of chocolate. Want some?" He started to reach into his pocket.

"Nick, I don't need to eat chocolate. I am chocolate," Ralph said, and stepped back to allow Nick to observe his magnificence.

Nick barked a laugh.

"You're too much."

"You mean, as in rich, dark chocolate? That's about right."

"Have a good night, my bald friend," Nick said, trying not to smile at the old joke. He should have known better than to offer Ralph chocolate.

"Well, I would ask you to share some of your hair," Ralph said, staring at Nick's eyebrows, "since your body must think it's winter year round. But your snow-white hair wouldn't compliment my complexion. Bald is beautiful, baby," Ralph said, as he ran a hand over his smooth scalp.

Nick guffawed and clapped Ralph on the shoulder. "You should reconsider. I'd hate to see your skinny butt frozen to your steering wheel in the parking lot when winter rolls back around."

"Funny!" Ralph replied as he turned to go back down the hall. "Not really. Have a good night, old man."

"You're older than me."

"But you look it."

Nick just shook his head and chuckled. Ralph had been working at the shelter for as long as he could remember, and they'd become fast friends, having the same sense of humor. Ralph was a teacher, literally and figuratively. He'd taught junior high right out of college and took a summer job at the shelter to help make ends meet.

Falling in love with the people in this place, he never went back to mainstream teaching, and some ends were just never met. Now he assisted folks who were at the shelter long term. He helped them get their GEDs, and apply for jobs. He even tutored some of the older kids while running the Saturday "Lean" program, which brought high school students to the shelter to tutor elementary-aged kids.

Ralph believed education could boost self-esteem. Sometimes they needed to be reminded of what they were capable of. Being in a position that landed you in a shelter would knock anyone down quite a few notches, and fast! It didn't matter who they were.

God wanted Nick here, and lucky for him, it was where he wanted to be too.

Ralph's official title was an 'advocate.' There were twenty to thirty advocates employed by the shelter, and every single guest or family was assigned one to help them adjust to their stay at the shelter and assist them with their journey to leave it. An advocate's job was simply to help the guests develop a plan to get back on their feet, and Ralph had the highest number of program completions.

Nick knew his God-given talent was listening. The staff and the guests treated him like a counselor even though he didn't have a degree, never set appointments, and didn't have an office. He simply listened when people talked. God often gave him the right thing to say. If he had a dollar for every time someone said some variation of 'That's just what I needed to hear,'—he'd be rich. Nick sensed the hurt of others, and hurt with them. He and Ralph were a good team.

Krystal's hurt projected from her like a billboard; her eyes betrayed her when she smiled. Hidden emotions and deep thoughts permeated her being. She wasn't your typical fourteen-year-old girl.

Patience was a virtue, so he'd wait. As much as he wanted to help everyone, he knew God's timing was key. Krystal was a fortress, and if he tried to be too helpful too quickly, she would likely not return. He noticed she seemed quite amused by his Santa appeal, and that was always a great icebreaker.

Nick turned off all the kitchen lights on his way out the back door. Parked right outside the door, Nick folded his tall, stocky frame into the little, red VW Bug. He knew a big man like him looked a little silly driving this car, but he didn't care. If it made people smile, he was glad he'd given them a reason to. He even found a sunflower at the dollar store, cut the plastic stem down to size, and put it in the vase that came with the car. It was cheery, and he liked cheery.

Chapter 7

$\mathcal{S}$unday morning, all of her siblings were at the breakfast table when Krystal went upstairs. Her mom had made a big breakfast as usual, and they mowed it down as if it would be their last meal. The aroma of the Mexican sweet bread wafted to Krystal's nostrils, prompting her stomach to growl. Everyone snickered except her.

"Eat fast, Krystal," her mother said. "Your Tia is already on her way."

Krystal sat down at the small, round table without replying and loaded up her plate. One thing that hadn't changed was her mother's culinary skills. No one could even come close. This morning, she served up scrambled eggs, tortillas, and a chilé sauce. The scrambled eggs had finely diced onions, jalapeños, and tomatoes. A small saucer held a sliced avocado. Krystal and Esme were the only two out of the kids who would eat avocados. Rosie and Jaime had decided they didn't like avocados without giving them a chance—they didn't know what they were missing.

"Mom, I'm done. Can I play the game until Aunt Maria gets here?" Jaime asked.

"No. Put your plate in the sink and put your shoes on," Josefina replied.

Jaime groaned. He was always the last one to get his shoes on. If they were waiting for any reason, it was usually because of him.

A horn blared outside, and Krystal recognized it as Maria's. Sofia began wailing in response to the noise that ensued.

Right on cue, man, that kid cries a lot!

Krystal started shoveling food into her mouth.

"All of your plates in the sink," Josefina ordered in a rush. "Go, go. See you all tonight, mijos." She then rushed into the other room to go scoop Sofia up.

Krystal grabbed a piece of sweet bread, wrapping it in a paper towel so she could eat it in the car. She let Rosie do the bulk of the talking while they all waited on Jaime. Finally, he was running up to the car. Krystal thought he might fall since he hadn't bothered to tie his laces.

"How is everyone doing in school?" Maria asked.

"Good!" Esme and Rosie responded in unison.

"I got A's in almost everything," Rosie said, bouncing in her seat.

"Oh, look at you, smart girl," Maria replied. "What about you, Jaime?"

"It's okay, I guess," he said, looking out the window on the pretense of disinterest.

"Come now, that doesn't sound positive," Maria said, sounding concerned. "How are your grades?"

Jaime looked at his lap in silence as if pondering a response.

"Jaime is stupid," Rosie said, and snorted. Esme giggled, but knew better than to comment.

Maria and Krystal both looked at Rosie sharply. Maria had to do it via the rearview mirror, but Rosie didn't miss a beat.

"Sorry," she said. *She isn't, but what can you do?*

Jaime glared at his twin before returning his eyes to his lap. He loved his Tia Maria and didn't want her to think he was stupid.

Rosie was unconcerned.

"Are you going to eat that?" she asked, pointing at the sweet bread Krystal was still holding. Krystal gave it to her without answering.

Maria tried a different approach.

"What's your favorite subject? Is there anything you like the best?"

"Math," Jaime said. "I do really good in math."

"That's great!" Maria gushed, flashing a big smile into the rearview. "Math is tough for a lot of people, so to be good at it is wonderful, and to like it is even better." A quick over-the-shoulder glance at him showed her his mood had brightened. She was happy to see the small smile lift the corners of his mouth.

Aunt Maria had been giving the kids a ride every Sunday since the move. As busy as she was, Maria loved her family and would do anything she could to help them. Krystal thought her mom was taking advantage of Maria. Why should she have to taxi them around when her mother was perfectly capable?

"So, now, tell me which ones you dislike the most?" Maria coaxed.

Jaime's countenance fell a bit. "Reading mostly, and writing too."

"Why don't you like it?" she probed.

"Because I'm not good at it," he mumbled, and slumped back into his seat. Krystal thought he might disappear into the cushions if he could.

"Different people have different challenges, Jaime," Maria began. "When I was your age, I wasn't good at science at all. I had to work harder than most of the other kids to pass, but my hard work paid off. Just keep at it and don't give up."

As a confidence booster, Maria started shouting out some appropriate second grade math problems. Jaime didn't miss a beat, and neither did Rosie when she started chiming in with answers. The sweetbread was long gone.

Krystal sat silently throughout the entire ride. She had never felt selfish about her attitude and actions until today. Her little brother didn't think he was smart and Krystal knew better than that. She even knew she was smart. Her grades only sucked because she didn't do all of her work and didn't care to. Seeing her brother shrink down at Rosie's words made her heart wrench. *Didn't siblings always taunt each other? But he was taking it to heart, and that wasn't good.*

It was easier to see Jaime acting like everything was okay like he usually did. Guilt engulfed her; she felt responsible for his lack of esteem and for not helping him. But how could she help him when she couldn't help herself? Shouldn't her mom be helping him? She doubted her mom knew he was even struggling.

Resting her forehead on the window, she wished for the millionth time she just wasn't here anymore. She was so tired of dealing with all the drama, all the emotions, and the stress. She wasn't suicidal...wasn't trying to kill herself when she cut. But if she disappeared, died in her sleep, or even got hit by a bus, she would be okay with it. She certainly wasn't scared of physical pain; she was so lost, so hopeless, and she couldn't explain it if she tried, not even to herself. It was just all of the feelings and she was tired of feeling.

An overwhelming desire to cut flooded her. *A few more minutes.* She began tapping her foot. *Just a few more minutes.*

The front tire bumped the curb when Maria pulled up to Roberto's house, causing the bobble-head puppy on the dash to get whiplash. Exhaling, Krystal unbuckled her seatbelt and got out of the car, heading directly for the front door, when Maria called out. "You know the drill, guys! I want a hug from everyone."

If this had been her mother, Krystal would have ignored her and headed straight in, but she couldn't bring herself to do that to Maria. Besides, it would cause more commotion than it was worth. Biting her lip, she waited her turn.

The kids lined up in order of age every time. Rosie was first because she loved hugs and there was no way she'd let Jaime be first. As mean as she could be to Jaime, she had that much and more love and hugs to give away. She was never bashful about dishing out the hugs and kisses to family and friends. Jaime and Krystal were probably the only ones who weren't direct recipients of Rosie's overflowing affection.

That hadn't always been the case. Rosie used to love Krystal. Used to hold her hand when they were at the grocery store. A lump formed in Krystal's throat, and she swallowed hard. Silently, she filled her lungs with air and exhaled through her nose. It helped a little.

Jaime gave Maria a hug and Krystal overheard Maria's whisper in his ear. "We will talk later about helping you with reading and writing, okay?"

He nodded, and once the hugs ended, they walked up to the gate. Roberto stood on the porch. Lucky, their cat, waited for them next to his feet. Mostly he waited for Esme, who would scoop him up and love on him.

"I'll be back at eight like always," Maria called out.

Roberto nodded appreciatively, then smiled. "Thank you." He held up his hand.

All the kids walked up to greet their dad with hugs, except Krystal. She walked straight into the house.

"*Adonde vas*, Krystal?" he asked, wanting to know where she was going.

"To the bathroom," Krystal called back as she kept moving. She passed through the living room and then into the dining room where the door to the restroom was on the left side of the room. She went in, closed the door, and pushed the lock in on the knob. She checked the door to make sure it wouldn't open.

Knowing it wouldn't be hard to find something to use in here, she opened the door to the medicine cabinet. Right in front of her eyes was her dad's straight razor. She reached for it when she saw the box of blades on the top shelf and the razor they belonged to. Opening the box, she pulled one out and could see her reflection in the sliver of metal.

Her dad's bathroom, their old bathroom, was small and unoriginal, but they'd done their best to make it nice. The tub was on the far side, then the toilet, and the sink.

The mauve walls had been more appropriate when the number of girls outweighed the number of boys in the house. Small rosebuds adorned the center of each tile on the floor. Her mom had picked the tiles, her mom and dad had laid them, and she'd done the majority of the painting. She'd even done the custom border by hand. They'd done the entire project in one Saturday and then ordered pizza that night because everyone was tired and famished.

Krystal sighed. Maybe it would be better if her dad moved. That way, she wouldn't see ghosts of the family past every time she was here.

She closed the lid on the toilet, sat down, and pushed her sleeve up.

Chapter 8

Monday came quickly and Krystal was miserable with a capital M. Actually, just capitalize all the letters and shout it out. Her BFF was MIA and she just didn't function the same without her here.

Where the heck was Em, anyway? Brandon was in this class and ever since she'd seen him at the shelter, being around him was entirely awkward.

Em had even noticed his recent attention to her and started teasing her about it.

'He's cute and nice; that's a pretty good combination,' she had said. 'You should talk to him. Maybe I'll start seeing you in something a bit more feminine than a hoodie.'

"Repeat after me, class," Ms. Eichorn said loudly, interrupting Krystal's thoughts. Krystal rolled her eyes. Ms. Eichorn noticed and her eyes shot darts at her.

Oops.

"*Ill fait beau,*" the teacher enunciated in a perfect French accent.

Everyone repeated, including Krystal.

"And what does this mean?" she asked. Multiple people offered the answer. "Correct. It means 'It is beautiful!'"

No, no, this is not beautiful. Krystal wanted to go…now. The teacher shot a sharp look at her. Krystal froze.

"Please, stop tapping your pencil." Ms. Eichorn paused for effect after each word.

Krystal sent the teacher her best apologetic expression. "Sorry."

For the hundredth time, she wondered where Em could be. Though her dad promised he'd be getting a phone for her soon, it hadn't materialized yet. Not speaking to her family did have plenty of repercussions.

In the old days, she would have constantly reminded her father of his promises. So much so that he would have sprinted to make the purchase just to have a little peace. How she wished she had it now so she could call and find out why Em wasn't there.

When the bell finally sounded, Krystal couldn't get up fast enough. She grabbed her books and headed for the door. Her long legs carried her out of the room ahead of most of the class. Eagerness did the rest.

"Krystal, do you have a second?"

Krystal stopped in her tracks. She knew who it was before she even turned around. *What? Did he run to catch up? Oh man,* she thought, *this is all Em's fault for not being here.*

"Sure," she replied. She waited and wondered what he was going to say. Could he see how flushed she was? She hoped not. In these moments, she always told herself that her darker skin didn't tell on her.

"Well, I know this is…" he stopped for a second, absently rubbing his temple, trying to figure out how to say what he wanted to.

He clearly felt as awkward as she did. Of course he would! Less frazzled now, the awkwardness lifted and she calmed a bit.

"Brandon, I'm not going to say anything to anyone. I promise."

Brandon exhaled in pure relief and smiled. Dimples Krystal had never noticed before appeared.

"That's what I was hoping," he admitted. "We are, well…my family is going through a tough time right now, obviously. I know if you were going to say something, you probably would have already done it by now. Obviously, you haven't because no one has said anything to me." He paused, then said quickly, "Anyway, I couldn't stop thinking about it and just wanted to clear the air."

"How long have you been staying there?" Krystal instantly panicked. She didn't even realize she was going to ask, and it was definitely none of her business. "Sorry, I didn't mean…."

"It's okay. We're not staying there. We just eat dinner there most nights. My dad died last year, and my mom is having a tough time with all the bills. We have to move into a smaller place after the house sells; then things should start getting better, financially anyway." His gray eyes drifted down to his shoes.

Krystal could tell selling the house bothered him.

"I'm really sorry, Brandon, about all of it. Was your dad sick, or…?"

"No, he was the healthiest person I knew," he said, as he shifted his book bag to the other shoulder. Looking down, he rolled a lost pebble around with the toe of his shoe, keeping it within the square tile. "He loved to run and went out one evening before dinner to jog around the neighborhood. He was hit by a car…drunk driver. It was a Friday," Brandon said and looked up at her again, "guess they got an early start on their weekend."

"How awful."

"Yeah." He sighed. "Anyway," he said, changing the subject back to where they started, "I'm on the baseball team and I would hate for the guys to find out about our situation; I'm not sure how they would handle knowing. They aren't the most mature kids in the world."

Completely able to relate, she nodded. "I totally get it."

Brandon smiled just enough for it to turn up the corners of his mouth.

"See ya later. And thanks."

Krystal stood there for a second processing everything that had just happened. She was genuinely sorry for his family's current situation. To lose your dad and wind up eating at a homeless shelter…poor Brandon.

On another note, she'd had him in class for this whole semester and never noticed how cute he was. Em was right. Well, she was noticing now. Krystal was tall for her age, but Brandon stood at least an inch or two above her. She could still see his light blue sweater way down the hall as he headed to his next class. She'd noticed he was wearing chucks too. They had a lot in common.

Krystal sighed. That's enough of this day! Other than a quick stop by her locker for her bag, she didn't waste any more time contemplating what to do next. There was nothing new about her skipping a class here and there.

Krystal had time to burn and went to the library. It was only a half-mile from the school, and she liked the library's sitting room where all the comfy chairs were. The idea of sitting alone with her sketchpad and no one to bother her sounded quite appealing.

She selected a couple of art books and went up to the second floor of the library. The entire floor had been redone the year before and it was awesome. It had every form of seating imaginable, from couches, chairs, desks, and even beanbags.

It smelled like a library should. A clean scent made up of books, live plants, which were in every corner, and the bright spring flowers resting on the windowsill, tilted toward the sunlight.

Krystal settled into an oversized, soft, brown leather chair. Faux leather, most likely. In this section, the comfy chairs were arranged in groups of mostly twos and fours. This one was alone with a matching footstool, which sat next to the windows overlooking her school's bell tower.

Wonder what class Brandon is in now?

She always thought Topeka High was especially awesome, structurally speaking. It was probably the best-looking building in town and was a landmark of the city. The mighty Trojan statue stood guard out front and center at all times. There were multiple generations of graduates in the city, and they were proud of their school.

As an artist, she appreciated the beauty. She didn't appreciate the gazillions of stairs she had to climb every day, however. To give people something to look at as they all climbed the stairs, she drew flowers and other designs on the backs of her chucks. She considered it a public service, especially since lazy daisies such as herself were prohibited from using the elevators.

After spending the next half hour drawing a certain boy with dimples to die for, she started flipping through all the different drawings she'd done recently. Some had been ideas for her storytelling piece. One idea had been a young girl sitting in front of a vanity mirror; her expression was wide-eyed and frightened. The only things reflected in the mirror were the objects in the room. There was a bed, the painting on the wall above the bed, and the back of the chair in front of the table that held the mirror.

The next one showed a man who stood in a desert looking forlorn. His hand positioned over his eyes as if to shade them from the sun as he gazed out in the distance, searching. His other hand hung at his side; in his hand he held a photo by the corner—a family photo. She didn't pick that one for her project either.

The drawing she chose was a reverse of the Dia De Los Muertos, which means Day of the Dead. It's a day designated to remember the dead, kind of like Memorial Day, except it was for anyone they wished to remember.

During this time of year, many photos and art pieces started popping up of young beautiful girls adorned in masks of skulls. Sometimes they were pictures of skulls or skeletons in various levels of adornment with pretty colors and flowers. While Krystal didn't relate to it the way some of her extended family did, she did like the art aspect of it.

Instead of drawing the typical beauty with a skull mask, she had drawn a figure sitting in a beautiful red velvet chair. The top of the chair's wooden frame was intricately carved with blossoms. Long, dark hair had been twisted into a long braid that fell over the right shoulder of a female figure. A tiara sparkled against her hair.

The girl wore a beautiful white gown that many might have mistaken for a wedding dress. But the girl was dressed for her Quinceañera, her fifteenth birthday, her coming-of-age celebration.

Krystal's eyes scanned the embroidered details in the lace. She'd spent a long time on the intricacies, probably too much time for a sketch, but she'd gotten carried away. She'd hidden the girl's hands in the folds of fabric and lace as she sat forward in anticipation of something.

She would've been beautiful, but her face was a skull. On the corner of a table, visible in the bottom right-hand corner of the drawing, was a mask. The mask was of a beautiful face. This drawing sat on her easel in Mr. Z.'s class gradually taking shape in a much larger format.

Though her family was still deeply rooted in the tradition of throwing a Quinceañera party to celebrate turning fifteen, Krystal had already told both of her parents not to bother. The custom of choosing a beautiful gown and spending an evening in the company of family and friends would be a waste and an embarrassment.

Neither of her parents argued the point. Neither wanted to deal with extended family. Her fifteenth birthday wasn't until September, and she'd rather spend it with Em.

Flipping to her most recent sketches, she smiled when she looked at the picture of Nick she had drawn. He was standing in the doorway of the kitchen, hands on his hips, a smile on his face and a twinkle in his eye. She turned the page and looked at the old man and his dog. She had drawn them the way she'd seen them the first time; him hunched slightly forward and the dog's face stoic and alert.

Suddenly, a thought struck her, and she sat up quickly. Em wasn't there today. Perhaps she was sick? If she were sick, would the rest of Em's family go to the shelter the following day? Surely they wouldn't all miss. Somewhat surprised by her feelings of disappointment at the thought of not going back the next day, she smiled. The Topeka Rescue Mission was full of misfits, and she fit right in.

She stood to gather her things, glancing at the clock on the wall. More time had passed than she'd thought.

Could really use that phone right now. It was nearly four; she needed to get home and call Em.

Chapter 9

Krystal could hear Rosie and Jaime playing in the backyard as she walked up to the house. They sounded excited and out of breath. Esme's laugh rang out next. Curiosity tugged at Krystal, but she decided to head in and just peek out the back window instead.

She'd just opened the front door when she heard a car pull up. She glanced over her shoulder and saw her Tia Maria's car. Maria saw her in the doorway and waved, and then she waved her hand motioning for Krystal to come out to the car.

Krystal went back out to see what her aunt wanted. Before she even reached the car, Maria started talking.

"Krystal," she said in a hurry, "I'm glad I caught you. I just want to drop these by for Jaime. I'd planned on talking to him, but I just got a call about a case and have to go. I'm sorry. Do you think you can get him started with these?"

"Sure."

Maria handed Krystal a book and several comic books. They all had a common theme - skateboarding. How clever of her aunt to pick the one thing Jaime loved to do that didn't require him to hold a game controller in his hands. Well, he did have one skateboarding game but he preferred the real deal.

Jaime's love for skateboarding started when he was six. Their older cousin Jorge, who was nine or ten at the time, had already mastered some pretty serious moves for just being a kid. After spending time with his older cousin, everyone noticed Jaime had a natural talent for it. For his seventh birthday, Roberto bought Jaime his own board and safety gear. Jaime was over the moon that day, claiming it the best day ever in his whole life.

It occurred to Krystal she hadn't seen Jaime on his board in a long time. Krystal looked up, and lines creased her forehead. When was that last time he had it? He usually brought it along on Sundays. Had it been weeks? More than a month?

He used to go to the skate park in Oakland with Jorge, but now that they didn't live on that side of town anymore, he couldn't. Jorge's family wouldn't drive across town to pick him up and then have to take him all the way back. It would be a double trip across the city and back. Besides, Jorge was their cousin on their dad's side. She didn't think they'd be interested in picking him up at the Man's house.

Maria was still speaking in a rush.

"Please ask him to read for at least fifteen minutes every night out loud. It would be great if he would do it with one of you, but if he won't, let him do it alone for now. Tell him I will be asking him questions about what he read on Sunday."

Maria smiled at Krystal but then her brows came together.

"Are you doing okay, Krystal? You're always so quiet lately."

Krystal fielded generic inquiries such as these like a pro. 'I'm doing fine' or 'Things are good' had become second nature. No one wanted the truth and certainly didn't want you to spill your guts to them. They wanted to stay off the hook and not be involved, but still have given you the pretense they care.

Krystal imagined what it would be like if she answered the next generic 'How are you?' with something like, 'Oh you know, the usual. I about had a nervous breakdown this morning so I sliced my arm open with a piece of glass. I still hate my life but at least my head doesn't feel like it's going to explode this minute. And how are you?'

It was ludicrous, but the thought made Krystal want to giggle.

Maybe that wasn't completely correct concerning her Tia Maria; she knew she cared. However, she had no intention of confiding in her.

"Yeah, I'm doing fine," she said and added a smile for a bonus.

It wasn't convincing. Maria studied her face. Krystal shifted under her gaze. So this is what an insect feels like under a microscope… She transferred the books to the inside of her other arm. They weren't heavy but she needed to do…something.

"We need to talk sometime soon, Krystal. You know you can call me if you ever need anything or just to chat, right?" Maria asked.

Krystal nodded.

Krystal's hands were full, so Maria grabbed her forearm instead and gave it a 'thank you' squeeze. Krystal visibly flinched at the unexpected pressure on her fresh wound.

"I'm sorry, did I hurt you?" Maria sounded a bit alarmed.

"No, I'm okay," Krystal quickly said.

"What happened to your arm?" Maria asked.

Krystal fought the urge to roll her eyes and groan.

"I fell on it weird in gym. It's sore is all; it's not a big deal. I'll tell Jaime what you said." Krystal wanted this conversation over so she said good-bye and started walking back up to the house.

As she hoped, Maria accepted her answer and hurried away. Krystal was glad her aunt had somewhere else to go; otherwise that conversation may have lasted way too long. Krystal sat the books down on the kitchen table with a thud.

A glance in the living showed her mom sitting on the edge of the seat in the recliner. Leaning all the way forward, her elbows rested on her knees and she was clapping her hands. Sofia was lying on a princess blanket sprawled out picnic style.

On her belly, Sofia was fascinated by Josefina's clapping hands and was laughing and kicking. Tiny fists were grabbing the blanket as she tried to push herself up. Suddenly, she rolled onto her back. Josefina was thrilled and praised her wildly. Sofia was now free to clap too. Those big brown baby eyes were lit up in wonderment. Completely engaged in the song Josefina was now singing, she flipped herself back over, and Josefina swept her up above her head, bringing her part way down for a kiss, then back. Krystal almost smiled but caught herself and didn't.

Disgruntled and confused, Krystal turned away and went to look out the back window in Esme and Rosie's room. Peeking through the blinds, she saw what all the commotion was about in the backyard.

A brand new trampoline sat in the middle of the lawn. It was so humongous that the nice-sized yard now seemed dwarfed by the contraption. It reminded her of how Nick looked in the tiny room at the shelter. The base alone looked to be three feet high and who knew how tall the net that encircled it might be. All three kids were on it.

Esme was doing jump kicks on one side, Rosie was jumping and twirling simultaneously, and Jaime, Mr. Athletic compared to the rest of the gang, was doing forward and backward flips.

They're going to break their necks.

Just then, she saw the Man sitting in a lawn chair drinking a glass of soda as he watched the kids play. He looked…happy.

Ugh!

Krystal stiffened and turned away from the window. Leaning against the wall, she placed her hands over her ears and closed her eyes as she attempted to mute all the hurt and anger that filled her. It didn't help. She imagined how good it would feel to break the window and stop all their fun.

When she opened her eyes, what she saw pricked her heart and left a tiny hole. Her anger drained out of her, leaving her shaken. Esme had taped a picture on the wall above her bed.

A drawing she had done for Esme two Christmases ago. Things had been uneasy at home. She and Esme were fine-tuned to their parent's quandary. To cheer her little sister up, Krystal had drawn a picture of a lady firefighter in bunker gear holding an ax. Her skill had improved a hundred fold since then.

Krystal recalled that day years ago, they were leaving for school in early October. She was almost eight and Esme had just turned six. Their dad had an appointment that day and was going into work late. Instead of them taking the bus as usual, he told them he was taking them for breakfast at McDonalds and dropping them off at school. They were thrilled of course. On the way to the car, they were startled by a panicked sound from above their heads. They glanced up and could see a young gray tabby cat on branch high above their heads

"Daddy!" Esme cried, "He needs help!"

"He got up there somehow," Roberto said, "He'll find his way down."

That answer didn't cut it, and Esme was in instant tears.

"You can't leave him up there. What if he falls?" She started sobbing.

Roberto had looked at his little girl whose shoulders were rising and falling with each shudder.

"He's a cat; he'll land on his feet." Three times he told her to get in the car, but Esme was unmovable. She planted her bottom on the top step of the porch, crossed her arms, furrowed her brows, and stuck out her bottom lip.

Roberto took in the scene, softened his stance and then laughed. Of course he could have picked her up and forced her in but the rest of her day would be ruined. He told Krystal to go wait on the porch with her sister and surveyed the tree. There was no way he could get up there.

"The cat is at least thirty feet up," he said out loud as he stood with his head tilted all the way back.

Roberto rubbed his forehead and then pinched the bridge of his nose in thought. He went in and called the fire department, explaining that if they didn't help he'd have a six-year-old to answer to and it wouldn't be pretty.

Firefighters arrived in less than ten minutes. The flashing lights and big red engine drew neighbors out of their homes to watch the rescue. Roberto, embarrassed by all the commotion, watched as the firefighter scaled the ladder that extended from the fire engine. The poor cat didn't even try to back away. The little thing knew help when he saw it. The fireman picked him up and the cat burrowed into his chest, hooking his claws into the fireman's jacket and hanging on for dear life.

Once his boots hit the ground, the fireman disengaged the claws and handed the cat, who was mewing songs of thanks, over to Roberto.

"He's not ours," said Roberto.

Esme was on her feet, jumping up and down.

"Can we keep him, Daddy?" she'd begged.

With the firefighters and neighbors watching, Roberto sighed. Krystal knew he wouldn't say no. He told Esme they would try to find the owners, and if no one claimed him, they could keep the kitty.

He and the girls, especially Esme, thanked the firefighters profusely. Esme stared in awe. When she got a glimpse of the firefighter who'd been driving the big engine, her little sister's eyes grew to the size of a baseball. The lady firefighter looked at the girls, winked and waved good-bye as she drove off. Hooked from that moment on, Esme declared in front of the neighborhood that she would be a firefighter when she grew up.

Esme had since learned firefighters do a whole lot more than rescue cats out of a tree. In some cities, they aren't even allowed to go out on calls for cats. That didn't deter her at all; it only intrigued her more as she perused the newspaper to read up on daily fire department calls. Krystal fully believed her sister would be a firefighter when she grew up. As she left the room, she thought about a new drawing she could do for Esme.

A phone call to Em confirmed they were returning to the shelter the next day. Apparently, Em had a dentist appointment that she had forgotten about until her mom reminded her this morning. Em had pretended to be offended that Krystal didn't call because she missed her. "Well, you didn't miss me either," Krystal said, "who called who first?"

The house immediately became clamorous as the kids and the Man came in from outside. Their cheeks flushed from playing and jumping.

"We're starving," Rosie touted.

"Yeah, we are," Esme agreed.

"Did you have fun?" Josefina inquired, already knowing they did.

"Yes!" They all chimed in with varying degrees of exhilaration.

"It was awesome!" Rosie exclaimed.

"You should have seen my flips, Mom!" Jaime breathed heavily, still winded from all the acrobatics.

"They loved it," the Man confirmed. "You should have seen them when I was waiting outside after school. They were so confused. Once I told them there was a surprise at home, all I heard on the way back was about how much of a grandpa driver I was being. I mean…I was doing at least 25 miles per hour!"

Josefina laughed heartily.

Krystal busied herself by getting a glass of water. Was she ever going to be able to deal with him being involved in everything? Why was he trying so hard? He'd already reeled her siblings in hook, line, and sinker. Didn't the thought ever once cross the kids' minds that it should be their real father doing these things with them? Didn't they miss Dad?

"Did you thank Eliseo?" Josefina asked the kids. "It took him a long time to put that trampoline together for you today."

The Man's schedule sometimes varied. He was a mechanic and owned his own shop. Krystal had once heard him tell her mom that within a year of opening his shop, he'd already had more than enough work coming in. With his business growing so rapidly, he'd had to hire a receptionist and two other mechanics, one full-time and one part-time. 'It's because you're such a good business man,' Josefina had said, playfully patting his cheek. 'You're so honest and such a hard worker.' Krystal had wanted to barf, hearing her mom gush over him that way.

"Thank you!" the kids sang out in unison.

"See," Josefina said to Eliseo. "Aren't you glad you didn't tell them the same day you bought it!"

"Oh yeah. Work has been busy, and then Susana," his sister, "had car problems too." He rolled his eyes. "Putting it together with these monsters around would have been chaotic. Concentrating on the instructions would be nearly impossible with them chirping like hungry baby birds asking when I would finish." Eliseo made talking puppet gestures with his hands in the air. He and Josefina laughed together.

"All of you go wash your hands and faces," Josefina directed. "Esme, you go first so you can set the table."

"I'll do it," Krystal said and instantly wondered why she'd offered. Her mom's eyes flashed a look of shock, but she quickly recovered.

"But I'm going to eat in my room," Krystal said quickly. "I have stuff to do." After Sunday's revelation that things were difficult for Jaime, she wanted to do something but had no idea what to do. It made her want to be around him and her two sisters, but she didn't know what to say to them.

"Thank you," Josefina said.

For some time now, her mom knew she wasn't going to get any help from Krystal. For the most part, her mom had quit trying. Krystal assumed it was to keep from upsetting the entire house. Oh, but as soon as Josefina needed her to call her dad, the battle commenced.

Krystal put down a plate, fork, spoon, and a cup of ice at each place. The small table only seated four. Josefina and the Man sat on barstools at the counter; many times

Josefina ate on the go. Usually she multitasked. Between preparing meals and tending to Sofia, she stole bites in between tasks.

The Man came in carrying Sofia and sat on one of the barstools. Sofia was on his lap, her back resting against his chest with his right hand securing her little body. Holding Sofia's bottle up with his other hand, Sofia wrapped her tiny fist around one of his fingers as she drank her milk noiselessly. Her chin lifted, and her eyes kept floating upward so she could watch her dad while she drank.

It would have been a sweet picture if it involved someone else's family, rather than her broken one. She could see the Man was trying, but instead of making things easier to digest, it was harder. Even more regretful for offering to set the table, she hurried and finished as the kids began serving themselves.

Jaime noticed the books that were still in the middle of the table and Krystal saw his eyes light up; he knew they were for him. She relayed Maria's instructions to him. He regarded her a bit strangely and just nodded.

Probably because he hasn't heard me say this many words at once that weren't being yelled. Guilt intermingled with her aggravation. She knew her brother and sisters didn't deserve the bitterness from her. They were too young to understand.

"Put the book away until after dinner," Josefina told him.

"I want to read one," Rosie piped up.

"No!" snapped Jaime. "They're mine."

Rosie's answer was sticking her tongue out and making a face at him. Then she just couldn't help herself.

"Stoopid!"

Josefina swiftly popped Rosie on the back of the head. Esme nearly choked on her pop trying to keep the giggles in her chest from bubbling out. Her eyes shined with laughter.

"Stop it!" Josefina reprimanded all of them at once and pointed at their plates. "Eat!" The room went silent. Krystal noticed the Man was pressing his lips together, trying not to smile.

Everyone was sitting except her mother. Krystal fixed her plate of enchiladas and sopa—Mexican rice—and poured a glass of soda. She made a beeline for her room without another word. Her appetite had vanished along with her urge to draw Esme's picture or help Jaime with his reading. But instead of throwing her plate down and stomping off like she would have done in the recent past, she made a much less dramatic exit.

Once in her room, Krystal sat the plate of food on her dresser. She carried her soda over to her bed and took a long drink before placing her glass on the bedside table.

For the first time since she began cutting, there was this niggling doubt making her uneasy about it. Any other day, it wasn't a consideration; it was like she was on autopilot. The relief was addictive, and she'd never felt guilty about it though she'd questioned her sanity on multiple occasions. The only real inconvenience there'd ever been was keeping her scars covered.

So why was she thinking about it now? The simple fact she was now questioning one of the few things that helped her to keep going every day was burdensome.

Irritated, she took a shower and put on shorts and a long-sleeved, plain white t-shirt. Even in her room, she was careful to keep her arms covered in case of an unexpected visit, which never happened. Sometimes, she didn't know why she bothered to cover her scars. She could walk through the living room in her bra and underwear and her mom probably wouldn't even notice the unmistakable signature of anger and sadness that decorated her body.

Awareness shifted her guilt to resolve, and she granted herself permission once again.

After retrieving her glass and towel, she sat on her bed with her back against the headboard. She drew her legs up and pushed the left leg of her shorts down as far as she could.

Knowing she had to wear shorts in gym, she had to be careful whenever she cut on her thighs. Most of the time, she preferred her arms, but not tonight. Pushing all thoughts from her mind, she found her escape.

Chapter 10

At school the next day, things felt a bit more normal with Em's presence. On their way to Biology class, Brandon passed them in the hallway.

"Hey, Krystal," he said.

"Hey," she greeted. Oh boy, she knew what was coming next and blushed in anticipation.

"O-M-GEE!" said Em in the loudest whisper Krystal ever heard.

"Shhhhh," Krystal grabbed Em's sleeve and whispered furiously, "Calm down!"

"Well, it seems like me being gone one little day made a great big difference!" Em said as a huge cheesy grin invaded her face. "Thought you didn't like any boys at this school," she said in a singsong voice.

"Put your teeth away," Krystal said dryly. "It's not what you think."

"Um, Brandon is cute and out of all the boys in this school, if you were going to like one, he'd be a good choice. K, I award you with my seal of approval," Em said.

"Keep your seal, crazy one," Krystal said. "Why do you so readily approve, anyway?" Did she have some sort of information that caused her to act so silly about it all?

Em's reply came in a quick hushed tone. "Two years ago, while we were still at Robinson Middle School, these two bullies, Raymond and Josh, had this kid named Charlie cornered in the boy's bathroom. Charlie has autism and he always carried this one toy with him everywhere he went; it was a toy figurine of Raphael from The Teenage Mutant Ninja Turtles. Well, Raymond and Josh had taken it from him and were waving it up in the air. By the time Brandon came along, Charlie was in hysterics; he was groaning loud and pulling at his ears. Brandon grabbed Raymond by his shirt and snatched Charlie's toy and gave it back to him. Charlie bolted, but the other two boys ganged up on Brandon. Thankfully, the coach heard some noise when he was walking by and was able to break up the fight. Brandon must have held his own, though, because all he came out with was a few scratches. Raymond, on the other hand, had a bloody nose and Josh had a nice goose egg on the back of his head. A boy named Larry had been in one of the stalls and saw it all."

Em just succeeded in making Krystal like Brandon even more.

"So what happened to them after that?" Krystal inquired. "Why didn't Larry try to help if he was in there the whole time?"

"He was probably scared. Raymond and Josh were really mean. But Larry did tell the principal everything that happened," with a side nod towards the general population of students she added, "as well as the rest of the school. Everyone but Charlie and Larry got expelled."

"So, Brandon got in trouble for helping Charlie?" Krystal asked, appalled.

"Yeah, but his suspension was only for a couple days. Principal said that he should have gotten help instead of confronting Raymond and Josh on his own, blah-blah-blah." Krystal rolled her eyes. "Of course I disagree with that, too," Em continued, "Charlie was able to confirm what happened. Charlie finished the year, but I haven't seen him since."

"Wow," was all Krystal could think to reply.

"Okay, just answer me this and allow me to remind you that I am your best friend and you have to be honest." Em stopped walking, grabbed Krystal by the front of her hoodie, mockingly imitating what Brandon had done to Ray in the seventh grade. She got in her face nearly nose to nose, scrunched up her face, and in an emphatic low whisper she asked, "Do you think he's hot?"

Krystal couldn't help but laugh. Palming Em's forehead, she pushed her about a foot back.

"Get off me, you weirdo."

Em audibly cleared her throat. Krystal ignored her.

"Ahem!"

"Oh, for goodness sakes! Yes! Okay?" She must have been as red as a cherry, because her ears were on fire.

"Thought so," said Em smugly, and pretended to be polishing her nails on her shirt. She followed through by looking them over and blowing on them.

Em was unrelenting with her prodding for details and Krystal didn't know what to say. Betraying Brandon's confidence was not an option, but Em was most likely going to see him at the shelter at some point. Now that she thought about it, she wasn't even sure Brandon knew Em was the one she volunteered with at the shelter. *Ugh, dilemmas!*

Lesson learned from the previous Tuesday, Krystal came prepared. Before they got out of the car, she unzipped her hoodie and took it off, leaving it in the backseat. Underneath she wore a simple long-sleeve black t-shirt. On the front were pink flowers in a swirl formation.

Em let out a whistle.

"Been a long time since I've seen you in anything but a hoodie!"

Krystal sighed loudly.

"Okay, okay," Em said, "I'm done. But just ditching the hoodie was a huge improvement! You look cute, my little Goth friend."

Krystal laughed. Em was the only one allowed to make any cracks at her, but she was pushing it tonight.

"Don't make me steal your makeup bag and hide it so that you never find it!" she warned with a smile.

Em put a hand on her chest and made a ridiculous expression in her attempt to feign shock.

"Hold that pose!" Krystal took Em's phone right off her lap and snapped a pic. The two girls fell into a fit of giggles. "You have to send me that one when my dad finally gets my phone."

"Come on, girls," Sharon said. She and Mike were in the front rolling their eyes and laughing at their silliness. Zach wasn't with them today. Mike and Sharon arranged for him to volunteer in a different capacity. He would help assemble backpacks for kids whose parents couldn't afford all their school supplies each year and get to work with kids closer to his age.

The scene outside the shelter was much the same as it was last Tuesday. Mike rang the buzzer. Glancing around, Krystal didn't see the man with his dog anywhere.

The door swung open.

"Hey!" said Nick as if he were surprised, "You came back!" Laughing at his greeting, they filed in like ducklings with Krystal at the tail; Nick winked at her and said, "Good to see you!"

Today they learned a little bit more about setting up. Krystal and Em discovered their age dictated what tasks they could perform. They learned where all the utensils were kept and made sure each dish had the appropriate serving piece with it. Plates were carefully stacked next to the serving line, and they made sure enough soup cups filled the bin. Silverware sat on carts in two corners of the dining hall. Along with the silverware, napkins and a variety of condiment packets filled the carts.

Donations counted for most everything they used. During their tour, Nick said almost everything the shelter was able to accomplish resulted from donations from the hearts of numerous caring people in the community.

"You girls ready to rock and roll?" Nick asked.

Krystal smiled and Em giggled, both nodding in unison.

"Well let's get this party started then." Nick headed off to open the doors of the dining hall.

Mel already had the soups in place. Tonight his hair was in groups of short spikes, and she could see the tattoo behind his ear was a small set of praying hands.

Krystal peered into the pots. Clam chowder and vegetable soup. She wrinkled her nose. Blech and blech. She wasn't a soup person.

The first round of guests consisted of people staying at the shelter. The second round served people from the community who came in for a meal. That's the round Brandon would be in.

She wished there was something more she could do. If things were normal, she would ask her parents to help his family but she wasn't sure how Brandon would feel about that. She wondered about his extended family. If her family was struggling, food wasn't something they'd have to worry about. All their friends and family would bring them meals left and right. Extra rooms and couches would become immediately available for as long as they needed. Heck, her family would probably start arguing over who got to host. They'd all want to do it. She knew because that was exactly what happened when her Tio Beto got hurt and couldn't work for nearly half a year. Everyone chipped in.

Taking their places at the soup station, Krystal was still lost in thought over Brandon's circumstances and feeling some anxiety about seeing him.

"What's going on in your head?" Em inquired when she noticed Krystal staring into her pot of soup motionlessly.

"Just thinking about some of the things people here must be dealing with," she said. It was mostly true. She felt very affected by this place, an unexplainable connection she couldn't pinpoint.

"I know what you mean," said Em. "After last week, I tried to imagine what it would take to put my family in this situation. I've never wanted for anything. Mom always has us doing things to help other people. We adopt a family every Christmas and Mom lets Zach and I pick out gifts for kids in the family. It's different seeing it like this though…people who don't have their own bed or pillow. That's why I get tired of some of the kids at school who act the way they do. They are so unappreciative of what God has blessed them with."

"Then why hasn't God blessed these people the same way," Krystal asked under her breath.

"What?" Em asked and looked up.

"Nothing." Krystal sighed. She scooped up clam chowder and set it down. When the cup she'd just sat down was immediately snatched up, Krystal picked up her pace. Out of the corner of her eye, she saw the old man in line almost right in front of her, pushing his tray along with one hand. He looked up and their eyes connected. A bit embarrassed at being caught, she smiled shyly.

His weathered face with its lines and wrinkles held untold stories, and his soft blue eyes lit up when she smiled.

"Thank you," he said directly to Krystal. She couldn't hear him above the commotion, but it was easy to read his lips.

"You're welcome," she mouthed. He nodded. Krystal was curious about what his story was. *He must be staying here at the shelter since he is in the first round of diners. That means his dog gets to stay here too,* she reasoned.

Krystal and Em were scooping in silence when, from behind her, Nick spoke.

"Need a break?" His hearty voice caused her to startle. "Sorry," he laughed. "Thought I might give you girls each five minutes or so. Just have to go one at a time." That was odd, Krystal thought. They didn't have a break last time, and they hadn't been working long. The entire shift was pretty short actually.

"I'm okay," Em said with a smile, "but thanks."

Krystal rose on her tiptoes and saw the old man sitting in almost the same spot as last time.

"I could use a few minutes," she said to Nick. Surprised at her boldness, she took off her gloves and headed for the old man. When she was close, she almost froze. What am I going say? She thought. Her mind was racing for words. He must have felt her presence because he turned his head to look over his shoulder, smiling when he saw her.

"Hi there," he said. "You make great chowder."

Krystal laughed, knowing he didn't really think she made the soup.

"I can't take the credit for that."

"What's your name?"

"Krystal."

"That's a nice color in your hair, looks like a flower petal. If I still had hair, I'd give it a whirl," he said with a twinkle in his eyes. "Want to sit down here, Krystal?" He motioned to the empty spot on the other side of his dog.

The idea of him sporting pink anywhere made her laugh.

"Sure. Can I pet your dog?" In school one year, she learned to not approach service dogs in any way, no matter how cute they are. When they are working, they stay focused on what they are doing for their person.

"Why, yes. This here is Peety." When he heard his name, Peety's ears perked up. "Sit, Peety." Peety sat to attention. "Turn and sit, Peety," the old man pointed at Krystal. Peety stood up, turned to face Krystal, and sat down. He was staring right at her at full attention. She could see the intelligence in his eyes. His classic look told her he was a German Shepherd, but his uniqueness hinted at mixed breed. Gray hair on his muzzle and doggie brows said he was no longer a pup.

"He's awesome," she said in awe.

"Greet," the old man commanded his dog. Peety raised his paw to Krystal. Looking at Krystal, who had taken Peety's paw, he said, "Now hold your hand out flat with your palm down. Like this." He showed her by holding his hand in the air. She did what he said and held Peety's paw from the top instead of holding it for a shake.

"Now treat her like a lady, Peety." At the command, Peety dipped his nose down and touched it to the back of her hand like a kiss.

"I love him already!" she exclaimed and scratched Peety's head and behind his ears. "He's such a good boy. What's your name?" she asked, realizing she still only knew Peety's name.

"Walter. Just call me Walt."

"It was super nice meeting you, Walt. I better get back to my soup." She stood, still smiling—couldn't have wiped it off if she'd tried.

"Nice to meet you too, young lady. Thank you for what you're doing here," he said, holding out a hand.

Krystal shook his hand—he cupped her hand with his other. She looked at his hands…hands that might look like her own grandfather's. She'd never met her grandfather, but she'd seen pictures of him in his earlier years. Walt's were old hands, lined and rugged. She thought how if she drew his hands, they'd tell their own story.

"It's no big deal," Krystal replied.

"Oh, but it is," Walt said seriously. "Don't ever feel like the time you're devoting to help people is no big deal. What you're doing is special. That makes you special. Remember that."

Krystal stood a little straighter. She had an unexpected urge to give him a hug but rejected the idea. Maybe she'd been as affectionate as Rosie once, but that was a long time ago.

"I will," was all she managed before waving and going back to the kitchen. After washing her hands, she resumed her position at the soup station.

Nick looked down at her, smiling.

"I see you met Walt. God's magic's got ahold of him too. He's been around here for a long time. Great guy."

Krystal didn't doubt that Walt had an amazing story, but she did doubt whatever it was Nick liked to call God's magic. That was the second time she'd heard him say it. *How can he believe in magic when this place is bursting at the seams with struggling people,* she puzzled. Every day he saw people who didn't have homes at all or didn't have enough food at home to feed their families….

The last thought broke into her mental rant. She knew they were going to be on the second round of guests any time now. Brandon would be showing up any minute. Consciously keeping an eye out while she was scooping, she started thinking about her parents. They had plenty of food, but not enough of other things. Not enough to keep the family together. She felt disconnected from all of them, and it was like they didn't notice most of the time or plain didn't care. She looked out at the faces coming through the line. There were smiles, gratitude, forlornness, and indifference all within steps of each other.

"Soup, kiddo," Mike said.

"Sorry!" Krystal tried to focus, but her mind disobeyed.

"Hey, space case," Em laughed. "I bet I know why you're so distracted." That got Krystal's attention. Em wasn't entirely wrong, but she wasn't going to explain how out of context it was. After the next ten seconds she didn't have to. Brandon was in line.

What do I do? Her mind raced. I don't want to ignore him, but I don't want to draw Em's attention to him either.

In about eight more steps, he would be standing where Walt had been. Anxious, Krystal was scooping so fast that she had three cups setting out and realized she didn't have room to set the fourth one down. That left her hands nothing to do for at least five seconds, which felt like forever.

After finally deciding not to look over at all, she realized Em had stopped scooping and was looking toward the line. Slowly, Krystal turned her head the same direction. Brandon was looking back at Em. For a moment, all three of them were paralyzed. Then Brandon shifted his eyes to Krystal's; he gave her a tight smile and moved on. Krystal knew what that meant. It meant, 'why didn't you tell me?'

"You knew?" Em asked quietly.

"Yeah, I saw him here last week. That's what we talked about at school," she admitted. "I would have told you but he specifically asked me to not tell anyone. By the time I realized I should have told him we do this together, it was too late."

"I'm sorry, K. Maybe you should see if Nick will take your spot again and go talk to him."

"Not while he's eating. I doubt he wants to talk right now. We only have about twenty-five minutes left, maybe after." Krystal's heart was in her stomach. Guessing Brandon felt humiliated, she wanted him to understand that Em was not a threat to his secret. He would still be uneasy with yet another classmate knowing, but at least he'd understand that no one was judging him.

When the shift ended, Krystal started to help Em clean up.

"I got this," Em said.

"Thanks," Krystal said and looked her best friend in the eyes.

Em gave her a lopsided smile.

"Love you too, bestie."

Krystal took a deep breath and headed out to the dining room. Looking around, it didn't take long to see Brandon wasn't there. Her shoulders slumped but she scanned the room one more time to be sure.

Ugh, definitely gone.

Either he ate fast or not at all—hopefully just fast. The thought of him skipping dinner made her sick.

She ambled back to the kitchen to help Em clean up. Em frowned knowing Krystal's quick return wasn't good news.

"Great job, girls," Nick said. "You did such a great job in fact, I wonder if you two would be interested in another volunteer opportunity."

Krystal was interested before even hearing details. But without Em's parents, she didn't have a way there. As much as she wanted to do whatever it was, she didn't want to ask her mom to bring her and absolutely refused to ask the Man.

"We are moving our daycare to another part of the building and need help getting it ready," Nick said. "It involves cleaning, painting, arranging, and all sorts of other tasks. We need help on Saturday mornings for the next three or four Saturdays."

"I wish I could," Em said, "but our choir group has several performances coming up over the next couple of weeks. We've been working hard to put them together. If it weren't for that, I'd be glad to help."

"Totally understand," Nick said. "Are you available, Krystal?"

"Yes, but I don't know if I could find a ride."

"That's not an issue at all. We have a van that goes around each weekend and picks up our teen volunteers. If you're okay with that, I need your mom to sign a permission slip, and we'll add you to the list."

Krystal considered forging her mother's name.

"Most of the teens help tutor some of the younger kids who are staying here at the shelter," Nick explained. "You can ride in and out with them. We do have a short list of rules for our young volunteers; I'll give you a copy so you can read it over."

"Okay," Krystal said. It'd be much better than trying to find ways to occupy herself at home, especially with Em being extra busy.

"Wonderful," Nick said, "I'll give you a permission form before you go. Have a parent sign it and bring it with you on Saturday. I'll go ahead and add your address to the schedule. One of our office ladies will call you at home to tell you about what time to expect the van."

The next day at school, Em and Krystal worked out a plan of diversion. During French class, five minutes before the bell, Em would ask to go to the bathroom. That would give Krystal the opportunity to talk to Brandon alone and make it less awkward for him since Em wouldn't be there.

Em's performance was Oscar worthy. Crossing her legs and pleading with Ms. Eichorn, the teacher actually made her ask again in French before allowing her to go! Em's expressions were priceless. She looked comically distressed with her drawn-in eyebrows and her exaggerated mouth that was a cross between anguish and a pout as she squeaked out *je peux aller à la salle de bain?*

Em had made it a point to waddle out with her knees together while hugging her books to her chest. Once out the door and out of Ms. Eichorn's view, Em put a hand on her hip, striking a Beyoncé pose then gave Krystal a thumbs-up. If it weren't for her anxiety over the circumstances, Krystal might have fallen out of her desk laughing. She made a mental note to award Em the *most flamboyant* award for the day. But then she knew Em would say she took that award every day. It was true.

Minutes later, the bell rang. Brandon made it out the door several kids ahead of her. Oh no, she thought, he's avoiding me. But he wasn't, he was leaning up against the wall to the right of the door when she exited.

"That was quite a show," he said. His eyes were shining with humor. "I'm honored."

Krystal giggled. *Oh, I sound stupid.* She stopped immediately.

"If Em were here, she would take a bow. I'm just glad you didn't make me run to catch up," she said.

"You would have run? Man, I should have kept going. Would you have leaped over all the others to get to me?"

She rolled her eyes playfully.

"Don't push it." Pausing before she continued, she was relieved he didn't seem upset in the least. "Look, I'm sorry I didn't think to tell you about volunteering with Em. Honestly, I don't know how you two missed each other the first time around. You don't have anything to worry about though. She's cool and would never blab; she's always kept my secrets."

"What are your secrets?" he asked. "Seems like you know a lot about me while I know nothing about you."

Walked into that one!

"Nothing exciting," she said.

Luckily, he let her off the hook.

"Last time I just saw the back of her head, but I was looking at you, so I didn't pay attention to who she was."

Her heart started pounding. It was loud in her ears. She hoped he couldn't hear it.

"Sorry, didn't mean to make you blush."

"I'm not blushing," she said. *Stupid, stupid.* Why did she giggle and say dumb things when he was around?

"Can I call you?" Brandon asked.

Did her heart just stop? She wasn't sure.

"Don't know if you're into guys who have to eat at the local food kitchen but…."

"Stop. You don't have to make light of any circumstances on my account and I'm not judging," she said very seriously.

He mimicked her tone.

"I was just going to say, I'm a cheap date if you ever want to go to dinner."

Krystal couldn't help but laugh. The bell rang, and she knew they were late for their next class.

"Oops," he smiled and then said, "Sometimes it's better not to take the rough stuff so serious. While I can't say I'm not embarrassed, I can say I think I have a pretty decent grip on reality and I'm better for it."

"I know what you mean," she said. But she didn't.

Krystal scribbled her number on the corner of a notebook page and tore it off. *Ugh. That was so sloppy!* "If you meet me out front after school, I'll walk you home," he offered as he took the paper from her hand. His fingertips grazed hers.

Goosebumps broke out over her entire body. For once, she was thankful for her long sleeves. Somehow, Krystal got her senses back and found her air.

"I'll be there," she said and hurried off, daring a glance over her shoulder. Intense heat blasted her cheeks; he was still there, smiling after her, not caring about being late.

Em was in her gym class, which was the last one of the day. Krystal was bursting with the need to talk to her bestie, but missed her chance for a locker room lowdown because she was so late.

After changing into shorts, she found Em in the gymnasium with the rest of the class.

"Note?" Mrs. Grimm asked.

"No," Krystal responded.

"That's a tardy then."

Krystal didn't care. Today was aerobics, and she saw Em in the last row and went to join her. Whispering rapidly, she gushed out as much info as she could before the warm-ups ended.

Krystal couldn't find her normally quiet and composed demeanor. Infiltrated by Brandon, her naturally monotone voice had forgotten itself and her whispers changed to owl screeching.

Em was ecstatic for her.

"Just calm down and be cool."

"Easier said than done," Krystal said. Her lack of self-confidence was glaring.

"He already likes you," Em whispered. "Just be you."

"Ladies. Is there something pressing you need to share with the class?" Mrs. Grimm inquired dryly.

Krystal and Em stood next to each other in the back row with their heads together while everyone else was doing jumping jacks. Their backs straightened at the query.

"No," Em answered for the both of them. "Sorry!" Immediately they joined in on the jumping jacks.

Before leaving the locker room, Krystal stopped in front of the mirror to check her hair. Combing through it with her fingers, she checked her teeth. Nothing stuck. For the first time, she felt a little self-conscious about her hoodie. Brandon was a semi-preppy dresser. He didn't seem like the type who would like someone who dressed the way she did, not to mention the pink hair.

She took a deep breath and chided herself. Why did it matter to her? Because you didn't like him before, she answered herself. Or he didn't like you before. Or you just didn't know that he might like you before…. *I never considered the possibility.*

"Oh, shut up," she said, scolding the reflection in the mirror.

"Whom are you talking to?" Em asked, startling her.

"Don't sneak up on me."

"Sorry," she laughed. "But you know I didn't sneak. Call me tonight, okay?"

"Okay."

Maybe I'm just reading too much into this, she thought. He probably just wants to be friends. *No one besides Em and I know what he's going through. Who am I kidding?*

She walked out the front doors of the school and saw him sitting on the rail that followed the steps down to the ground level.

"Hey." Brandon smiled.

"Hey," she said.

Once she stopped psyching herself out, talking to him was easy. They talked about her classes and teachers, her family—she gave him the Reader's Digest version, her art, and her volunteer work at the shelter.

Every time she tried to change the focus back to him, it failed.

"Nope, I want to hear about you. We can talk more about me later." She wished she lived four miles from the school instead of four blocks, because they got there way too quickly.

"Thanks for walking me home," she said.

"If was fun; unfortunately, I can't do it every day. I blew off baseball practice tonight." He grinned.

"What?" she exclaimed. "I wouldn't have taken you for the skipper type."

"I'm not." He laughed. "Not normally, anyways, but it was worth it." He started walking backwards down the sidewalk. "I'll call you after dinner; I have to make sure I get back to the school before my brother comes to pick me up. He might choke me if I'm not there." Putting his hands around his neck, he crossed his eyes and stuck out his tongue.

She giggled again and waved bye.

Walking in the house, she realized she was still smiling and paused. Oddly, she didn't feel like going to her room just yet. Maybe now was a good time to get her mom to sign the permission slip.

A peek in the living room showed her mom relaxing in the recliner. Sofia was in a funny contraption Krystal hadn't seen before. It almost looked like a car seat but was thin and leaned back at an angle. It held Sofia in place securely, leaving her little legs and arms free. Whenever she moved, it bounced with her; the kid loved it.

"Did you have a good day?" Josefina asked. Looking at her mom, she realized a small smile had crept onto her lips while she had been watching.

"Yeah, I guess," she said, letting the smile go. "What is that thing?"

"It's a baby bouncer. Eliseo's sister brought it over since her baby is too big for it now. It would have been nice to have when you all were babies. Especially Rosie and Jaime. Aye! They were all over the place."

"That's cool," Krystal replied in her dry monotone voice. Uneasiness had started creeping up as soon as her mom asked about her day. This conversation was probably the most normal one she had with her mom since they'd moved in here. But she had no interest in reminiscing about when the kids were little and got right to the point.

She gave her mom the short version of how she had spent the last two Tuesdays and how she planned to spend the next several Saturdays.

"I won't need a ride or anything, but I need you to sign this," she finished, handing her the form.

"Krystal, I'm proud of you for volunteering," Josefina said as she opened the drawer on the end table next to the recliner. Selecting the first pen she saw, she signed the bottom of the paper. "I understand poverty. I saw it everywhere in Mexico, except there was no place that could help so many where I lived."

She could see the distance in her mother's eyes as she remembered things from long ago. Krystal wasn't interested.

"I'm going to work on some stuff until dinner." As she headed down the stairs to her room, she heard Esme, Rosie, and Jaime making an exceptionally rambunctious entrance, even for them.

"Can we keep him? Please, Mom!" she heard Rosie plead. Krystal went back up the stairs to see what the commotion was about.

Esme stood in the kitchen, cradling a kitten that looked like it still needed its mama and had the raspiest mews ever, his little voice scratchy.

"He sounds like he needs water," Krystal said from behind them.

"Will you put some on a saucer, Krystal?" Josefina asked. "I don't know," she told the three sets of begging eyes. "I would have to take care of him while you are at school and he is not even old enough to eat real food yet."

"Mama, please?" Esme begged, sitting the cat down by the saucer of water. The cat didn't have a clue what to do with the plate; he obviously wasn't weaned yet. Esme dipped the tip of her finger in the water and put it to his mouth. Looking up, she said, "I will do everything for him every day, except when I'm at school. I promise. I can get up extra early to feed him in the morning before I go to school too." No one doubted her words.

"I'll help her!" Rosie exclaimed. Everyone's doubting eyes turned toward Rosie. "I will," she said, trying to sound more convincing. "That way we will have one here and then one at dad's house!" The reality was, she wouldn't even feed Lucky when asked, much less get near his litter box. All eyes shifted back to Josefina.

"Where did you find him?" Josefina asked exasperated. She knew the kids just got off the bus.

"We saw him on the street when the bus was stopping," Esme answered.

"Don't go into the street, but go look and see if there are more babies out there," she directed.

Esme did as asked and came back a few minutes later to report she couldn't find any other cats.

Minutes later, the Man walked through the door and greeted everyone, planting a kiss on Josefina's temple. Krystal's eye twitched at the sight, but she forcibly ignored it.

"What's going on here?" he asked.

Three voices started talking simultaneously. Despite the jumbled confusion, the kids managed to get the short story of finding the kitten that doesn't know how to eat yet, while exclaiming their desire to keep the tiny beast. The Man looked amused at their excitement and raised his eyebrows. "I see. Hang tight, I'll be back in about fifteen minutes."

"Okay, kids," Josefina said. "I have to get dinner on if you want to eat anytime soon. Jaime, you go do your reading. Rosie, you take the kitten for now and get some newspaper from the recycle bin. If he looks like he is going to go potty, make sure he's on the paper."

"Okay!" Rosie said, jumping up and down—pleased her job was taking care of the kitten.

"Esme, please feed Sofia. She needs her rice cereal. You can do it in here while I start dinner."

"Okay," Esme said quietly. Krystal could tell she wanted to be the one to take care of the kitten. Feeling a tug of guilt that her mom didn't bother asking her to help; she surprised herself by asking, "Is there something you want me to do?"

Josefina's eyes registered surprise.

"Yes," she said, practically whispering. Clearing her throat she said, "If you could just peel about six potatoes while I start the rest, that would be very helpful."

Before the last of the potatoes were peeled, the Man returned. He had gone to the vet who was a short distance down the road from the high school. He'd bought cat milk and a tiny bottle. He showed Rosie how to feed the cat. Apparently, he'd done this before.

Krystal finished and asked if there was anything else.

"No," her mom replied. "Thank you for helping, dinner will be ready in about a half an hour."

The kids were informed they could keep the kitten and the Man would go to buy supplies after they ate dinner. Rosie and Jaime pleaded to go with him. Rather than joining the chorus of the beggars, Esme sat quietly. Krystal knew her little sister was planning on having the kitten to herself. *High-five, smart girl,* Krystal silently approved.

Agitation at the scene surrounding the new kitten increased by the second. It was difficult to get past what the others were obviously not seeing. She thought about Lucky and how even the poor cat went from a full family to an empty house the entire week while her dad was working.

One time, Esme had asked if she could take Lucky home to the new house and was vehemently told no by their dad. He'd already lost his entire family to the Man; he wasn't giving up the cat too.

Watching the Man do things her dad would normally do wasn't getting any easier. Worse, he was likable, but if she ever liked him that would make her the worst kind of traitor. No way could she betray her father like the others already had.

It would be a whole lot easier if he didn't like her siblings at all. Why couldn't he just be a complete jerk? Did he do nice things because he really liked them or to impress her mom?

When she looked up, she caught her mom watching her. A regretful look crossed her mom's face for a split-second before Krystal turned away and went down to her room.

She sat on the edge of her bed and picked up her sketchpad, turning to the next clean page. Instead of thinking about her family, she thought about Brandon's smile. Butterflies danced in her stomach. She picked up the charcoal pencil. Her fingers knew just what to do and went to work.

"Dinner's ready, wash your hands!" her mom called through the house. Movement erupted above her head as if a herd of starving elephants just spotted an apple tree across the way.

Krystal blinked away her art-induced fog. That was half an hour? It felt more like three minutes! Looking over her work, she had an urge to kiss the lips she'd drawn. Since her lips would smear the fresh charcoal, she settled for drawing two hearts, one in each corner at the bottom of the sheet.

Disappointed he hadn't called yet, she frowned. *He's probably too busy or maybe he just doesn't want to,* she thought and went upstairs to get her food.

Back in her room, she set her plate on the dresser. *Don't think too hard,* she told herself when thoughts of why Brandon hadn't called kept intruding. It had been a pretty good day, and she didn't want it to be ruined.

Tearing off a piece of a tortilla, she scooped the chorizo and potatoes in it, making it just the right size to fit in her mouth. She tasted the spicy chorizo first, and then the combination of jalapeños, onions, and potatoes her mom blended brought her appetite back to life. She cleaned her plate.

Krystal worked at her easel, lost in thought. She jumped when her mom called down the stairs.

"Phone is for you, Krystal!" Then in a lower voice, she said, "It's a boy."

Krystal's heart flipped in her chest. She hadn't even heard the phone ring, but that wasn't unusual. When she was working on her art, the rest of the world might as well not exist. She met her mom at the top of the stairs to get the phone.

Brandon called. True to his word, he called. They talked about everything. His mom thought they might have a buyer for their house. More about her art. His baseball. Family. Their French teacher. Em.

Two hours later, they said goodbye and hung up. Leaning back on her pillows, she thought she might float up to the ceiling. Had someone told her two weeks ago she'd meet a super cute guy at her school who would like her…she probably would have punched them for saying something so outlandish.

The phone beeped next to her. Krystal picked it up and saw the low-battery light blinking. Running the phone back up to the kitchen to place it on the charger, she realized how quiet the house was.

The clock on the wall showed it was well after nine, so she knew Rosie and Jaime had already been ushered off to bed. Flashes of light from the TV told her someone was in the living room. She recognized the scene from the movie *Ladder 49*. Well, that was a telltale sign of who belonged to the feet extending from the rocker. How could Esme enjoy watching it with the volume turned so far down?

"Does Mom know you're still in here?" Krystal asked.

Esme started at the voice behind her and looked a little guilty.

"Yeah, I was feeding Lucy." Sure enough, the box with the newspaper was off to the side of the recliner, and the cat that had been snuggled down was now mewing and trying to walk up Esme's shirt towards her shoulder.

"Lucy? I thought it was a boy?" Krystal asked with raised eyebrows.

"Eli says it's a girl."

Eli? When did the Man gain nickname status with her little sister? Krystal rolled her eyes.

"Shouldn't you be going to bed?"

"I will when this is over," Esme said in a matter-of-fact tone. Her expression warned…don't even think about trying to get bossy.

"Come down to my room for a minute when your movie is over," Krystal said and walked away. She could imagine the confusion Esme must be feeling right now and sighed. *Big sister doesn't talk to you in forever, and now she tells you to come to her room,* she mused. She wouldn't blame Esme for ignoring her completely.

Ten minutes later, Krystal could hear the soft footsteps on the stairs and inwardly smiled. Esme's curiosity must have gotten the best of her, because that movie wasn't even to the halfway point when she was up there.

Standing in the doorway, Esme held Lucy with one hand, the wiggly kitten endlessly aimed for the shelter by her neck and under her hair.

"Knock knock," Esme said and waited to be invited.

That made Krystal sad. What little sister ever needed an invitation? She wasn't exactly thrilled about how clear some of the broken things were becoming, like the relationship with her siblings. But she longed to make amends.

Waving her in, Krystal could see Esme's eyes taking in the room around her.

"I like your lights," she said.

Krystal figured her siblings had at least snuck down to her room from time to time, but apparently Esme hadn't. Remorse poked at her again.

"Thanks," Krystal said. "I have something for you and I want you to see it, even though it's not finished yet." Esme's right eyebrow went up.

Though it was ridiculous, she felt a bit awkward. It had been ages since she'd spent any kind of time with anyone in her family.

Krystal walked over to the easel and turned the drawing around that she had traded so much sleep for, as she'd worked late into the night. She watched as Esme's eyes turned into the size of a half-dollar and her mouth went into an O.

"It's not done yet. I just started on it late last night," she explained. "It'll be done in another day or so."

Esme gasped. "Thank you, Krystal. I love it! I totally love it." Esme used her cat-free arm to wrap around Krystal's neck. In seconds, the lopsided embrace undid miles of the distance Krystal had created over the past months.

"I'm glad you like it." Krystal smiled, watching as pure delight played over Esme's face. Her own heart swelled.

The drawing, once again a lady firefighter, with her face tilted upwards to the smoke-filled sky stood courageously. Only a little imagination was needed to see that she could be surveying a burning building or her paramount decision at the scene of a blaze. Her shoulders were back, and her hair was tied in a messy knot at the base of her helmet.

The finest thing about this new drawing was the firefighter was Esme. It wasn't hard to capture her nearly twelve-year-old sister's profile. Pensive and dreamy was a natural place for Esme, who was awestruck with this gift.

Esme needed to get some sleep. It was way past her usual bedtime, so after she bid Esme and Lucy goodnight and gladly accepted another hug, Krystal crawled into bed too.

Exhausted, her last thought before drifting off was she should add Lucy to the drawing, maybe on Esme's shoulder. It would be a tribute to Lucky too.

The rest of the school week went by in a flash. Eager to see Brandon each day, she didn't consider skipping even once. Any doubts Brandon had about Em knowing his secret had dissipated. Em had been included in his circle of trust.

Things had been going quite well for Krystal until all the teachers began talking about finals. An alarm sounded in her head. The fact was that school was over in a month, and her grades were wrecked. The last thing she wanted was to repeat her freshman year. But there was no way to turn things around this close to the end of the school year. Her best friend would move ahead without her and what would Brandon think about her failure? Would a junior even be interested in a repeat freshman? She inwardly cringed.

"Why don't you talk to all your teachers?" Em suggested. "Maybe they'll work with you. Let you make up some of the past homework or do some extra credit."

"I don't know, Em. They'd all want to know why I'm so interested in trying now. They would think I'm trying to scam them, or would expect me to tell them my life story. I shouldn't have to explain all of that."

"Krystal," Em said authoritatively, "I know what you've been through is rough. But it's not uncommon. You don't have to give them all the details, but if you want help, you do owe them something. Honestly, you don't have anything to be embarrassed about."

"You don't think it's embarrassing that my mom cheated on my dad, had a kid with the guy she cheated with, and moved us all in with him? Not that you'd have anything in your life to compare that to," Krystal snapped. Instantly, Krystal felt remorseful. The hurt look on Em's face made Krystal feel like pooh on the bottom of a shoe. "I'm sorry, Em."

"It's okay. I'll see you on Monday." Em forced a smile.

Krystal rested her chin in her palm. Em had never once said or done anything to minimize Krystal's feelings so for her to do that to Em was downright mean. And Em was right. If she wanted to try to finish the year with anything better than a bunch of D's and F's, she was going to have to bring something to the table.

Before dinner that night, Krystal called Em and apologized again. Her bestie being the forgiving person she was told her she wasn't mad at her, she loved her and then told her to quit acting like a butt. Fair enough.

Resolving to speak with her teachers on Monday, she put it out of her mind. She sought Jaime out in his room after dinner and asked him to read to her for about fifteen minutes. Afterward, she told him about a skateboarding park Brandon had mentioned upon learning of Jaime's love of the sport during one of their long talks. It was called the Mouse Trap, and while it wasn't within walking distance, maybe there was a way Jaime could go every now and then.

Rosie, who had been eavesdropping right outside the door, was ready for Krystal's spotlight to shift her direction.

"Do you want to hear me read?" Rosie asked as she headed straight for Krystal and landed in her lap, knocking the wind out of her.

"Sure," Krystal wheezed, trying to get her breath back.

Krystal was astonished by Rosie and Jaime's instant acceptance of her sudden involvement in their day. How did they forgive so easily?

While she was judging them for not caring about all the changes, they were more affected than she knew. However, they were enjoying the positive things life was delivering to them. It didn't mean they weren't hurt by it all, they just weren't harboring anger the way she was. They deserved more credit than what she'd given.

She thought about Jaime and his problem with reading and writing and wondered if it had something to do with not seeing their dad as much. Jaime had always devoured his father's attention and approval, and now he was limited to one day a week to soak it in.

Rosie, on the other hand, had been in more trouble at school recently. Maybe it wasn't unusual for her to needle Jaime, but it was unusual for her to be in trouble for hitting at school.

Krystal silently sighed. Had she really been so blind?

Rosie started to reach for the book Jaime had been reading when he snatched it from within her grasp.

"You can't read mine," he snapped.

"I didn't want to read your stupid book anyway," she retorted.

"Rosie, you really have to stop using that word," Krystal heard herself saying. "Let's go find one of your books in your room." Leaving the room, she turned to Jaime. "Aunt Maria is going to be so happy this Sunday when she hears how well you're doing." His ears turned a little pink at the compliment. *I know the feeling, little brother.*

Inside Rosie and Esme's room, Krystal saw the picture she drew for Esme in the place where the other had been. Esme was stretched across her bed stomach down and feet up in the air, crossed at the ankles, working on what looked to be a math assignment. She promised herself she would spend all her evening time working on her own homework. About ten minutes into the reading of a Ramona Quimby book, Krystal heard her mom calling her name.

She went into the kitchen where her mom was mixing ingredients in a bowl. Krystal surveyed the kitchen—flour, sugar, broken eggshells, oil, and baking soda were strewn about the counter. She knew there would be cake tonight. *Yum*, she thought, licking her lips.

"Yeah?" she asked.

"I need you to call your father and let him know Rosie won't be there this Sunday. She wants to go to her friend's birthday party."

Krystal stiffened. Two seconds. That's all the time it took for her mom to ruin everything. Why did she think her mom would try harder since she was trying harder? That obviously wasn't the case. If she had to get used to all the changes, then shouldn't her parents have to too?

"I don't want to call him for that. He's going to be upset if Rosie doesn't go. Why don't you call?"

"Look, Krystal. It's how things are right now. Please do as I ask and call." Her mother stopped mixing and looked right at her. "Eliseo has taken Sofia with him to the store; it's better to do the phone calls when he is not here. Having you make the call is more comfortable for me. This extra drama is unnecessary."

"Drama? Being your mediator is stupid!" Realizing she just used the word she told Rosie not to, she glanced at the door to make sure her little sister wasn't listening. "Why don't you try to make things easier for me for once?" Krystal hissed, trying to keep her voice down.

Without waiting for an answer, she snatched the phone out of the holder and dialed her dad's number. Sure enough, he wasn't pleased. His responses didn't surprise her, they consisted of, 'I only get to see my kids once a week,' and 'why did she tell Rosie she could go….'

Blah, blah, blah is what Krystal heard. Next, he asked, "What time is the party?" Then said he had plans for them all but they could wait until the next Sunday and he could pick Rosie up from the party." Come to find out, the party was at two in the afternoon. Two extra phone calls later, it was decided that Rosie would go to her dad's as normal and just take her overnight bag and the birthday gift with her. Roberto now had the address to the party where he and the kids would drop her off. She would stay the night with her friend and go to school with her the next morning.

Krystal was left weary and angry, and she was tired of feeling that way. She went down to her room and shut the door. Outrage was lodged in her throat. She wanted to scream but couldn't. Instead, she sat down on the edge of her bed and cradled her head in her hands, placing her palms over her eyes.

The urge to cut hit her like a Mack truck. She started shaking her head from side to side, saying no. For the first time, something inside her warred with the desire to cut. It was like having an angel and devil on her shoulders, except the fight was deep inside.

Her need to cut was overwhelming, but there was something else. A sudden pull told her it was wrong, told her she shouldn't and should stop forever. She thought of her two sisters and Jaime. How would she feel if they cut? The thought made her sick.

With her palms still over her eyes, she tangled her fingers in her hair, pulling until it hurt. Her tears refused to be impeded; they ran over the sides of her hands and down her arm.

Pulling back her sleeves, she looked at her arms. It might have looked like a cat attack, but her cuts were neatly placed and most all of them were approximately the same length, like a prisoner marking time.

The wounds were more healed than she had seen in a long time. All of the cuts were completely closed. The oldest ones were a white color now.

The fierceness of the urges had decreased some, for tonight anyway. She'd cut less in the last couple of weeks.

When she did do it, she chose her thighs or stomach now. The last one on her arm was still red and inflamed, but it had scabbed over completely. Tons of anti-itch cream had helped keep her from scratching herself raw during the healing process.

She just wanted her arms to heal now…to find whatever her new normal was and get her life on track. Recently, she felt like she had more things to look forward to. As stupid as it might seem, she wanted to be able to wear something prettier. Her hoodies were getting way too warm for the weather, and she only had so many long-sleeved t-shirts.

Sadness took complete control, and she lifted her head from her hands. Who was she kidding? Her arms would never be normal. There'd always be a memorial of her pain reminding her forever of what she'd done to her body.

Rising, she walked over to her dresser. She hated herself for being weak. Maybe holding her jagged heart would be enough. Opening her book, it was laying there, her faithful friend and dreadful enemy; it knew secrets no one else in the entire world would even believe were possible.

She brushed her fingers over it, and then picked it up. Just a little cut, she told herself, just enough to help me calm down. Besides, it was her body, anyway. If this was what made her feel better, why should she deny herself the relief?

Krystal turned towards her bed; a light tap sounded at her door and startled her out of her reverie. Guilt washed over her and she dropped her fragile heart back in the book and snapped it shut. As she put it back on her dresser, she called out. "Come in." Quickly, she fixed her sleeve.

Esme stood there. Her little sister now donned in pink fuzzy pajama pants and a white sleep tee with a yawning bunny on the front. The pink in his ears was the same fuzzy material as the bottoms. Her hair was pulled into a ponytail at her nape with an oversized pink scrunchy. Lucy was curled up in the crook of one elbow.

The sight of her little sister drew out some of her shakiness. Silently, she inhaled and exhaled, mentally pushing all her problems away—for now.

Krystal smiled at the picture before her.

"Think she'll ever walk on her own?" Esme giggled, putting Lucy on the floor. Lucy started walking around Esme's feet, in and out, in a figure eight. "Well, she's got you pegged as mama," Krystal said. "At least she's smart."

Esme's eyes brightened at the compliment.

"What are you doing?" she inquired as she sat down at the foot of Krystal's bed. Having her little sister getting close again was a gift. Krystal vowed to herself that no matter what, she would not close them out again. She was their big sister, and she was going to act like it. It didn't matter if she couldn't get along with her mother—she was hanging onto them.

"Nothing important, I'm glad you came down." They talked for nearly an hour. Esme told Krystal how much she liked her pink bangs and how she would love to have some just like them. Krystal learned about the boy Esme had a crush on at school and was shocked Esme had crossed over from the 'boys are gross' phase.

Krystal took Esme's ponytail down and braided her hair. When she finished, Esme had a braid that started at each temple and met each other in the back, joining for the length of her hair. Pulling the braid and the lose hair back; Krystal bound them together with the pink scrunchy.

"Now you can sleep with your braids in and they should still look pretty good tomorrow," Krystal said.

"Too bad we don't have school tomorrow," Esme said, touching the braids and letting out a big yawn, which made Krystal yawn too. They laughed.

"Oh yeah. Well, we can do it again Sunday night," Krystal promised.

Esme tilted her head back to look up at Krystal. "Thanks," she said.

Krystal started to say no problem when she looked up and saw Lucy in a squatted position.

"Ahhhhh," was all she could get out before the little cat pooped on the floor.

Chapter II

The van arrived on time just as the lady said it would. The side door slid open, and Krystal started to step in.

"Good morning!" the driver greeted. "My name is Ralph and I will be giving you a lift today as long as you can answer me this."

The other teens had stopped talking and were grinning as they waited expectantly.

Krystal's eyes quickly scanned the interior. It was a fifteen-passenger van, and there were four other teens already in the back. One was a girl from her school who was in her art class.

"Okay," Krystal said shyly, wondering what he could possibly need to know.

"What do you call a bear without teeth?" he asked.

She laughed at the unexpected inquiry. Whatever she had been expecting, that wasn't it. The answer hit her a second later.

"A gummy bear?"

"Ding ding ding. All right! Welcome. We have four lovely knuckleheads back there so far." A good-natured uproar stirred from the teens. "Casey, Sarah, Max, and Liz."

Everyone either said hi or smiled at her. She couldn't help but smile back; their upbeat air was palpable in the van. She recognized Sarah from her art class, though they'd never spoken. But then again, before Brandon, she didn't speak to anyone besides Em.

Sarah said hi to her first and immediately complimented her art.

"You're seriously gifted! Most of us are a bit jealous. We know you're Mr. Z's favorite." Sarah smiled. "Can't blame him for getting excited about you, though. You make him look good."

Krystal was glad Sarah smiled. Otherwise, she would have wondered if animosity lurked behind those words, but there clearly wasn't any. Sarah was just being nice, and Krystal inwardly flinched that she hadn't given her a moment of time all year long.

"Thanks," Krystal said. They chatted about school as they stopped and picked up seven more teens. The van was starting to resemble a rolling can of sardines.

Ralph repeated the van-boarding question with each teen he picked up. Though she didn't talk a whole lot, she was having fun, and this was just the ride in. It made her wish she were tutoring instead so she could stay with the group. But Ralph might want to see her grades first. If he saw those, she probably wouldn't be allowed to tutor a kindergartener, much less an older kid.

The question about the bear was funnier with every stop. She learned that if the teen didn't know the answer, the rest of them were allowed to help even though Ralph had threatened them with walking to the shelter. Ralph said it was because if he had to wait for them to walk, he'd have to do their work.

At their last stop, the van was pretty rowdy, with eleven teens and Ralph all laughing it up. She recognized a few of the other kids from school. None of them acted spoiled, snobby, or stupid, which is what she'd assumed of the majority of the school. Seems like she might have been the snobby one.

Once at the shelter, she stayed with the group while Ralph led them into the tutoring room and left them to another staff member.

"I'll be back shortly. Go ahead and get any supplies you think you'll need together. Your kids will be with me when I come back." Ralph gave them a thumbs-up, and they all returned the gesture and then laughed. Krystal realized she hadn't stopped smiling since being picked up.

"I'm going to show you to your area, Krystal. We are so happy to have you here and appreciate your help," he said with a smile. "An important thing is never to walk around on your own. It's not to scare you, and we haven't had any incidents involving teens or children, but we have guests with various challenges, and we are very serious about your safety."

Krystal nodded at Ralph's more serious demeanor. She knew he didn't want her to take the rules lightly. During the stroll to the daycare, Ralph asked her questions about her family, school, and hobbies. When she answered art was a hobby, his eyebrows went up.

"I heard Sarah mention art in the van. What kind of art?" he asked.

"Well, I like to draw and paint," she answered.

"How good are you?"

Krystal could admit she was good, but she didn't ever gloat. That would be tacky. She settled for extreme modesty.

"I do pretty good."

"I doubt 'pretty good' is what has made you the teacher's favorite."

Krystal could see his wheels turning, but he didn't say anything else, and they were at their destination. He opened the door and allowed her to proceed first.

"Hey, St. Nick, I brought you an elf!" Ralph called out.

"Was that a crack at my hair?" Krystal asked, giving Ralph a sideways glance. She was teasing, but Ralph's eyes got big for a second.

"Oh no, those pink bangs are fantastic. I just have the habit of calling all of Nick's volunteers elves since he insists on looking like Santa all year round. If I were going to change my hair color, I might go with green since I'm always on the go. Haha." Ralph laughed heartily at his own joke.

"You'd have to find hair first, Ralph," Nick jabbed. "He's just jealous. His skinny self couldn't pull this look off if he tried." True to form, Nick was wearing a white t-shirt, red painter's pants, and black shoes. Krystal doubted he ever wore any other colors.

Ralph looked at Krystal and pointed his thumb at Nick.

"He keeps up the Santa look so he doesn't have to stop eating cake." Krystal's eyebrows went up. She wanted to laugh but wasn't sure if it was appropriate, so she pressed her lips together and smiled instead.

Nick laughed at her expression and patted Ralph on the back when he said he needed to get back to his kids. He turned to Krystal. "Well, I hope you stick around now that you know what it's going to be like in here."

"It's been great," she said.

"Good!" Nick said enthusiastically. "Glad you can put up with us. Let me show you around. This entire unit," he said, gesturing widely, "is an area we built on to the property. Right now, our daycare unit is a fraction of this size. With the growing numbers of guests with children, we needed a lot more room to be more convenient for our daycare volunteers." Krystal looked around as Nick continued to explain. "Currently, snacks and meals have to be prepared in the kitchen and wheeled over on a cart. That can be hard some days, especially if we are short staffed for any reason. You've seen how fast-paced dinnertime is; breakfast and lunch aren't any calmer. So we made a list stating what we would need to accomplish this mission, we shared our wishes within the community, and God came through."

Krystal's eyes darted over to Nick curiously.

"An anonymous donor provided all the funds we needed to build on this unit and buy the additional supplies. So far it's looking like there won't be much of a difference between what was given for the project and what we've spent."

Nick led her to the farthest room to the left, which adjoined the one they were passing through. On each side of the doorway, the wall had large square windows that let you see into rooms from either side. He explained this room would be for infants. As they stepped into the infant room, there were two gray-haired men putting the finishing touches on the largest changing table she'd ever seen.

"That is going to be a changing table with drawers," Nick explained when he saw her staring at it.

"It's huge," she said, not bothering to mention she knew what it was.

"Well, it will hold all sizes of diapers and any supplies you might need for changing. It has a built-in diaper disposal at the end over here," he said, while knocking on the wood. "There will be padded walls and bumpers for the area where the babies are changed. It will be structurally safe and almost impossible for a baby ever to roll off. Almost," he reiterated, "—babies are slick Lil' Boogers."

Nick put his hand on one of the men's shoulders.

"This here is Ned and the uglier one over there is Frank." Frank just grinned and rolled his eyes at the age-old introduction.

"These two can build anything they set their minds to. We are incredibly blessed by the work they do for us," Nick said seriously.

"We do it for the Lord," Ned said, nodding once.

"We'll work 'til God makes us quit," Frank laughed. Nick beamed at the two grandfather-aged men.

Krystal followed Nick into the room they'd started in. He explained this room would be for walkers to age two. There was yet another adjoining room on the other side, which would be for ages three and four. All three rooms' walls aligned perfectly.

"We have a completely separate unit for school-age children. It'll be empty during the day while school is in session, but will fill up after school and be extremely busy all summer long. Our daycares are all open year round since the parents all have very different schedules…gets pretty hairy at times," he said, wide-eyed as if the thought scared him.

Krystal smiled at his expression, but she wanted to laugh. His bushy eyebrows already looked like caterpillars over his eyes, but when he made any expression at all, it was like they were on a roller coaster ride. And Nick was very expressive.

"All three of these rooms will have different themes," he explained. "We'll be cleaning, painting, decorating, bringing in furniture, and then stocking supplies. We hope to have this all completed in the next two to three weeks."

She noticed another door off to the side of the room for the oldest kids.

"Oh, let me show you this one, I almost forgot." Nick opened the door to a brand new kitchen. It was tiny, but it had all the necessities. "The only thing being wheeled over on carts will be the supplies to keep it stocked," he said enthusiastically.

"Nick," a female voice called from the main room.

"That would be Jane," Nick said as he turned in the direction of the voice. "She and her husband will be helping as much as they can. It's a big job, but with the four of us, we should be able to get it done." Going back through the door between the second and third rooms, Krystal saw a young couple standing near the entrance.

"Krystal, this is Jane and Lenny," Nick introduced.

They all greeted each other with rounds of 'nice to meet you.'

Jane was a tall, slender woman in her early to mid-twenties whose hair was short and Afro-textured. Krystal thought she looked like a model with her bronze skin and huge, almond-shaped eyes; she was stunning.

Krystal's hands itched. If she'd had her sketchpad in hand, she would have just plopped down on her bottom and drawn her right then and there.

Lenny was also tall, but more skinny than slender. He looked as if he'd just stepped out of the seventies. His paisley shirt and high-waisted jeans somehow complimented his wavy ginger hair resting on his shoulders. His thick mustache might have been comical on someone else, but it fit him. Krystal would have never imagined these two individuals together had she met them separately, but they did suit each other, somehow.

"Well, let's roll up our sleeves and get to it," Nick said. Krystal knew it was just an expression, but she felt incriminated all the same.

They carried in buckets of soapy water, sponge mops, and regular sponges. Cleaning was the first order of the day. Krystal and Nick started in the baby room, and Jane and Lenny started with the older kids' room. They'd meet in the middle.

Ned and Frank sauntered out, bidding them a good day as the little crew of four got started.

Before Krystal started dunking sponges, she flipped up the edges of her sleeves. She could expose a little more than two inches of her wrist before she reached the first scar. She sighed.

As they worked, Nick told her some fascinating stories from his time at the shelter. She learned about all of the different hats he wore. He was officially the kitchen manager but he also conducted tours, led projects, and listened to guests, workers, or visitors when they needed to talk. He went on to explain how Ralph gave up a teaching career to work at the shelter, accepting a drastically lower salary. She also learned Jane and Lenny were once guests who met during a Sunday service in the chapel. Two very different circumstances landed them in the shelter three years before.

"Whether you're a volunteer, employee, or guest, no one who comes through those doors leaves the same. I can see that in your case, too." Nick said assuredly. "Love is God's magic."

Krystal blushed a bit. She didn't know if she would say 'love' was what attracted her to this place.

Krystal mentally sifted through all the people she had met in her short time volunteering. She stopped when she got to Walt and Peety. They certainly made her smile. She asked Nick about them.

"Well, like I said before, he's another one of our 'God's magic' stories," Nick said. "You should ask him to tell you. It's a long one."

He looked up and caught a fleeting expression of doubt in Krystal's eyes.

"Do you believe in God?" he asked in an inquisitive tone. There was no accusation in his voice at all. He was just genuinely interested in what she thought.

"Yes. I don't know. I mean yes, I believe there is a God. I don't think we got here because matter and anti-matter kissed each other."

Nick's bushy caterpillar brows crawled all the way up his forehead. "That didn't sound like a fourteen-year-old at all." He guffawed and slapped his knee. Krystal relaxed at his demeanor. Knowing she wasn't being judged put her at ease. Nick wasn't going to scold her for her thoughts, and besides, she wanted to talk about it.

"I guess I just don't get all the magic talk," she said simply. "All you see every day are people without homes and food. But at the same time you are always smiling and talking about how magical God is. Sorry, it doesn't make sense. I don't get how God can be about love when so many bad things happen, and so many people are hurting."

They had both stopped working while she was talking. Nick grabbed the stools Ned and Frank had been using and offered one to Krystal.

"Have a seat, Krystal. If you don't mind," he said. She did. Quickly and silently. She was eager to hear his response now that she finally got to verbalize her thoughts.

"Here is the best answer I have to that question. Can God make everything and everyone perfect?" he asked theoretically. "Of course God can. But imagine that world, Krystal. Imagine the world where nothing is ever wrong." Krystal did. "What do you think would happen?" he asked her.

"Nothing," she answered. "It would all be okay. People wouldn't be hungry. Everyone would have a home. Families would stay together." She paused and then almost whispered, 'just like they should.'

Nick looked at her. Krystal felt like he could see her very soul.

"Fair enough," he replied.

"But think about it this way. God is love…loves us and wants our love in return. We weren't made as robots, right?" She nodded agreement. "Right," he said again and nodded for emphasis. Krystal noticed Nick's expressive nature meant he used his hands a lot when he talked. "We are given free will to choose our paths and make our own decisions. Sometimes we make good decisions." His hands went up. "And sometimes, bad ones." His hands went down. "Without the negative things that happen to us, we would never appreciate all the good. The hard things in life help make us who we are. If everything were easy, we wouldn't value or cherish anything, because to us, it would be an entitlement. God doesn't promise us life will be easy, but God does promise us it will be worth it." Nick paused. "Make sense?"

Krystal nodded again. She didn't like that it made sense, but she understood perfectly.

"Stick with this place and I promise you'll start seeing God's magic," Nick said. "You'll see the stories of where people came from, how they found their purpose, and how they arrived."

"Arrived?" she asked.

Nick's shoulders shook with his chuckle, then he shrugged.

"I like to say arrived instead of 'ended up.' Ended up has a ring of finality and a negative connotation. But arrived!" He emphasized with flair, whisking his index finger into the air, "Well, that's something else. Arrived is a realization that you've come to a turning point, your knowledge base has been increased, and there's always room to grow," he ended, with a hushed tone.

If Krystal were honest, she liked listening to Nick talk. How she felt about what he was saying was yet to be determined. It made sense, to a degree. She wouldn't tell him the words he spoke moved her. They made her heart beat faster and made her mind race with wonder. It was too much to sort out immediately.

"Will you make a deal with me, Krystal?" he asked.

"What deal?"

"Each night, before you go to bed, you say one prayer; even if you don't feel like it or it makes you feel funny. Write it out if you want to." Nick whisked his finger in the air. "Whatever works best for you…."

"Okay," she agreed.

"Well, okay then," Nick said. "I thought I was going to have more trouble than that." He chuckled again.

He's so…happy. It was contagious. "We should probably get back to work; Jane and Lenny probably think we're being lazy."

Krystal wouldn't admit the only time she had spoken to God in the last year had been out of anger. Memories of her family going to Sunday services ran through her mind. Her mom used talk about God and Jesus a lot. They used to say grace before dinner, and their mom would pray with them at nighttime before bed when they were younger.

When had it all stopped? She couldn't say, but she remembered one night before cutting she looked up and told God—If you're there, really there, you'll fix this. But days and weeks turned into months and nothing happened. It wasn't going to happen.

Nick sent a sideways glance in Krystal's direction.

"You still okay?"

"Yep."

Nick squinted. It was like he was deciding if he believed her. Is he a mind reader, too? "Just thinking about what you said," she tacked on for good measure. It was the truth, after all. Nick didn't persist and she was glad he left it alone.

Once they finished, Jane and Lenny said their goodbyes for the day and Nick walked Krystal over to the room where the others were getting ready to leave.

"Do you have a hard time making so many friends here and then seeing them go?" she asked, thinking about some of the stories of past guests he told her while they were working.

"Sometimes," Nick answered. "You've probably heard the poem, The Wind?" She shook her head no. "Do you like poetry?" he asked.

"Sometimes." She didn't like the sappy love stuff or the kind written in riddles. But she'd read some cool poetry.

"Well, you should read that poem. It beautifully expresses the relationship of people passing through each other's lives. But to answer your question, it's bitter sweet. This place," Nick swept his hand out before him and looked at his surroundings. " It was never meant for permanence; it's a rest stop. Most people are at their lowest low when they walk through those doors for the first time, and I have the beautiful job of helping to lift them back up. Others, like Jane and Lenny, I don't have to miss because they come back to serve as many others have."

The ride home wasn't quite as rowdy as the first. All the teen's tummies were rumbling and Ralph made it worse by talking in depth about delicious food he could think of.

"You're killing me," Max cried, with one hand on his stomach. "That's just pure evil."

"I can't help it," Ralph said, feigning innocence. "You know how it is when your mom or grandma bakes brownies. The smell floats through the house and you can't wait til they're done so you can eat one. You take them out of the oven and can't bear to give them time to cool. You just sink your teeth into that warm, sweet chocolate. It melts right in your mouth, I tell ya!"

Everyone groaned.

"Stop acting like you're suffering," Ralph said into the rearview. Amusement lit his eyes as he held up a brownie and took a bite. "Knuckleheads."

For the rest of her Saturday, Krystal spent time with her siblings, all except Sofia. Jaime read to her for a solid thirty minutes; her mind was wandering most of that time, but she helped him with the harder words right on cue, so he never noticed. She praised his progress and asked him if the writing felt a little easier yet? He shrugged, and she told him it would take a little time and to not get discouraged.

Rosie, who'd been pecking around waiting for her turn, saw her opportunity, grabbed Krystal's hand and pulled her into her bedroom. "I want to play Mary had a little lamb for you," she said. She pulled a long pouch from under her bed that held her school issued recorder.

Uh oh, Krystal thought, this is going to be interesting. It was. Rosie blew out her rendition of Mary had a little lamb and by the seventh note, Krystal had to force herself not to squint her eyes or cover her ears. Dutifully, she clapped her hands when it was over and refrained from telling her to practice more. She didn't see Rosie becoming a musician, so why encourage her?

"That sucked!" Jaime taunted, as he stuck his head in her room, then ran.

"Shut up, Jaime!" Rosie yelled, putting her recorder down to give chase. Krystal threw her hands up. She was going to intervene until she heard her mother's raised voice in the other room.

"Rosie! Apologize to your brother for punching him," Josefina scolded from the other room. Krystal shook her head and went down to her room.

Taking out a fresh notebook, she settled onto her bed. She'd made Nick a promise and she intended to keep it. Although she wasn't ready to admit it, something deep down inside her wanted to talk to God.

Dear God,

I'm writing because I promised Nick I would. You probably know that already. I'm not exactly sure of what I should be saying. Can't really say I know you are listening…or reading, but I'm going to pretend you are. Don't most people talk to you when they want or need something? Well, I'm pretty sure you can't give me what I want so I won't bother asking again.

Nick thinks you're so full of magic. He's kind of nutty, but I really like him a lot. He's really cool about stuff. Everything he does is for you. He even gives you the credit for the good things he does. I don't get it…. But he would be a cool grandfather to have. I've never met my grandparents, only one of them is still alive, and I've only spoken to her on the phone. If what Nick said is true about you being magic, let me see it.
—Krystal

At the shelter, Nick's shift was over. He thought about his talk with Krystal that morning. It was obvious she was a pro at hiding her feelings. He wished he could say just one thing that would convince her of how much God loved her. But he knew he was on God's time, not his own. If he said too much, too quickly, he'd likely have her running for the hills. It was her journey to work through, and he couldn't stand in the way of that.

He walked into the chapel and stood there for a moment; he couldn't remember the last time he had seen it empty. There was almost always someone in here, even if there was no church service or bible study happening. He knew he didn't need a special room or building in order to pray, but since it seemed to be empty just for him, he'd put it to use. He laid his jacket over a chair in the back and walked up the aisle to one of the benches near the altar, and kneeled down.

"Lord," he spoke aloud, "Thank you for every single thing today, for every blessing you've given to all those who have ever walked these halls. I'm so thankful for every opportunity to show others my love for you. Guide my steps every day. Help others to see you working in me. Search my heart and remove anything that doesn't belong. Use me, Lord, to reach Krystal's young heart. Help her to know you, so that she'll love you too. In Jesus's name, Amen."

When Nick walked out of the chapel, he saw Ralph speaking to one of the guests. Ralph held up his index finger, signaling Nick to wait.

"Thanks for waiting, ol' timer," Ralph said, as he strode over.

"Ha! No problem. I always have time for a friend, even the wrinkly ones. What's happening?"

"Nothing much. Just wanted to talk to you about Krystal real quick." Nick's eyebrow went up. The young lady seemed to have made an impression on everyone. "Did you know she's into art?" Ralph asked.

Feeling a little guilty, Nick shook his head. Now that he thought about it, they didn't really talk about her much at all. Maybe she'd done that on purpose. She's pretty slick if that was the case, but then again, he knew it wasn't hard to keep him talking.

"Well," Ralph continued, "you and I talked about several options for the walls in the daycare unit, but I think you should let Krystal paint them. It may take a week or two longer than using basic stencils or stick-on art, but I bet she'd enjoy it. It just feels like the right thing to do," he said, pointing at his heart.

Nick understood the message behind what Ralph was saying.

"Perfect! Ralph, that's perfect! God's already working." God was always several steps ahead of him, and he preferred it that way. The timing of this project was perfect for someone with artistic abilities. He and Ralph decided they'd get together the next day to hash out the details.

Chapter 12

Sitting on her dad's couch the next day, Krystal had a big smile on her face. In her hands was the phone her dad had finally bought her. To top it off, he'd purchased an iPhone, just like Em's.

She'd asked if she could stay behind while the others took Rosie to her friend's house and he'd said okay since they were coming back shortly.

Krystal programmed in the few numbers she ever had cause to dial—Brandon's and Em's mainly, then she texted Brandon her new number. Seconds later, her phone rang.

Sliding the bar to answer the call, she laughed into the phone.

"Hi! You're my first caller ever on my new phone."

"Do I get a prize for that?"

"Sure, I'll draw you a gold star," she said, then giggled.

"I tried to call you yesterday, but your mom said you were working?"

"Oh yeah, I didn't tell you. Nick asked me to help out at the shelter. I'm helping them get the new daycare ready."

"That's cool. Speaking of the shelter…that is one of the things I wanted to tell you yesterday. Mom sold the house so we are moving out next weekend. Thankfully, you won't be seeing me there anymore."

"That's such good news! Well, mostly right? I know you'll be sad to leave your house." He was quiet for a moment. "Are you okay?"

"Yeah—and it is good news, it might help being in a new place. We'll see." He stopped talking for a second, then abruptly said, "Anyway, the real reason I called you yesterday was to ask you something."

"Ask me what?" His voice had changed. He sounded weird and that made her nervous.

"Well, I know Emily has the best friend status already." Krystal went from nervous to high alert. She thought she knew where he was going with this, and her heart was pounding.

"But…" he continued before pausing again.

But what? She wanted to shout at him, but didn't. Her heart was about to beat its way out of her chest!

"I was thinking I could settle for boyfriend status if you're okay with that."

Excitement washed over her. Her body was tingling from the crown of her head to her toes. And boy was she warm. *Whew! I can't get a fever that fast, can I?* She put a hand on her head. Why did it feel like someone was using her stomach to make popcorn?

Krystal opened her mouth, but nothing came out. Nada. Zip. Nothing!

Did he really just ask her to be his girlfriend? She wanted to shout YES, but it was stuck down in her throat somewhere. The silence must have given Brandon doubts about her answer.

"Um, either way, you're my best friend even if you don't want to be my girlfriend." A long pause and then, "Hello?" she heard him say. "Are you there?"

"I-I-" she stuttered, "uh-" *Speak!* she silently screamed. But she couldn't speak, so she hit the end button on her phone.

She went down on her side like a lumberjack just yelled, TIMBER! Squealing first, then laughing, she found her voice. Brandon wanted to be her boyfriend, and he considered her his best friend!

Realization of what she had done dawned on her, or rather, popped her upside the head. *Oh my gosh! I just hung up on him!* Sitting up, she put her hand on her forehead and gasped. "I am an idiot!"

Fumbling through her phone, she somehow managed to call him back.

"Hello," he answered unsurely.

"That would be awesome," she said, elated, all her senses back. Brandon laughed.

"I'm glad," he said, sounding relieved. "You had me worried when you hung up on me."

"I'm sorry! I'm just so surprised."

"Surprised? We've been hanging out as much as possible and talking on the phone for hours. Why would you be surprised?"

"Well—no, nothing, it's nothing." She didn't quite mean for the truth to try to slip out.

"No, tell me."

"You just seem like the type of guy who might like a girl like Em. I mean…I just don't seem like your type. Not that I'm saying you should like Em like that…ugh, I'm so bad at this!" Her face was on fire, and all she was doing was fanning the flames. "What I mean is—"

"You're just the right girl for me," he interrupted. "Just the way you are. Oh, and don't think I'm chicken. I would have asked you in person, but I never really get to talk to you alone except for a minute here and there. Soon as we get moved, we should go to the movies."

"Yes, we should," she said.

Later that night, she wrote:

Dear God,

I think this writing thing might be easier for me if I make it more like a diary but directed at you. So here it goes. I'm exceptionally happy today. Not just because I got a new phone, but also because Brandon asked me to be his girlfriend.

I'm feeling better too, even before Brandon asked me. Is it weird that sometimes I don't want to feel better? Sometimes I feel guilty if I feel too happy. I start thinking about my dad and how he spends so much time alone. How Lucky is by himself all day while dad is at work and how my family will never be whole again. Anyway, it's just not fair. I'm going to stop for now because I am ruining my own good mood and I'm trying to change how I handle my feelings. Goodnight.

—Krystal

Chapter 13

Monday was a whirlwind for Krystal. For the first time, Brandon had taken her hand as they walked. Proudly, she wore the blush that spread through her the moment their fingers touched.

Though it would be challenging, she was excited about the future. She had to make a huge difference in the last three and a half weeks of school.

In order to pass her classes, and be a sophomore with Em, she'd have to work herself to death. Failing wasn't an option.

She regretted how low her grades were, but she knew she wouldn't let that happen ever again. Her main goal was to pass everything and improve as much as she could in the short time that was left.

That morning, she had arrived early and found the counselor assigned to her. Ms. Lightly had advised her to speak with all her teachers between today and tomorrow and report back to her. Together they would work out a plan that would hopefully keep Krystal from failing any classes her freshman year.

At the end of the first day, Krystal was mind blown at how responsive her teachers were to her. They were clearly thrilled she'd taken an interest in her grades, and while it wouldn't be easy, they were more than willing to work with her. She'd been given extra credit assignments and chances to turn in old homework for full credit.

After school, Em went home to get everything she needed to spend the night at Krystal's house. Being genuinely excited for the changes she saw in her best friend, she was going to do everything she could think of to help her get through the last leg of the school year.

It hadn't escaped Em's notice Krystal was trying to wear hoodies a little less since Brandon came into the picture. The weather had been beautiful this last week. The temps had never dipped below 70 degrees during the day, and the few times she saw Krystal actually take her hoodie off, she was wearing a long-sleeve shirt underneath. She had to be burning up, Em thought. But whenever she made a comment, Krystal either shrugged it off or changed the subject.

Em started sifting through some of her clothes. She giggled to herself knowing Krystal would threaten to punch her if she tried to give her anything too girly. She hoped Krystal wouldn't get too upset by her giving her anything, period. If Krystal's family was struggling financially, her friend might be offended and see it as a donation.

She focused on tops that would go well with skinny jeans. And chucks—she sighed at Krystal's lack of fashion sense.

Em had a pair of chucks too, but for goodness sakes, would it kill her bestie to mix it up a little bit? She found a few stylish tees and a couple of blouses that would pair well with jeans and put them in a bag.

"Ready to go?" Sharon asked.

"Yep," Em said, flashing a big smile at her mom.

Her arrival couldn't have had better timing. She was famished, and Krystal's mom was almost done with dinner; it smelled amazing.

She'd only been to Krystal's house a few times with her parents to pick Krystal up or drop her off. Krystal had stayed the night at her house a few times, but was always reluctant to do so, which Em never understood. It was almost like Krystal didn't want to be anywhere but home even though she said she hated being there too. *Oh well,* Em shrugged off the thought, *things are getting better, and that's what's important now.*

Things were certainly different here than at home, Em thought. Her house was calm the vast majority of the time, unless Zach had a friend over.

Krystal's house was a constant whirlwind of activity. Krystal's mom was cooking, directing, and chatting all at the same time while her boyfriend was tending to the baby. Em couldn't remember his name. Had Krystal ever mentioned it?

Esme was walking around with a kitten up on her shoulders. Josefina told her to put it down and go wash her hands. Jaime was asking his mom to play the game and huffing when he was told no. Rosie looked up at her.

"Want to come see my room?" she asked.

"She doesn't want to see your room, Rosie," Krystal said in her usual monotone voice.

"Of course I do," Em said, throwing Krystal a look that said—don't make me the bad guy. "How about right after dinner?" She asked looking down into Rosie's eager little face. Rosie nodded and smiled in agreement.

"All right, it's ready," announced Josefina. "Sit down, everyone." Mostly meaning the younger ones.

"We're going to eat in my room," Krystal said. Rosie looked disappointed she wouldn't get to have Em's full attention for the duration of the meal.

"Okay, you two go ahead and fix your plates first."

Krystal and Em each grabbed two homemade tortillas off the top of the stack and then scooped carnitas and grilled veggies into them. Em's mouth was watering. She didn't really know what the side dish was other than recognizing corn and black beans. It was mixed with a creamy sauce and contained finely diced bits of something green. *Maybe bell peppers,* she thought.

"Whoa!" Em exclaimed as she looked around Krystal's room. "You get all this to yourself?"

"Yep."

"This is freaking amazing!" Em twirled around. "You are so lucky!"

"Your room is just as cool. It's just extra princessy," Krystal snickered.

"Whatever! Because I am a princess," Em declared, tossing her hair dramatically, then snickered and said, "Totally joking."

"No, you're not." They both laughed.

Ten minutes later Krystal and Em both had tears streaming down their faces, but for two very different reasons. Krystal was laughing so hard she snorted. Em was fanning her face with her tongue hanging out in between sips of the milk Krystal had so gallantly retrieved for her when water just wasn't doing the trick.

"Them peppers is hot!" Em breathed, quoting Shaggy from Scooby Doo. "Whew! My body is a thousand degrees Fahrenheit!" What she thought were bell peppers were actually hot serranos.

"Wimp."

"I guess," Em replied with one last tongue wag, wiping her nose for what seemed like the hundredth time. Her stomach hurt from eating and then laughing so hard.

"What do you want to do first?" she asked.

"Probably French," Em panted.

"Do you girls want ice cream?" Josefina's voice carried down the staircase.

"Yes!" Em shrieked and shot up off the bed and made a beeline for the stairs, not even bothering to wait for Krystal.

"I've never seen you move so fast," Krystal said when she reached the top of the stairs. Krystal was holding her side.

Josefina looked at both girls' red-rimmed eyes and just smiled. Em smiled back even bigger when Josefina broke out the fudge, whipped cream, and sprinkles.

The girls ate their ice cream upstairs with everyone else, and afterward Em took her obligatory tour of Rosie's room. Recognizing Krystal's work on Esme's side of the room, she stared at the girl firefighter that was obviously an older Esme. Her friend's skill never ceased to put her in awe.

Back in Krystal's room, the girls dutifully spent the rest of the evening on homework and studying, only stopping once for a few minutes when Brandon called.

When they finished, Krystal's brain was on overload. French was going to be the hardest class to recover in, but she resolved to do her best. Her English homework would be time consuming, but not nearly as difficult. Mr. Hughes had given her an entire list of work she'd missed that semester and had the option of completing. She highlighted three that were worth the most points and decided she'd start with those.

Krystal and Em worked together to complete outlines for three papers. Two of the papers were from earlier in the semester. The third, a current assignment, was a two-page paper focusing on a current event. Krystal was eager to write an article about being homeless in America.

Because they were easy assignments, she completed three short essays. They weren't worth as much, but she figured the points would add up fast. She submitted those by email.

"Oh! Hey, I almost forgot," Em said as she rose and stretched out the aches from sitting in the same position for so long. "Now don't go getting cranky on me, but I brought you something." She walked over to her pink duffle bag and started pulling clothes out.

Immediately, Krystal knew Em had brought clothes for her. Her tear ducts activated. Scared she would cry any minute, she swallowed hard. She couldn't wear them...any of them. Every single one had sleeves above the elbow. Why was Em bringing these to her, anyway? She hadn't known her before she started at Topeka High, never knew how she used to dress. All Em knew was the hoodie and jeans Krystal.

This is why she didn't make it a habit to stay the night at Em's. Now she regretted letting her come here. She had one secret no one else in the world knew and it had to stay that way. No one could ever know.

At that very moment, a thought, or maybe it was a voice, resonated in Krystal's head. It said, 'I know.' Krystal gasped. It was so strong and she knew it wasn't coming from her. Then again more softly, 'I know.'

"What's wrong?" Em asked, looking wounded. Krystal was reeling. She heard that message loud and clear and looked around. It wasn't really a voice—it was just there, in her head. But it was so clear it might as well have been spoken aloud.

What did that mean? '*I know.*' Was it God telling her that her secret wasn't a secret? What else could it be? She saw Em eyeing her warily and shook it off.

Krystal sighed and turned to her friend. "Look, Em…. Thanks, but those aren't my thing," she lied. They actually were her thing—exactly her kind of thing. Pretty without being all frilly, something that would look nice without a lot of work.

Both Krystal and Em felt defeated. Krystal wanted a fresh start, but that wasn't going to happen. These scars would never go away, and they would probably take all summer for all of them to heal to white and be a little less noticeable.

Krystal knew she could never completely expose her arms. There would always be someone who would notice. All of the happy she had been experiencing washed down the drain in her ugly concrete bathroom.

Forget it, she told herself. *Forget it all. Forget Em and Brandon. Forget the shelter and Nick. Forget my family.*

'Never forget.' There it was again! Krystal looked around and then wondered why she did. It wasn't anything audible. She knew it was coming from within somehow. Maybe she'd finally gone crazy? It made her feel better to consider it, the voice, the non-voice, was God because that would mean she wasn't loony.

"What's wrong with you?" Em sulked. "You look like a scared rabbit." Shoving the shirts back in her bag, she said, "I should have known you wouldn't take them, anyway. I'm going to go change."

While Em changed behind the pulled curtain in the cement fortress, Krystal moved fast and put on a long-sleeve, white t-shirt with sweatpants. She was already sitting on the bed when Em slid the curtain back.

Em eyed her warily.

"I feel like I'm missing something, K." Krystal's heart froze, wondering if her friend had figured her out. But then Em said, "You can't wear hoodies all spring and summer long. The weather's been warm and you have to be sweating in those hoodies. Frankly, that's kinda gross."

"I just don't wear stuff like that, Em." Krystal sounded exhausted.

"Are you just too proud to take them? Is your family having money problems? You can tell me," Em pushed.

"No, we're not," Krystal snapped. "My family has plenty of problems, but that doesn't seem to be one of them." Forcing herself to calm down, she spoke softer and tried to change the direction. "Don't go having your feelings hurt over it and all. I appreciate the thought, really I do. You've always been the nicest person I know, but I don't need your clothes. I'm tired. Can we drop this and go to sleep?"

Em's shoulders visibly slumped.

"Yes," she answered. "You suck for not taking them, though."

"Well, I'm sorry I suck," Krystal replied. She hoped making Em laugh would move them away from this topic forever.

After she was sure Em was asleep, Krystal eased back the covers and slid down the side of her bed to a sitting position. Turning on the flashlight function on her phone, she lifted the edge of the fitted sheet and eased her notebook out from between the mattress and box springs.

Dear God,

Was that you tonight? Talking in my head? Probably not, I'm probably just crazy. Either way, it freaked me out.

I wish I could just explain to Em and everyone else and stop hiding. But I can't. I will never be able to do that. They would be hurt and it would cause so much drama. It's just not worth it.

Why does everything have to be so complicated? I didn't used to feel guilty about cutting until things got a little better. Honestly, I didn't think about there ever being a day I would care what someone thought if they did find out. In some ways, it was easier to be mad all the time. I used to daydream about how my mom would react if she walked in and caught me. How it

would serve her right, and she would understand how much everything was all her fault. But now, I have to make sure she doesn't know. I really don't want to hurt her like that anymore. She's been acting like she cares more recently, and I know she really does. Except when it comes to my dad…the day I turn eighteen is the day I stop talking to my dad for her. But that's a long time away. Ugh, it really was easier to just always be mad, even though it was lonely…not as much after I met Em but still lonely. I don't know what to do.
—Krystal

She carefully put the notebook back in its hiding place and got back in bed. As she was starting to drift, there was one last word that was placed in her mind— Love. Then sleep came quickly.

Chapter 14

Em woke first and was disoriented for a moment before she realized she was at Krystal's house. Fumbling for her phone that was lying on the floor by the bed, she pushed the button on top to see the time. It was 6:59 a.m.

It was brighter in the room than she would have thought for being in the basement. Spilling in through the ground-level windows, which were directly above the bed, the light reflected in Krystal's oversized mirror. It seemed to illuminate most of the room, with the exception of the bathroom area.

Moving slowly, she pushed the covers off and sat up. Knowing she needed a lot more time to get ready than her bestie, she thought she'd better get a head start. Not everyone was willing to wear a hoodie and jeans every day…or refuse gifts, for that matter. *Okay, let's not start the day sulking,* she told herself.

As she inched off the bed, she looked at Krystal to make sure she wasn't disturbing her. Em froze. Blood drained from her face, leaving her usually rosy cheeks pale.

Krystal was lying on her side facing Em, with one arm tucked under her head and the other resting on her stomach. She slept soundly. The bend in her elbow had pulled her sleeve just far enough so that Em could see a swollen, pink rope-like mark running across her best friend's forearm. Everything became 'Krystal clear.'

Not even knowing what she was about to do, Em reached out, hooked her fingertips in the sleeve, and yanked the sleeve down almost to the elbow. She was horrified at what she saw. It looked like an animal had savagely attacked her, but Em knew better.

Krystal's hand was yanked from beneath her head, and she woke up disoriented. She looked up at Em's horrified face.

"What's wrong?" Alarmed, Krystal sat up. Her arm was hurting where Em's nails had raked her cuts, but the truth of what had happened still hadn't registered.

Following Em's eyes, she saw her exposed arm and her heart stopped beating. At least she wished it would have. Her wounds were shouting her secrets. She squeezed her eyes shut, covered her ears, and laid her head down on her knees that were now pulled up to her chest.

Never had she heard Em cuss before. Practically shouting, Em's rapid-fire questions were becoming hysterical. Realizing someone might hear Em, Krystal grew even more alarmed.

"Shhhh!" she hissed. "Stop! Stop!" Krystal said, putting her hands out between herself and Em. "I don't do it anymore, Em," she lied fiercely. She hadn't been doing it as much, but she hadn't stopped completely either.

"It doesn't look like it to me!" Em replied, wild-eyed.

"You've got to calm down. Trust me. I don't do it anymore," Krystal said in a pleading voice. Panicked, she didn't know what to do. What if Em tried to run upstairs to tell her mom? She'd have to stop her. How would she do that? Sit on her? Duct tape her mouth closed? Krystal said a silent prayer for her friend to keep her secret.

Em was standing slack-jawed with one hand on her forehead. "We need to get you help. Are you trying to kill yourself?"

"EM!" Krystal exclaimed harshly. "I'm not trying to kill myself."

Em stopped abruptly, and the girls looked at each other.

Em became eerily calm. "You know, it's so obvious now that I know. I don't see how I missed it this whole time. Oh gosh, I am so stupid," she said, shaking her head side to side.

"You're not stupid, Em. There was no way for you to know. I didn't want you to know." They stood staring at each other in silence. Em's tears returned and were rolling down her cheeks. A shrill blast of sound caused both of them to jump. Krystal's alarm sounded. It was 7:15 a.m.

"Let's get ready for school and I'll explain everything. I promise," Krystal beseeched her friend. "C'mon, we have to leave in twenty-five minutes to get to class on time and I can't be late, not anymore." Hoping Em would let things go until they were out of the house, she moved to get her clothes together.

"How are we both supposed to get ready in twenty-five minutes?" Em snapped.

Krystal had to laugh. At least Em was thinking like herself again.

The morning was rough. Em looked like she'd been run over by a truck. Krystal felt bad about that. Em had only managed to get dressed, wash her face, and brush her hair and teeth before they were called upstairs for breakfast. Normally Josefina didn't call her for breakfast, but with a guest in the house, she wasn't letting Em out unfed. That meant Em ended up with less than fifteen minutes to get ready.

Krystal had been worried for a minute Em might say something to her mom or in front of her mom, but she didn't. But on the walk to school, Em had a million questions. She conveyed a combination of concern, betrayal, and anger. Her mixed emotions led to two more outbursts. It took all Krystal had to calm Em down.

Krystal could see Em was trying to figure out if she should tell someone. Krystal did her best to convince her that wasn't necessary.

Krystal told the story of how her cutting begun before fabricating details of how she'd quit completely.

They'd sat on a bench in a very small park located in the middle of a cul-de-sac a few blocks away. At one point, Em started crying again. Krystal did too. She'd never spoken out loud about her cutting, and it was like pouring salt in a wound.

Em made Krystal show her both arms. Krystal did— then Em turned away.

"I feel sick," Em said. "I love you, Krystal, and I don't ever want you to hate me, but I might ask to see your arms sometimes." Sighing deeply, Em stood up. "As long as you're really over it, I won't tell anyone. But, you realize you won't be able to hide it forever. If you start doing it again, I will tell. I will get help." Stressing the word 'will,' she continued, "I'm going to be praying for you. You should pray too."

"I kinda have been," Krystal confessed and went on to tell Em about the promise she'd made to Nick and the way she'd been writing her prayers out. She wanted to tell her about the thoughts…voices…whatever it was in her head the night before, but that information might drive Em straight to the school counselor. She couldn't risk it. Instead, she said, "Honestly, I just don't know what to say, and I ramble about things."

"Just talk to God the way you do me or anyone else. There isn't a certain way to pray. Don't think you have to sound all poetic and stuff, because you don't. God is already working on you, and you don't even seem to know it. That's why you aren't cutting."

If guilt could drown you, Krystal would have died right then. Lying to Em was physically painful. But had God really been trying to help her? Either God was speaking to her or she was truly out of her mind insane and hearing things that weren't even audible.

They'd missed the majority of their first-hour class. Krystal apologized to her teacher and assured her it had been for good reason. The red rims around her eyes were probably pretty convincing since Mrs. Sails let her off the hook without any fuss. Or maybe it was because she had homework to hand in after last night's efforts. Either way, it was a blessing her teacher didn't recant on her promise to let Krystal make up her work. She couldn't be late again.

Chapter 15

It had become a habit for Krystal to look for Walt when she arrived at the shelter. Spotting him halfway down the street, she waved. Walt saw her and waved back. She wished she could go talk to him, but followed everyone to the back door instead, so they didn't have to wait on her.

They rang the buzzer and Nick's smiling face greeted them as the door swung wide open. Intermingled spices wafted into their nostrils as they entered.

"Hello, everyone," he bellowed in his usual cheeriness. Just looking at him could put just about anyone in a better mood. He was a big ball of happy. "How are you wonderful folks today?" Smiling back, they all greeted him at once.

This was their third week volunteering at the shelter, and they all knew the drill. First they donned aprons, gloves, and hairnets. Next, they checked their stations. Krystal stored a purple folder she brought with her in the cabinet under the soup station.

Mel brought their soups over one at a time, placing them in the wells. He now had blond streaks running through his hair. He certainly stood out with his tattoos, gauges, and dyed hair. Remembering Nick said Mel used to be a guest at the mission, she realized they'd never asked Mel to tell his story.

Everything was running smoothly and on time today. Feeling a little braver, she decided to ask Mel herself.

"Mel, Nick said you used to be a guest here, do you mind me asking what happened?"

The minute she asked, her ears grew hot. What if he didn't want to talk about it? Sometimes people pretended to not mind when they really did. She knew all about that. But his smile put her at ease.

Em looked up, surprised Krystal asked the question, but listened intently. Mike and Sharon turned around too.

"We would love to hear your story, Mel," Sharon said.

Mel smiled at his small audience. Krystal saw Nick shoot Mel a wink from across the kitchen.

"Well," he began, "about six years ago we moved here for my dad's business. I started Topeka High in the middle of my sophomore year. I'd always been a good athlete, but I was especially good at football, and I made quarterback my junior year. My skills in football got me a lot of attention from my peers and from some colleges. By the end of the year, I was getting conditional scholarship offers as long as I kept performing well and kept my grades up.

"I'd always had plenty of friends, but I became more popular than ever. I was invited to every party imaginable, and I went to most of them. Drinking became something I needed to get through my day, and by my senior year; I was an alcoholic and kicked off the team. One of my friend's older brothers worked in a liquor store, and he'd sell to me as long as I bought some for him too.

"Long story short, my parents were not the nurturing sort, and never had been. After several warnings, and me wrecking my car twice, they kicked me out. My parents were…well, still are wealthy people, and I was bringing the wrong kind of attention to the family. When they kicked me out, they took the credit card they'd given me and my car keys. My dad threw a duffle bag at me and told me I could take whatever I wanted from my room as long as it fit in that bag. I'd had about seventy dollars in my room. I took that with some clothes and a bottle of Jack I had hidden under my bed.

"My parents forgot to take my phone, so I was trying to text and call some of my friends. No one would let me stay with them because of my erratic behavior. They said their parents wouldn't go for it. I blew through my money in a matter of days. I spent it all on alcohol, none on food. One of my friends told me I should stay at the Mission. I don't remember doing it, but I must have walked to North Topeka. Two homeless men who stayed down by the river found me behind the Great Overland Station." The corners of his mouth turned up at the memory. "They must have felt sorry for me because I was so young. They took me under their wing, and even though some of the others had alcohol, they wouldn't give me any. Forcing me to detox, they dealt with my shakes, hallucinations, puking, screaming, and cursing for days.

"They fed me soup and whatever else they cooked over the fire…kept making me drink water and tea. It felt like an eternity, but after four or five days, I started feeling a lot better. But they wouldn't let me go anywhere for about another five days. They told me if I tried to leave, they'd call the police and tell them I robbed them." Mel grinned though his eyes shone with tears. He laughed. Putting up his hands in a comical surrender, he continued, "I wasn't sure if they were serious, but I wasn't going to test them! I'd had enough trouble up to that point. They were all I had in the world."

His tone grew serious.

"When I tried to call my parents, I found my phone had been shut off. The guys let me cry on their shoulders and then told me I had to get back to life. They brought me here and once I registered, I had a bed to sleep on, a place to take a shower, and regular meals once again. It felt like an eternity since I'd been at my own home, but it had only been a couple of weeks. The director tried to call my parents and talk to them, but they weren't interested. I was already eighteen and they made it clear they no longer had any legal obligation to care for me.

"As a condition of my stay at the shelter, I went back to school and got a job. During my stay here, I saw so many miracles; it was inevitable I accepted Jesus as my savior. I'm a completely different person. Between God, my friends down by the river and countless people here, I'm now a Washburn student, working toward a bachelor in fine arts with an emphasis in education. Part-time, I work as a tattoo artist and I spend as much time volunteering here as I can. God used Walt and Johnny to save my life and this place to give me a new life. Even if I could go back and change it all, I wouldn't."

Krystal reeled. That was hard to believe. Who wouldn't go back and fix mistakes? She sure would if she had the chance.

"Not even the alcoholism?" she asked.

"Not even that. Without that struggle, that experience, I wouldn't be who I am today. I wouldn't have met the countless people who've touched my life. I wouldn't trade my experiences for anything. My life had been empty—now it's full."

Krystal was stunned. Unconsciously, she lowered her head in thought.

"What a beautiful story, Mel," Sharon said softly.

"An amazing testimony," Mike said, "and you still have your whole life ahead of you."

Krystal had been listening intently, but then it dawned on her that Mel mentioned Walt's name. Her head shot up.

"You mean Walt, who has Peety?"

"Yes," Mel smiled. "That old man is like a father to me."

"He stays here now, right?" she asked.

"He does," Mel answered. "He's a veteran and lived by the river for a lot of years. He suffers from PTSD from his days in Operation Desert Storm. The guys by the river helped him the way he and Johnny helped me. Because of Johnny's health issues, Walt knew he needed to move from the river and so they both came in together. If it hadn't been for that, he'd probably still be living out there.

"Living indoors around so many others was quite an adjustment for him. The VA offered Walt a service dog on the condition he lives someplace where the dog would have shelter. Peety helped Walt through the transition; that's for sure. Walt and Johnny helped each other until Johnny passed away last year," Mel said, getting a little teary eyed again. He cleared his throat and sniffled.

Krystal's eyes were holding back unshed tears.

"I'm so glad you guys let animals stay here. Peety makes Walt happy," she said.

"We do when they're service animals or guide dogs," Nick said from behind. "If they aren't, we have a special program where family pets are taken care of until the family is back on their feet."

Em, who had been silent the entire time, spoke up.

"You all are amazing. Most people probably don't know how much you really do here. I know I didn't. People should know. You should make sure everyone knows," she declared with conviction.

"Shout it from the rooftops, eh?" Nick said, matching her enthusiasm."

"Yes!" Em replied and laughed. "Really."

"Well," Nick said. "Our director wrote a book. It's called *In Darkness, a Light Still Shines*. You should read it sometime."

Sharon and Mike nodded.

"We will," Sharon said. "We all love to read."

"We're just spreading God's love around the best we can," Nick said. "People need to understand how unconditional God's love is and the changing power it holds. Just today, one of our ladies, that has been staying here for the last two years, moved into a place of her own. When she first came here, she was using Meth and was physically and mentally ravaged by the drug. Now she is working in an office downtown and helping other addicts on the weekend. Anyone who used to know her during her days using wouldn't even recognize her now."

Em's family and Krystal stood in awe and wonder at the stories of healing. Nick chuckled as they all nearly sighed in unison.

"We'd better get ready—we have to open the doors in just a few minutes."

"Thanks for sharing your story, Mel," Sharon said, giving him a hug, "I feel blessed for hearing it."

As people began to pour in, Krystal felt weightless. Thinking of Mel's statement saying he wouldn't have changed his past choices, she couldn't help but wonder how she might be able to change things around for herself. Maybe there was something to this God thing.

Her eyes were constantly checking for Walt and Peety to come through the door. Once they were in line, she made eye contact with Walt and gave him a big smile. He looked downright tickled as he held up his hand in acknowledgment and smiled back at her. Catching sight of the hearing aid in his left ear that she hadn't noticed before, she wondered if it was due to age or from the war. Right on cue, Nick startled her when his voice boomed from behind her.

"Need a break, Krystal?

Krystal just laughed.

"You know I do." She squatted down and retrieved the folder from under the soup station. "I'll be back in a couple minutes."

"Take your time," Nick smiled and winked. Krystal was starting to get the idea of the wink. It kind of translated to 'I know, or I get it.' The thought sent a shiver down her spine as she thought about the correlation to the messages in her mind the night before.

"Hi, Walt!" Krystal greeted.

"Hello, Krystal! How are you this fine day, young lady?"

"I'm good. How are you and Peety?" Peety's ears twitched when he heard his name. Krystal reached down and scratched between his ears.

"We are having a good day," Walt said. "I felt well enough to take him on an adventure to go visit some friends."

"I bet he liked that." Krystal wondered if the adventure took him down by the river.

"We both did," Walt chuckled.

"Well, I can't stay long, but I wanted to give you this." Opening the folder, she pulled out a piece of paper.

Walt took the paper she held out and stared at it in silence. He looked up at Krystal.

"Did you do this?"

"Yeah, I've done others too," she admitted, "but I wanted you to have this one. She watched as his eyes filled up. "I didn't want to make you sad," she said and patted his hand.

"Oh, you didn't—you didn't." Grabbing a handkerchief out of his pocket, he wiped his nose. "You have a talent that is beyond words, young lady," he said seriously. "You should show me some of your other work someday."

"Thanks," she said as she looked at her shoes. "Maybe I will bring in some of my drawings sometime."

Walt stared at the portrait in his hand, of himself and Peety. "I can't stop looking at it. You made a funny-looking old man look beautiful somehow…and my Peety, he's my heart. It's a precious gift from a precious girl." He looked Krystal in the eyes and said, "Thank you."

"You're welcome." She stood knowing she should get back. "Hey, Walt, would you mind telling me your story sometime? Maybe you can come by the new daycare next Saturday. I'll be volunteering until close to lunchtime."

"I think I can do that." He gave her hand a squeeze and thanked her again.

Chapter 16

Between keeping up with her homework and make-up work, spending time with her siblings, gaining Em's trust by proving she was no longer a threat to herself, and of course talking to Brandon…life was crazy. It was already Friday night; the days were just flying by way too fast, every spare minute filled with something important…. But she was having a great time.

Krystal hadn't cut since the morning Em found out. It certainly helped to have someone hold her accountable because the urges had not subsided completely, but something else made her want to stop. Maybe there were multiple things, but she knew God had a hand in it. There was something comforting about knowing God was paying attention to her.

Three phone calls to her father the night before to arrange for some insurance payments didn't even send her off the deep end. Though she wasn't thrilled, she kept her cool and didn't say anything mean to her mom.

When she finished, she'd retreated to her room and debated on whether or not to punch the wall. Since her wall was concrete, she settled for screaming into her pillow and then writing in her journal.

Her phone buzzed, pulling her away from her thoughts. It was a text from Brandon.

B: Hey

K: Hey

B: What r u doing?

K: Homework. What r u doing?

B: Standing in front of your house.

K: WHAT?

Krystal ran up the stairs as her phone buzzed. The message was simply, 'LOL.' Dashing through the kitchen, she glanced at her mom who put her index finger to her lips.

"Shhh, don't wake the baby."

"Sorry," she said.

Too curious about Brandon to get annoyed with her mom, she peeked through the glass in the front door and discovered Brandon wasn't kidding. Quietly, she eased the door open just enough for her body to fit through before closing it behind her.

Still in shock, she stood on the porch with her mouth agape. He had a big smile on his face and she couldn't help but laugh.

"Are you happy to see me?" he asked.

"Of course I am. Duh."

"You might be able to see me more often than just at school now."

Krystal knew she was still missing something. His brother wasn't waiting out front and it was nearly 7:30 p.m. He must have walked from the school. "Is baseball over?"

"For the day? Yes. I never have practice this late. For the year, almost."

"I'm so confused," she laughed and walked out to meet him.

"Do you trust me?" he asked.

"Yes, but I think you're having too much fun with whatever is going on." She couldn't help but giggle. "How did you get here?"

"Just close your eyes and give me your hand." Closing her eyes, she felt him take her left hand. As often as they held hands, she still got goosebumps at his touch. "Don't peek!" he warned.

"I won't."

After leading her down the sidewalk a short distance, he halted.

"Can I open my eyes?"

"Almost."

With the weight of his hands on her shoulders, he turned her a full ninety degrees to the right. Tensing with anticipation, she just knew he was going to kiss her. They'd never kissed before, other than him kissing her hand, but that didn't count. She held her breath and wondered if it smelled okay. *Why didn't I brush after dinner?*

"Okay, you can open them."

Krystal opened her eyes and was slightly disappointed, but relieved at the same time. He wasn't even standing in front of her so a first kiss was not on the agenda. At least she didn't have to worry about her non-fresh breath.

The only thing she could see was the house that was three doors down. She looked around. Nothing stood out.

"I don't get it...."

Just then, Brandon's brother came out of the house. He carried a small bag of trash and headed toward them after tossing it in the can.

She spun around so fast her hair brushed across his nose and he blinked. "Did you move into this house?!"

"You can be a little slow sometimes."

Brandon's brother walked over after throwing out the bag.

"Hi, I'm Travis."

She shook the hand he offered. "Krystal."

"Oh, I know. Brandon has mentioned you…a lot. Plus, I saw you at some of his practices."

Krystal smiled when Brandon's cheeks changed colors.

"Shut up, Travis," Brandon said. Travis snickered and turned to go in.

"You should bring her in to meet Mom."

Krystal heard her mom calling her name.

"I'm right here, Mom," she called. She saw Josefina walk out and look down the sidewalk. Krystal dropped Brandon's hand and motioned her over.

"Mom, this is my friend, Brandon. He and I go to school together, and this is his brother Travis. They're just moving in."

"Why don't you both come in and meet my mom," Travis said and led the way.

Brandon leaned in toward Krystal's ear. "Friend?"

"Shhh. She might freak out."

Before they left Brandon's house, Josefina had managed to invite them all over for dinner the next night. "It will give you a break from all the work. Moving is exhausting."

They hadn't been back in their house for two seconds when her mom turned around to face her. "He is your boyfriend, yes?"

Krystal's eyebrows went up. Since when did her mom get so perceptive? She wasn't even going to try to lie. "Yes."

"He's cute. Very nice too. You probably shouldn't tell your father and don't ever ask if he can see your room."

"Mom!" Her face flushed a deep crimson. "You don't have to worry about anything like that."

"I know you're a good girl." She kissed Krystal on the cheek and squeezed her shoulder before going into the living room where Eliseo was holding a sleeping Sofia.

Stunned by the affection, Krystal wasn't sure how to react. She ambled back down to her room to continue her homework, but not before texting Em the news of her new neighbor.

Dear God,

Somehow things are getting better quickly. Maybe even too quickly if that makes sense…I was so panicked when Em found out about what I do and was so scared she was going to tell. But she didn't. It helps to have one person who knows. I really don't even want to cut anymore but then sometimes I do. I'm scared I'm going to give in to it again.

Then, it was so cool Brandon moved in down the street today! Tomorrow he and his family are coming for dinner. I'm pretty excited about that. I have to make sure mom doesn't put serranos in anything. The only sad thing is I haven't had quite as much time to draw since I've been catching up on my assignments. I know that will change soon. School is almost out.

I'm going to bed, but I just wanted to say…thank you. I'm pretty sure you are the one helping me with all this stuff. Any chance you're willing to make my scars disappear?
—Krystal

Putting her notebook away, she thought about what Mel had said last Tuesday. If it were him, he wouldn't be asking for his scars to go away. But his weren't visible. She would see her scars every day for the rest of her life. Krystal closed her eyes and went to sleep. She dreamed of arms that had no cuts, marks, or scabs on them.

Chapter 17

"What kind of keys can't open doors?" Ralph asked.

Standing there smiling, she was thinking hard, but had no idea. Then the answer suddenly hit her.

"Oh! Computer keys. Oh! And piano keys."

Ralph's disappointment was apparent.

"You can board, but that wasn't the answer. I wasn't thinking of those when I picked this joke. My joke book was printed a long time ago." All the others in the back were laughing.

"What? There were no pianos when you were born?" Max asked.

Laughter erupted amongst the teens.

"Oh, knuckleheads got jokes, huh?" Ralph tried to keep a serious face, biting his lip so the corners of his mouth didn't turn upward. It wasn't the first time these kids have called him ancient. "Just wait until you're all my age; it won't be as long as you think."

"I'd guess we have something over thirty years!" Max said playfully but sarcastically. Now they were all guffawing, holding their sides, and wiping their tears.

"How old do you think I am?" Ralph exclaimed. "You know what, for your safety, don't answer that. We'll be to

Ben's house in less than five minutes; it's your job to think of a new joke before we get there." When they pulled out their smart phones to pull up jokes, Ralph just shook his head. "That's just not right."

Repeating last Saturday's routine, Ralph dropped off the teens to get ready for their kids and walked Krystal down to the new daycare center.

"Krystal," he said, "Nick and I have a proposition for you today. However, do not feel obligated to accept if you don't want to."

"What's it about?" she asked. Her curiosity piqued.

"You'll know in less than a minute." They rounded the last turn and she saw Nick standing in the hall waiting outside the main door. His expression was hard to read. *Mischievous? No,* she thought. *He looks a little anxious.* Nick winked at Ralph. Krystal smiled and rolled her eyes.

"Okay," Nick began, "Ralph brought to my attention that you're an artist."

Ralph piped in. "Sarah went on and on about how talented you are, said she heard the art teacher use words like 'gifted' and 'natural' when describing you."

Krystal felt her ears getting warm. "I guess so," she said, in almost a whisper.

"Bet your teacher never used the word 'boastful' when describing you. Is Modest your middle name?" Ralph laughed. "Krystal, God gave me a push to talk to Nick about your skill and then Sarah pretty much gave us confirmation I was hearing God correctly. So, let's see how you feel about what we're going to ask you to do. Remember, you can say no."

"Okay," she said and fell quiet, eagerly waiting for an explanation.

"Now if you do say no, and Nick starts crying, then don't feel bad or anything. He does that a lot."

Nick snorted out a laugh. "Oh, I only cry the nights you pick the music in the office or if you try to cook. But all the guests cry on those nights."

"What? At least I don't—"

"Ralph!" Krystal said, completely exasperated. She was trying to be cool and just wait, but he was really dragging this out. "Tell me already. You're killing me!"

Nick chuckled at Krystal's expression. Then he winked at her. "Well, let's show you what we've done since last Saturday first." He opened the main door and stood aside allowing Krystal and Ralph to enter ahead of him.

The first thing Krystal noticed was that the walls had already been painted.

"Hey, I thought we were going to start painting today." She would have been disappointed, but she knew a blank canvas when she saw one. She saw Nick and Ralph smile and eyeball each other. They thought they were so slick—it made her laugh out loud. "You two are something else."

"It looks nice, though," she told them and decided just to go with it and let them play this out. Now that she knew what they were up to, she was totally entertained by their craziness. She tried to keep a neutral expression, and then gave up. Smiling at them, she asked, "So, what are we starting with today then?"

"We are starting in the baby room," Nick answered and led the way. "Ralph and I were just wondering if you'd like to paint all of the daycare rooms for us. We were thinking something along the lines of wall murals."

The word 'mural' stopped Krystal in her tracks, and then her gaze went to a pile of supplies sitting next to the changing table. Staring at the items with her mouth ajar, she was dumbstruck.

Finally, the gravity of their request hit her and she lit up like a Christmas tree.

"Murals?" she practically shouted. "Are you serious? Are you really serious?" Holding her hands over her chest, she told herself, *be cool, don't act dumb.*

Painting murals was far beyond the sunshine and bears with balloons she'd thought they were going to ask for. She'd been fine with that, knowing it would be fun. But murals! Her excitement was palpable in the room. Surely anyone who walked in right now could just have reached out and touched it.

Nick and Ralph laughed and patted each other on the back. She knew neither of them had ever seen her display that much emotion. But it was Nick and Ralph; she didn't need to keep rigid control over herself with them.

"I'm overjoyed you're this excited," Nick said. "I was worried you'd turn us down."

"Me too," Ralph said. "The way your face looks now is how Nick looks when he gets the last cookie."

Nick and Krystal both laughed.

"Oh no. I'm not turning a mural down," Krystal said.

Looking around wide-eyed, Krystal took in all the jars and tubes of every color of paint you could imagine. Most of them were acrylics; tons of it…gallons, jars, and tubes. She saw brushes of all different sizes, a couple of paint pallets, drop cloths, painter's tape, sealant, mineral spirits, and lots of paper towels and rags. She knew what every item was for.

"Did you rob an art store?" She was joking about the robbing part, but she knew this must have cost them a fortune. A tinge of guilt came over her. She hoped they didn't go all out just for her on this. She knew how important every dollar was to the shelter.

"Funny you should say that," Nick said.

"Oh I wish I could stay for this part," Ralph said, "but I have to get back to my kids. I'm delighted that you're going to do this for us, Krystal." Ralph was using an

English accent for some reason. "I'll see you when it's time for us to take off."

"You're always off," Nick said.

Ralph opened his mouth to respond, but was cut short when Krystal gave him a big hug.

"Thank you!" Giving Nick a hug next, she said, "You guys are the best! Really. I'm in heaven."

"Well, now, I wouldn't say heav—"

"You're welcome," Ralph said, cutting Nick off with a grin. "We do whatever God enables us to." He gave Nick a thumbs-up and a wink before he closed the door behind him.

No sooner did the door close before it opened again. Jane and Lenny came in and greeted them. Following Nick into the big kid's room, they were given the task of assembling some of the furniture.

"Why was it funny I asked that?" Krystal asked when Nick returned.

"What? Oh, yes. Well," Nick said. "As you know, these supplies are very expensive. You might remember I told you what we were spending on the new daycare unit was coming out to almost the exact amount of the donation provided to do it all."

Krystal nodded.

"Well, Ralph came to me about you being an artist and suggested we have you do the walls instead of using stencils or stick-ons." Krystal's heart swelled again.

"But," Nick said, "when we sat down to figure the costs; we knew we just didn't have the funds. We knew we'd have to find another way to obtain the funds if we were going forward with this. We decided to talk to the director and put our heads together about how we might obtain what you would need. The three of us prayed together in his office, and he assured us he would reach out to some friends who may have the connections to help. As it turned out, he didn't need to reach out at all.

"The very next day, a local business owner, who owns a bakery of all things, came into his office. He stated that he'd received a large shipment of painting supplies, and he didn't know why. He didn't order them, and he couldn't figure out who sent them. He'd contacted the shipping company in an attempt to get them to the rightful owner, but they told him there was no record of that shipment."

Nick's excitement lit up his eyes, and he started talking faster. "He'd given them the tracking number on the boxes multiple times and received the same answer each time…no such shipments. For the last two months, they've been sitting in his back room. Last Wednesday, he went into his back room and saw the boxes sitting there in the same place they'd been since they arrived. All of a sudden, the message Topeka Rescue Mission was being repeated in his mind. He said it wasn't a voice, but he was getting the message loud and clear, and he couldn't stop thinking about us."

Krystal's heart went so still; she wasn't even sure it was still beating. She knew God was speaking to her. Thunderstruck, all she could do was wait for each next word as Nick spoke. Everything was in slow motion. She was aware of her breathing and the particles in the air, yet she didn't miss a single word.

Nick smiled knowingly. Except he didn't know. She'd considered telling him about her experience, but decided against it. For now, she just wanted to hear the rest of this story.

"So he asked Barry, our director, if he thought we could use the paints. Barry then told him the whole story of what we wanted to do, our discussion, and how we had prayed. That man sat right in Barry's office and gave his heart to God that day."

Nick leaned forward and put his hand out like a teapot.

"Turns out he'd been mad at God ever since he'd lost his wife. Now God was showing him he still mattered. Then he told Barry he brought the paints with him, so they grabbed a dolly and lugged them in. After all that, we only needed to buy the other supplies…brushes, et cetera. When we were done, we'd spent the exact amount left from the donation. Not a penny more, not a penny less."

Krystal's throat thickened, and her eyes filled. To prevent tears from spilling over, she rubbed her eyes. Sighing, she looked into Nick's eyes. "God's magic?"

"Absolutely." He nodded.

Chapter 18

Nick and Krystal spent nearly an hour going through the supplies and talking about the project. Feeling like a cloud was carrying her around the daycare, she was totally in her element.

Nick told her she should pray about what she'd paint. The only request they had was for one of the walls in one of the rooms to be a mural of a scene from Noah's Ark. That was just fine with her.

After discussing a multitude of ideas for the other two murals, she told him she'd work out some sketches and they could talk about them next Saturday.

Wishing she had her sketch pad now, she asked Nick for a pencil and paper. Normally, she kept it near, but she'd had no idea what this day was going to bring. They'd already decided Noah's Ark would go in the baby room.

There would be one wall in each room with a mural. The others would still be painted and decorated but not to the full extent of a mural. Instead, they would have cubbies, file cabinets, corkboards, and a chalkboard in the bigger kid's room.

A sudden realization alarmed Krystal, and sighing, she decided she might as well bring it up.

"Nick, did you say you wanted to have this done in three or four weeks?"

"Originally, yes. But we know you'll need a couple extra weeks and that's fine."

How was she going to tell him that still wasn't enough? Painting wall murals isn't something that can be accomplished in four or five mornings. Nick saw her disheartened expression.

"Tell me what you're thinking," he said.

"Well, it's not enough time. I know you need to get this daycare open as soon as possible, but this isn't something that can be done quickly." Normally, Krystal would have volunteered to stay for much longer on Saturdays to get more done but with all the school work she was trying to catch up, she couldn't give the time up right now. Explaining those very issues to Nick, his expression brightened.

"I'll tell you what," he said cheerily. "Don't worry at all and let me do some checking. Is it okay if I give you a call at your home tonight? God will work out the details. We've gotten this far, haven't we?" Nick was always the optimist.

"Sure," she said. "I'll give you my cellphone number." Before she had a chance to consider what Nick might be checking into, a familiar pair of frames darkened the doorway. Smiling was starting to become a common occurrence recently, and she couldn't help but do it again now.

"Walt!" she greeted. Walking over to him, she gave him a light hug and knelt down to greet Peety's bright eyes.

"Hey!" Nick exclaimed. "Fancy seeing you in here. Hope you're not looking for babies. We don't have any in stock yet." Krystal couldn't help but snort and roll her eyes. "What?" Nick feigned innocence. Krystal just shook her head.

"Well," Walt said, as Nick grabbed one of the lower stools and set it right next to the changing table so Walt would have some support for his back as he took a seat. As soon as he sat down, Peety did too. "Krystal invited me, said she wanted to hear my tale. After that beautiful picture she drew me, I'd hate to disappoint her."

"Oh, I would love to see that sometime," Nick said enthusiastically. He then gave Krystal a look that said…what about me. Krystal laughed and made a mental note to bring Nick one soon. She'd already planned on it, but she wanted to give him just the right one. Gifting her art was a way for her to show she cared without having to use words.

"We just made plans for Krystal to do some special work for us here in the daycare. She's going to do wall murals," Nick said as he waved at the walls.

"Well, I can tell you that you will not be disappointed," Walt said with certainty, nodding his head for emphasis.

"Somehow, I think I was the very last to know she was an artist!" Nick said, shaking his head. Krystal just stood by as the two talked about her right in front of her. Adults seemed to do that a lot.

Jane poked her head in to let Nick know she and Lenny finished for the day. "I'll be right back," she said, holding up a finger. She went back to the big kids' room and returned, rolling an office chair behind her that she and Lenny had assembled, and offered it to Walt.

Once Walt settled into the chair, he patted her hand and thanked her. Krystal could tell they knew each other. She loved the fact she was now a part of this band of misfits, actually, honored was more like it. They suited her so well she couldn't imagine going back to a life without them.

Nick sat down on one of the stools, and she sat next to Peety on the floor and patted his leg. Peety looked up at Walt as if asking permission. Walt simply pointed at Krystal and Peety pivoted, resting his head on her knee.

"Oh, you are so sweet, Peety," she said as she scratched behind his ears.

After what felt like a hundred years of listening to talk about how the Royals were doing so far this season, Krystal realized that if she didn't interject soon, Walt and Nick might continue until it was time for her to leave.

Trying to think of a way to interrupt without sounding rude, she considered…. *So, what brought you here, Walt? No, that wouldn't work.* She'd asked him to come after all.

After another couple minutes, she couldn't come up with anything, so she simply cleared her throat, but with effect. Both men stopped in surprise, and Peety looked up at her. Nick snickered in amusement, and Walt laughed out loud, bringing his weathered hand to his belly.

"That a girl!" Walt complimented, his shoulders still shaking with his chuckles. "You know how to get the job done. We're just two old wind bags."

"I'm not really THAT old," Nick said. "Not like Walt."

"Coulda fooled me with all that white hair," Walt said.

"Ahem!" Krystal looked pointedly at the two men.

Obviously tickled at her assertiveness, Walt decided he'd better get down to business. He shifted in his seat and Krystal watched as he assumed a more sober expression as his mind selected just the right place in time to begin recounting his journey.

"Well, I guess there's no place like the beginning," Walt said. Krystal smiled and nodded.

"I grew up here in Topeka with my folks. I was an only child. My father's family owned a furniture store, and mom worked at the library. When I was six, a new family moved in next door to us, and I became friends with their son, Christopher, who was a year older than me. We played together almost daily and sometimes people would shout nasty things out their car windows; things I didn't even understand the meaning of yet. Once, someone even threw a pop bottle at us. Luckily, they missed. In those days, pop bottles were all made of glass.

"That was the first time I became aware of how the world could be very ugly and life wasn't fair. You see, his family was black. I was too young to know anything about the civil rights or the Brown vs. Board of Education case that had been filed the year before, a case Chris's parents had testified in. My parents never raised me to judge people—all I knew was that he was my best friend.

"When school started, I was disappointed not to see him there. We stayed friends over the years, even though both of us took some heat for it; what we went through strengthened our friendship more than anything. A few years later we found ourselves in the same school. There were fights. Some we won and many we lost." Walt reached down and pulled up his pant leg. "See that scar?"

Krystal nodded, as familiar as she was with scars; she'd never seen one like this. Walt's leg had a permanent dent above his ankle nearly the size of a quarter. At the center, his skin was puckered, and the flesh around it was forever marred.

"During one altercation, a boy threw a tire iron at me and that's where it struck me. The pain was intense; I was shocked and relieved when I found out nothing was broken. Chris had to help me get home that day because I couldn't walk on my own. He was doing a little bit better than me, though he had an eye that was swollen shut.

"I started questioning God as to why this was allowed to go on. I stopped wanting to go to church when I realized all of the people there not only looked like me, but they sounded a lot like the people who gave us trouble. They wouldn't use the vulgar phrases you heard on the street— their words were subtle and tinged with self-righteousness. My mom tried to help me understand, but I saw so much hate in people that I couldn't figure out a way to forgive them like she said I should…like God tells us to. I couldn't stomach the ignorance, and blamed God for their actions as if everything was His fault."

Taking a deep breath, he went on. "While I was in my freshman year of high school, my mom became very ill, very fast. After we found out she had cancer, it wasn't much more than a month later that she was gone. The cancer was so aggressive they gave up on radiotherapy shortly after she was diagnosed.

"Seeing what she went through hardened my heart almost completely. Madder at God than ever, I decided I would never pray again. I couldn't understand why he'd let someone who'd been so faithful suffer so. My mom was one of the sweetest people I knew and even while she was suffering, she was telling me never to turn my back on God. At the time, I tried to appease her despite knowing I couldn't grant her wish, at least not then. Later I would recognize the blessing in the fact that at her worst point, she didn't suffer long, and we had time for goodbyes.

"Christopher graduated in '64 and moved away to attend Pittsburg State. He wanted me to go too, but I didn't. I wanted to stay close to my pops a little longer. I graduated the next year and attended Washburn." Krystal quickly did the math and realized Walt wasn't quite as old as she had thought.

"The next year, the June 8th tornado ripped through here and tore up much of the campus. I ended up spending much of my college career in trailers used for our classrooms. We nearly sweated to death for a while until they finally put in air conditioning units. Chris and I kept in touch through letters; I sent him pictures of the destruction from the tornado. He sent me pictures of the student march that took place in '68 to honor Martin Luther King after he'd been shot." Walt paused in thought, breathing softly as his mind moved though memories of long ago that were so fresh they could have been just yesterday. Nick and Krystal waited patiently.

"I haven't heard any of this before," Nick said, amazed. "I thought I knew your whole story but there is more to it than I thought. Take your time, my friend. We're not in a hurry."

I kind of am. Though she'd never say it aloud, she didn't want Ralph to come to take her home before Walt was finished. She remained quietly engulfed in the story Walt was painting. As he talked, images and ideas of drawings and paintings came to mind, but she didn't let herself get carried away. She was too interested to miss even a single sentence.

Walt blinked, then smiled. "Well, I met a girl my sophomore year in college and I thought it was serious. Her name was Wanda, and I was head over heels. When I asked her to marry me, she said yes. We agreed we'd marry after graduation. I didn't want to wait, but she thought it would be better for us to stay with our parents while we finished college instead of having to worry about money while we were still in school.

"The Vietnam War was already in full swing at this time. In '69 they announced the draft and my draft number was number one," he said as he held his index finger up. "My birthdate had been the first one pulled from the lottery. It was so unbelievable I walked around in a spell for days."

"The lottery?" Krystal asked, "What do you mean?"

"During the draft, the Selective Service, which is a government agency," Walt explained, "put every birthdate on a slip of paper and into a capsule. All the capsules went into a big container and were drawn out randomly to determine the order of the draft. The first birthdate they drew was mine, September 14th. I remember that moment like it was yesterday."

"Oh," was all Krystal said, trying to imagine what that must have been like. She'd never met anyone who'd been to Vietnam. If her own family had ever been involved in wars in Mexico, she knew nothing about it, never had thought about it, really. It was cool she and Walt both had September birthdays, but she knew now wasn't the time to mention it.

"My induction had been deferred until I finished college in 1971—then I had to go. I kissed Wanda goodbye and told her I'd write. She said she would wait for me, and we'd decided, well, she'd decided we would marry when I came home. The fact she wasn't in a hurry should have given me a clue, but it didn't. She didn't wait, not for long. Less than six months in I received my last letter from her telling me she was sorry, but she'd met someone else…said she couldn't deal with me being gone so long. At the time, I was incredibly hurt. She was all I had at home besides my pops."

It was so strange how this cute old man had transformed right in front of Krystal's eyes. The frailness she'd seen in him that first day disappeared, and she saw him in an entirely new light. He was just a man. An older man, yes, but not a weak, frail, or helpless man. He really wasn't even that little now that she thought about it. This was the real Walt.

"So, what happened in Vietnam?" Krystal asked.

"Honestly, not a whole lot. My unit was non-combat. We were all affected by our experiences; if you were there it was enough to mess with your head. The draft had turned a lot of us upside down. The Vietnam War was surrounded by controversy, and it was hard to listen to at times. But our unit consisted of paper pushers. I guess they considered us smart," he smiled. "I was, as long as it didn't have anything to do with a woman." He grinned sheepishly.

"We handled a lot of information, did a lot of reports, but never saw any action, never even fired our weapons once. In fact, the whole experience left me pretty naïve. Though I was completely altered by the draft, the political upheaval, and the horror stories I heard, I never really saw any of it for myself. Reading some of the reports that came through was almost like reading a newspaper or book that left you shaken.

"There was always a trusty reality check though; all you had to do was look outside. Once my two years were up, I went home. Nothing seemed worthwhile here anymore. I ended up enlisting in the National Guard. Figured I could still use my college degree and lead a somewhat normal life, but something about being a soldier gave me a sense of self-esteem and self-worth I wasn't getting anywhere else. Guess I needed to feel a little manlier after being dumped on my rump," he said, and guffawed.

Krystal looked at Nick and they both laughed with Walt.

"So, whatever happened to Wanda?" Krystal asked. "Did you ever see her again?"

"Yep, I did actually…didn't take long, neither. She was still here, but had gotten married to a guy I knew from college…saw her at the gas station with a baby on her hip. By the age of the child, I wondered if that was the reason for the 'break-up' letter. Maybe they'd met before I ever

left, I don't know for sure. Either way, it hurt like hel—"
Walt cleared his throat. Nick smiled and winked at him.

"It hurt to see her that day," he said in a more proper
tone. "I'd told myself I was over her, but actually seeing her
told me I'd been wrong."

That bit of information caused Krystal's stomach to
go sour. *What's wrong with some women?* she wondered.
Anger bubbled up, and she knew her ears might be telling
on her if they were turning red. She couldn't help thinking
of her mother and feeling disgusted at this Wanda person
who broke Walt's heart. She silently vowed that the
decisions she made in life, especially in regard to
relationships, they would always be honorable. She'd never
be one of these women who were selfish and thoughtless.
She'd never be a cheater.

Walt and Nick both noticed her furrowed brows.
When she saw them noticing her, she straightened and
made herself relax.

"Don't worry, Krystal," Walt said, as he reached down
and put a hand on her shoulder. "That ended up being a
blessing too, believe me. But that's a whole 'nuther story."
At his reach, Peety lifted his head and nuzzled his nose into
Walt's palm—he was definitely not in work mode now; he
was in lazy-dog mode. Walt gently scratched Peety's head
as he continued with his story.

"Life went on. I was working for the May
Department Stores using my Finance degree and making a
decent living. Over the years, I could probably count a
hundred times I felt God tugging at me, trying to get my
attention, but I wouldn't face it. I wouldn't face God. I was
always the nicest guy until someone knocked on the door to
talk about Jesus, or kept inviting me to church…didn't
want to hear it. My heart was so hard I slammed doors in
people's faces, literally and figuratively. The only one who
got away with it even a little was my pops. But he

eventually gave up too. I think he feared he might lose me if he kept pressing.

"Those were some years." Walt sighed heavily. "I had my day job and then I had my side career. My part-time military career was my alter ego. I didn't want it to resemble my everyday life, not even remotely. I enjoyed being in the National Guard and I liked making the extra money, too. I became a Signal Corps officer and moved up the ranks over time as openings became available." He paused, took a breath and began again. "In July of '75, I met my wife."

Krystal's head snapped up. "You got married?" For some reason, she assumed Wanda ruined him, and he'd been alone ever since. Eager to hear the rest, she stretched her legs and then folded her knees back to sit picnic-style. Peety looked at her accusingly. He scooted closer and readjusted.

"Now, this part I do know," Nick nodded and waved his index finger in the air.

Just as Krystal had feared, she heard the main door and footsteps coming from the main room. Ralph's voice rang out before he reached the baby room.

"I'm missing one last knucklehead!" He reached the door, and his eyebrows went up when he saw Walt. "Walt, my man! How are you this fine day?"

"Just fine, Ralphy, good as can be." Krystal loved how easy they all were with each other. They looked like old friends getting together. Then she realized—that's exactly what they were. They'd all known each other for years and had become nothing short of family.

"Did a cat steal your cookie, Krystal?" Ralph asked. "Because you look like a cat stole your cookie."

Krystal laughed out loud.

"What does that even mean?" Peety looked up at her, mildly annoyed. She was laughing hard enough that she'd disturbed his slumber. "Do cats even eat cookies?" Ralph had obviously picked up on her disappointment.

Ralph shrugged his shoulders.

"Doesn't everyone eat cookies?"

"Why wouldn't they?" Nick agreed.

"I didn't say everyone should eat cookies," Ralph said, looking directly at Nick.

"I have to keep my shape!" Nick feigned offense, putting his hands on his stomach.

"We know, we know," Ralph said before he and Walt chimed in unison. "Round!"

"Nick really isn't round," Krystal said. Nick put up a hand for Krystal to high-five. She giggled. "But seriously, I'm not ready to go yet. Walt is telling us his story, and I want to hear the rest of it." She was trying to think of an alternate way home, but was hoping a certain someone would offer.

"I can give you a lift," Nick said. "No worries."

"Thanks!" Krystal exclaimed. His offer is what she'd hoped for. That was easy, mentally patting herself on the back, glad she didn't have to work too hard for it.

"Alrighty then," Ralph said, "Santa has you covered. I best get the rest of the beasts home," pointing his thumb in the direction of the teens. "It's no joke when it's lunchtime, they're scary when they're hungry. Such animals!" Ralph exited the room, but reached back in with one hand, and forming a claw, he said, "Rawr!"

All three of them hooted at Ralph's silliness.

Krystal hopped up on the stool Walt had originally been using.

"Back to July of 1975 when you met your wife!"

"Ha! Who knew you were the bossy type!" Nick laughed. "I'm getting to know you better and better!"

Walt was grinning ear to ear.

Krystal smiled mischievously, then looked straight at Nick…and gave him an exaggerated wink.

Nick lost it. He laughed so loudly, she wondered if he could be on the other side of the building. Suddenly, he turned toward Krystal and said, "You got me, didn't you?! You knew I'd offer a ride."

Her cheeks burned just a little, a very little. Instead of answering, she winked again. Nick reached over and clapped her on the back. "Have I told you that you fit right in?"

Totally taking that as a compliment. She was free to be herself with these two men who were both old enough to be her grandfather. That's how she would start thinking of these two, even though Walt had some years on Nick, he still made the cut. Ralph could be her uncle, she decided. She never knew older people could be this cool.

"How about we finish this story over some lunch? My treat." Nick suggested. As if on command, Krystal's stomach growled. "That was a yes from Krystal," Nick said, "What about you, Walt?"

"Sounds good," Walt replied. He sent a knowing look Nick's way and nodded his head as a way of acknowledgment. Her heart warmed. She was more perceptive than they gave her credit for being. She figured Walt needed a break. It probably wasn't easy for him to sit so long.

Krystal thought about it and decided she should call her mom and let her know she'd be home later. Nick called Ralph to let him know the plan and invited him to meet them for pizza after he finished his route.

"I had to leave Ralph a message," Nick said. "But he's really good at checking them. He'll be along if he can."

"Who's running the kitchen?" Krystal asked, realizing lunchtime meant the kitchen at the shelter would be buzzing.

"If I'm not there, then one of two people will be in charge; sometimes Mel and other times Akroor.

Krystal looked at Nick. "That's a unique name."

"He's from India. He's only twenty, but very mature and compassionate. He's working on a Psychology degree and came here to observe and write a paper for one of his classes. Next thing we knew, he was part of the team. He loves to cook. He makes wonderful Indian dishes from time to time, but can really cook anything. I'm surprised he's not going to culinary arts school instead."

The trio plus Peety made their way to Nick's car. When Nick walked to the door of the red Bug, Krystal's eyes went wide.

"No, you didn't?"

Nick smiled. He didn't think he'd gone too far.

"Yes, yes, I did."

Krystal, for the hundredth time that day, began laughing as they all got into Santa's sleigh. Peety sat with Krystal in the back.

"Where's Rudolph?" she asked.

"Under the hood!" Nick quipped.

Walt turned around in his seat to look at Krystal. "The first time I saw him walk to this car, I wasn't sure he'd fit, but it's rather roomy in here."

As Nick drove away, Krystal was wiping away tears from laughing so hard.

Chapter 19

By the time the time the pizza arrived, Ralph was coming through the door.

"Whoa, that was fast!" Nick exclaimed, "Are all the kids alive?"

"They're just fine," Ralph waved off the question, "only one needed stitches."

"Ha!" Nick bellowed, "And you think I have food issues."

Krystal and Walt looked at each other and shook their heads. Peety lay under the table by Walt's leg. Krystal had full intentions of sneaking him pizza crusts.

After some small talk during the meal, Walt sat back on the seat and nodded toward Krystal.

"I'd better finish this up, otherwise they'll make us order more pizza."

The group of them sobered a bit after the fun and food, anticipating the rest of the story. Walt began. He talked about one typically hot July day in 1975—he had taken his '74 International Travelall to the car wash.

"They're practically extinct now," he said, talking about his truck that would convert into what looked like an early SUV. As he was washing his car, a Jaguar XJ6 pulled up in the stall next to him. Unable to help himself, he stared at the sleek beauty of a machine. Walking to the end of the concrete wall, Walt peeked around for another look. The car door opened and the prettiest leg he'd ever seen stepped out. He started to yell, 'wait,' when *bang*! The car door swung into the concrete wall. She'd parked much too close. The next thing he heard was, 'Oh, dear.' It wasn't even his car, but he felt pained knowing it was now marked up.

Walt found out that the pretty leg belonged to an even prettier gal who turned out to be quite interesting, intelligent, and very funny. He was lighter than feathers while he was with her, unable to banish the ridiculous grin from his face as they spoke. They moved from the car wash to the Coffee Cup Cafe downtown and were there for several hours before finally exchanging numbers. They married in Vegas on December 21st of the same year and were back in time to spend Christmas with his dad and her parents.

"We were deliriously happy," Walt said, clearing his throat. "It's as close to love at first sight as you can get." His eyes were gleaming.

"What was her name?" Krystal asked.

"Ruth," he said, "my Ruthie."

They'd purchased a home right away and settled happily into married life.

"Don't get me wrong," Walt said, "we hit bumps in the road, especially when she started pressing me about how she thought we should start going to church. We argued some…had long talks about it, and eventually, I gave in…couldn't deny her anything," he said, with a sad smile. "Besides, I was a little less mad at God when she came into my life. She was a gift."

Walt told of how they tried to have a baby for years without success. Ruthie's inability to conceive was the major cause of her bouts of depression from time to time. The depression worsened whenever Walt was away on duty. They hated being away from each other. Years later, when they'd both given up on having children, Ruthie found out she was pregnant. After the shock had passed, they were ecstatic. Ruthie called the unborn baby their anniversary gift because she found out on December 21st, 1985, that she was three weeks along. Walt was thirty-nine and Ruthie was thirty-three at the time.

"Beth Ann was born on August 19th, 1986, and we enjoyed every minute of it. Those were the best years of my entire life." Walt's sad smile started vanishing little by little. "Then one day when Beth Ann was two years old, Ruthie took her to the mall to shop for new dresses for our family pictures. On their way home, a speeding car ran a red light and struck Ruthie's side, pushing our car into another. They were both gone before the first bystander made it over to the car."

Walt stopped, with shaking hands—he held his handkerchief over his eyes.

"Sorry," he said. "Sometimes, when I'm talking about it, it still feels like yesterday."

Nick, who was sitting next to him, placed a comforting hand on his back. Ralph cupped Walt's hands in his own. "They're with Jesus, my friend. You'll see them again. No doubt about it."

Walt took a moment to compose himself. "That's one of the things that keeps me going." Krystal sat quietly, trying to fight back tears and failing. Walt patted her hand from across the table. "Now I made you cry, but thank you for your tears." Krystal's throat was too thick with emotion to talk.

Continuing, Walt told of his deep depression. Taking time off from his day job and from the Guard, he had sunk so low, he'd contemplated suicide.

"But I couldn't do that to my father." He told them he stayed in his house for weeks at a time, barely eating.

Once he went back to work, he was a ghost of his former self and soon found himself unemployed. Selling the home he'd shared with his wife and daughter, he moved into an apartment.

"One day, nearly a year later, my dad was there on his regular weekly visit, puttering around my filthy, run-down apartment trying to pick up the trash. I felt a gut-wrenching kind of guilt and I nearly folded in on myself. My eyes were seeing clearly for the first time in ages; I saw how old my father had gotten. It was obvious Pops didn't feel well, and I knew that a large part of that was likely my fault. Not wanting to waste any more of the precious time I had with my father, I got cleaned up and took him out to lunch. We talked and cried together for what seemed like days. I vowed that no matter how I was feeling, I would make sure my father felt loved and knew how much I appreciated him. I kept that promise to myself. And in June of 1990, my father passed away quietly in his sleep." Walt swirled the water around in his glass, his eyes faraway.

"I crawled back into my cocoon then," Walt said. "I didn't have anyone else left that I truly cared about or who cared about me. So when Operation Desert Shield was activated, I volunteered to go. They sent me off for some additional training for the type of MSE communication and SINCGAR radio equipment. Somehow, I forced myself not to think about my life and lost myself in the training. I excelled. Afterward, I was deployed as a filler to the 1st Infantry Division, I was a Staff Sergeant E-6, in the Second Brigade, Second Battalion, 16th Infantry Regiment, Mechanized.

"My feet hit the sand well before Thanksgiving. When I volunteered, I knew in theory what I was signing up for. Heck, I'd been in the Guard for over fifteen years and I'd been around some, but knowing and experiencing are two different things. While I was well trained in my role, I was ill prepared for what was to come. The heat was like nothing I've experienced before, and that's with taking Vietnam into consideration.

"Before the combat phase, there was a lot of 'hurry up and wait,' maintaining equipment, pulling guard, a little training, monotonous duty, waiting for something to happen, with short periods of panic because of scud missile alerts or reports of enemy movements. Then, there was the constant guessing and gossip about when we were going to do something. Come January, we were holding our positions. As the Army deployed into attack positions at the end of Desert Shield, we were all spread over about a two hundred mile front from the Gulf west along the Saudi/Iraq border.

"In January, there was a lot of rain, so we were cold and miserable. But the rain helped shield our movement since our vehicles weren't kicking up miles of dust. The rest of the time we were baking in 120-degree temps during the day…then when it dropped to 75 degrees at night, it would chill you to the bone."

"Nights were pitch-black. If there was no moonlight, it was common to walk into parked cars. Most of the landscape was flat desert, very few hills, and a close horizon that made you feel boxed in on all sides. It seemed like the rest of the world had disappeared; you knew you could easily go crazy, if not for your team. There were only a few patches of sparse grass where nomadic shepherds had dumped seed for their migration.

"I got to know the others a little, but I was distant, let them do most of the talking. No one knew anything about my life other than the Guard and I was a volunteer. They'd ask why I volunteered, and I'd say something stupid like, because I was bored.

"When we attacked, the 24th Infantry Division was in the far west, and the whole front did a pivot until the

24th hit the Euphrates River. So, the units to the West moved much greater distances, faster than the units that started south of Kuwait. Iraq's landscape became much more rolling hills the farther north we moved, and the soil more granular, so we didn't raise as much dust, and breathing was easier. The attack was hard and fast. As a support soldier, I rode in a vehicle, and we were trying to keep up with the combat units. Until you saw the Iraqi tanks, you might have thought we weren't shooting at anything—that maybe real people didn't exist on the other side. No one to be affected by all of the bombs we were sending over. But then I started to see their tanks heading our way. While they were skilled soldiers themselves, they were easily demolished. Their tanks were very outdated and didn't protect them from our weaponry.

"We had been led to believe the Iraqi Army was a force of seasoned veterans, hardened through an eight year war with Iran, and equipped with top-of-the-line Soviet equipment, which we believed at that time to be as good as ours. And, they had the defender's advantages. They knew the land, had time to prepare, and had chemical weapons as well as being well-equipped with conventional weapons. What we saw was a different story. Many of them just walked over to us with their hands up in complete surrender; there was no fight in them. They were tired and hungry, and many admitted they didn't know why they'd invaded Kuwait. We were told Saddam wasn't feeding them, but even when he had tried to, we had ambushed their resupply convoys so they were starving out there.

"While I knew why our people were there, I was bothered by the high-fives some of the combat soldiers gave each other when they succeeded in hitting their target, which was almost always. It's like you aren't in just a different country; you're on a different planet. Sometimes you'd see what remained of the bodies that had been in those tanks or nearby vehicles and you knew that you held some of the responsibility. Some of those soldiers couldn't have been over sixteen.

"I stopped and wondered why I was there. Then I remembered, I'd volunteered. Many of these guys didn't have a choice about being there, but I had signed up. I'd felt sorry for myself, and there I was, still feeling sorry for myself, wishing I'd get picked off by a stray bullet.

"The experience provided a distraction, but the distraction wasn't any better than my reality had been at home. It was more suffering, more death. Thought after what I'd been through at home, I could easily deal with war, but I was wrong. Here I was with all these other people who had families waiting for them and not knowing if they'd make it back or not. I didn't have anyone waiting for me." Walt sighed, then took a deep breath. Everyone remained quiet.

"By the third day of combat, we were all beyond exhausted and filthy. Scared we were going to run out of water, we weren't drinking enough and we became dehydrated. I remember I was sitting in the back of a vehicle trying to fix one of the radios as we were driving. But I was so out of it. My eyes wouldn't focus so that I could see what I was doing. Then there was a sound, and like a dream, I tilted my head up and saw boots. They were my boots. I knew they were, because I had one of Beth Ann's ribbons looped through the top hole and tucked down in my boot.

"Everything was happening in slow motion. All at once I saw all the men from my vehicle in the air around me, some of them missing limbs. Finally, I hit the ground. I remember not being sure if I couldn't hear or if there was just no sound. Looking to the left, I saw one body and two more when I looked to the right. Soldiers were running toward me, but for some reason it was taking them ages to get there. I got tired of waiting, so I closed my eyes to rest.

Walt explained how he woke in a medical tent unable to hear out of his left ear. He learned he was the sole survivor out of all the men in the vehicle and he was anguished. It made no sense to him at all. Why would God let him live over the others? He should have been the one to die, not them. A sweet nurse told him he was blessed to have escaped intact and that an angel must have been looking out for him. He went mad, screaming out she didn't know what she was talking about and to shut up. He was crying and thrashing when a needle was plunged into his arm.

"Honorably discharged from both active duty and the National Guard due to the damage in my left lobe and also because of emotional instability, I returned home. Prior to deployment, I'd paid my rent up in advance. But now I just couldn't stay there. Grabbing my duffle bag—I shoved clothes, toiletries, and some personal items in before I walked out the door, leaving the rest of my belongings in that apartment.

"Making my way across many states, I lived on the streets. I talked to people from time to time, but never stayed long enough to get close. Money was never an issue; I had a substantial savings from working, investments, the Guard, insurance, and the sale of the house; my new simple life was easily sustained.

Walt stopped talking and looked at his small audience. There was a heavy stillness that surrounded them and no one wanted to speak first.

Krystal noticed the elderly couple at the next table had also been listening and were now sitting quietly, waiting for him to continue. Peety made a sound from beneath the table, almost like a sneeze.

"That means he needs to go out," Walt explained. "Excuse me."

Reflecting on the details, Krystal felt ashamed for feeling so sorry for herself for so long. While her circumstances were hurtful, she hadn't lost anyone to them; other than herself, that is.

"Can I ask what you're thinking?" Nick almost whispered the question.

Krystal looked at Nick first, then Ralph.

"Just that I need to get over some things that don't even compare to what others have gone through."

Nick inhaled and held his breath with a pensive expression. "Krystal, I do think perspective is important. Keeping things in perspective helps us to handle issues more efficiently, life more effectively. With that said, problems are problems, pain is pain, and hurt is hurt."

Krystal looked at Nick, trying to understand what he meant by that.

"What Nick is telling you," Ralph said, "is while your circumstances may differ from those of another, it doesn't mean the things that hurt you are less important than what hurt them. If you let God, he will use all your circumstances, painful or not, to help you grow as a person. Don't ever feel like you have to minimize your circumstances, because you're comparing them to someone else's."

Krystal nodded in understanding. At this moment, she had an intense sense of appreciation for all the things she'd learned recently and who she was becoming because of them. She knew God had been with her all along, putting the right people in her path, guiding her to this moment of understanding. Right here, right now. Somehow she needed to come to terms with her new home. At least, she now knew where to turn for help...to God.

Walt came back in with Peety and his backside barely touched the seat before Krystal spoke up. "So, Walt, what happened after you came back to Topeka? Why are you staying at the shelter?"

Nick and Ralph knew this answer, and they were anticipating Krystal's reaction when she heard it.

"Because I want to," he stated simply, and smiled.

"What?" Krystal's expression showed pure disbelief and all three men looked somewhat amused.

Walt's voice quieted considerably and he spoke in a hushed tone. "I could easily afford to live on my own. Money's not a problem. God has placed me in a unique position of having a lot of money with no desire of having worldly things. You see, early one morning while I was still on my journey, I was walking down a sidewalk in Houston. Across the street, I saw this woman and a little girl huddled together in the entryway of a store that hadn't opened yet. They looked just like Ruth and Beth Ann. Falling on my knees, I began to sob, and for the first time in a long time, I started talking to God. Once I'd cried myself out, there was a peace over me that I had never felt before, not in my entire life. It was like God was holding me. I stayed there for as long as I could and in the quiet, God told me to help that woman and her daughter.

"As I approached them, I stayed back a ways. My appearance wasn't exactly reassuring. I'd been hiding behind my scraggly beard and dirty face for so long. As long as I was unapproachable, people left me alone. When I told her God wanted me to help, she looked uncertain and a little scared. So I asked her to meet me in front of a nearby grocery store at 10 a.m. hoping she'd feel safer if she were around others and in public. In the hours before she arrived, I went to the store and bought a razor and then I went and bought some new jeans and a t-shirt and checked into a motel room to get cleaned up. The last thing I did was stop by the bank before meeting her. We sat outside on a bench and talked for a while, and she didn't look like Ruth at all and her little girl didn't look like Beth Ann. God had just showing me they could have been somebody's Ruth and Beth Ann. Know what I mean?"

Krystal nodded.

"She told me her story and I helped her get back on her feet. From that day on, I traveled around the same way I had been. But I was more open, letting God direct my footsteps, what to do, when it was time to help someone, and specifically how to help them. Financial assistance isn't always the best way to help a person. It depends on their circumstances. Sometimes you have to help people achieve things on their own.

"Eventually, I found my way home and met my friend Johnny. We pitched tents and lived by the river for many years. Both of us had been in the service and had a lot in common. Nightmares had plagued me for a long time after the war and sometimes still do, loud noises still put me on edge if they catch me off guard…sometimes has me ducking for cover, but that's okay. I'm living the life I'm supposed to be living and I'm truly grateful for it. I'd rather be here living around people for as long as I can, instead of alone in a house somewhere. Besides, it's easy enough to be alone when I want to be. Peety and I just take off for one of our long walks."

When they were all finished, Ralph headed back to the shelter and Walt and Peety rode with him, and Krystal went with Nick.

"You must be special," he said when they were stopped at a red light. Glancing over at her, he smiled. "I already knew that, though. God has big plans for you, my young friend."

She looked back at him, questioningly. Nick shrugged.

"You have a way with people, a big heart they can see and feel. Walt rarely tells anyone all the details he told you. Far as I know, Ralph and I are the only others he's told about his finances. Our director doesn't even know. You see, Ralph and I had to know because Walt will help some of our guests with their recovery when God gives him the green light, but he does it anonymously. He's still sharp as ever with numbers, so he helps out the shelter too. Helps us with budgeting for projects and sometimes audits our accounts to make sure everything is in order. He's been such a blessing to us over the years. Like many of us, he's more at home in this environment than he'd ever be in the so-called real world."

Directing Nick to her street, Krystal pointed, "This is it right here." A glance toward Brandon's showed his mom's car wasn't there. She wondered where they were.

Nick looked at her expectantly and she grinned.

"Would you like to meet my mom?"

"Why, yes, yes, I would!" he said cheerily. "Glad you suggested it." Good naturedly, Krystal rolled her eyes.

Nick met everyone except Jaime and the Man, who Krystal deduced must be together. Nick boasted about Krystal to her mother and thanked her for allowing her daughter to volunteer. After visiting a short time, he excused himself and headed back to the shelter.

Krystal walked him out and thanked him for the entire day.

"It has been amazing," she said sincerely before telling him she would bring some ideas for the murals the following Saturday.

As he was getting into his car, he stopped and looked back at her.

"I'll call you later with more details on the timeline for the daycare." Then he looked up again with a thoughtful look on his face. "Hey, let me know whenever you're ready to tell me your story."

Watching as he drove away, she was a bit troubled at the thought of revealing her secret to Nick and her euphoric feeling dropped some. There was no way she could ever tell him and that disappointed her, because she wanted to and knew she could trust him.

Turning to go in, she heard the familiar hum of the Man's truck pulling in. Jaime leapt out, obviously invigorated. Turning back to the vehicle, he slid out his skateboard.

"We went to the Mouse Trap! You remember the one you told me about?"

Not wanting to dampen his enthusiasm, Krystal put on a wide smile and told him that she thought that was awesome.

"Eli said he'll take me sometimes so I don't get rusty."

"Great," Krystal said, trying to sound chipper, ruffling Jaime's hair as he breezed past, heading into the house.

She looked up and her eyes connected with the Man's.

Contemplating what she saw, she inwardly sighed. She knew kindness when she saw it, especially after her constant exposure to it at the shelter. Giving him a tight smile, she turned to go in, missing his shocked expression.

That was the best she could do right now; him being genuinely nice just didn't make up for everything else his presence had done to her family. But she was sincerely glad he'd taken Jaime to the skate park, her little brother needed that.

Here she was, going down pity party road again. Silently admonishing herself, she thought of Walt's story. It showed her how blessed she was to have both of her parents in her life, even if they weren't together anymore. They were alive, and she could still hug them and talk to them and see their faces, even though she often chose not to.

The desire to forgive and move on was there, but she needed more time to work it out.

Chapter 20

Krystal had never been this busy in her entire life. Days and weeks rushed past at lightning speed, like she was perched on a unicycle, peddling away while juggling numerous rings in the air. Throw. Catch. Throw. Catch. Over and over again. She'd feel like a failure if even one ball dropped.

First there was homework, lots of it. Most days, she and Em went to Brandon's after school to do homework, usually staying until dinnertime. This was her way of staying on track while still spending time with her best friend and boyfriend. Her Tuesday nights were dedicated to soup scooping at the shelter. Nick faithfully gave her a break each week so she could keep up with Walt. Past her shyness now, she always greeted him with a hug and snuck Peety treats when she could.

Her evenings after dinner were reserved for her siblings. Once it was their bedtime, she would retire to her room to do more homework and study for finals until after midnight. Sleep deprived and stressed; she was completely worn out, but she kept reminding herself…just another week and a half and this will all get better.

Nick wasn't able to get much extra time on the murals because the director hoped to have the daycare open around the same time school was out. In spite of school being out soon, he was able to stretch the deadline to June 5th, which was an extra week. However, it no longer mattered, because Krystal had come up with a brilliant plan.

Deciding to speak with Mr. Z, her art teacher, and Sarah, who was also a volunteer at the shelter and in her art class too, they'd excitedly agreed to help her with the murals.

Mr. Z brought in a couple of other skilled, young artists who were eager to assist. The entire project would most likely be done the weekend after the last day of school.

While Krystal would have loved to take on the entire project alone, she knew sharing in the opportunity would be a win-win for everyone. If she was completely honest, she knew doing three murals would have been totally overwhelming.

She'd decided she would do the Noah's Ark in the baby room herself and let the others handle the rest, which left Mr. Z as the director. He and Nick had looked through her drawings and made the selections for the other two rooms. The toddler room got a Jonah and the Whale theme and the big kid's room was receiving a Daniel and The Lion's Den mural. An added bonus was that Mr. Z was giving the other students and her extra credit for their work. Unfortunately, art was the one class where she didn't need any help with her grade.

After looking through Krystal's samples, Nick raved about how gifted Krystal was. It touched her to see how enthralled he was with her art. 'You know natural talent is a gift from God, don't you?' He had questioned her seriously, but when he'd asked, the look on his face made her giggle. For good measure, she'd sent up a silent thank you to God for this experience and all the good things that had been happening as of late.

When Krystal told Nick she had drawn him numerous times starting right after the first night she'd met him, his response was nothing short of ecstatic. When she showed him some of the drawings, he'd gone quiet and was unconsciously holding one hand to his chest. He looked as if he might cry. 'I'm so honored by this,' he'd said. His favorite was a rendition she did of him greeting her and Em's family at the back door of the shelter. One arm was extended to the side from swinging the door open wide while the other was in the motion of a grand gesture to invite them in. All the love he carried with him was told through the story of the drawing, etched in each line and curve that formed his face.

Ralph had been teasing her about kidnapping one of his tutors for the murals. As retribution, he'd made her find several weeks worth of jokes that were guaranteed to stump all the other teens. After two failures, she found a riddle that did the job; not a single teen got it right.

With pointed fangs I sit and wait,
With piercing force I serve out fate.
Grabbing bloodless victims, proclaiming my might;
Physically joining with a single bite.
What am I?

At first, Krystal was unable to decide which was funnier, Ralph's increasingly dramatic delivery that could have been a narration by Dracula himself, ending with a *bwahaha*! or the glassy-eyed expressions on everyone's faces when he recited the poetic riddle that guaranteed a request for a repeat, ending with yet another befuddled expression.

Ralph won hands down, Krystal determined. Chase's reaction was the most hilarious though, looking as if he'd overslept.

"It's too early for all that," he whined.

What Ralph didn't know was she'd recorded his performance on her phone. Knowing Nick would get a good laugh out of it, she couldn't wait to show him. For the first time since Krystal had been volunteering, they were actually late to the shelter.

"Okay," Ralph said, "I'll stick to the not-so-hard jokes from now on so that we aren't late, but I'll bet they never look at a stapler the same again!"

Conversations with Nick were always a combination of meaningful and fun. Krystal was amazed at how well he could read her. He always knew when she was up for chatting while working or when she wanted solitude. This past Saturday, she'd broken down and explained her family situation to him. True to form, Nick listened well and understood all the different emotions that had plagued her. They had a long talk about forgiveness and how it can impact people's lives negatively if they withhold it. 'You're hurting yourself the most when you don't forgive,' he'd said. Nodding in response, she knew how true that was.

In retrospect, she'd been a coward. Willing to tell Nick about what her family had done, specifically her mom, while failing to reveal her shortcomings was wrong and she knew it. It was a repeat of what she'd done with Em. On the other hand, what Nick thought mattered to her and she didn't want to change how he saw her.

Because of the rides with Ralph, she'd become more social with the teens she rode with each Saturday. One of the girls told her she'd friend her on Facebook. When Krystal replied she didn't have a Facebook account, they'd all looked at her like she'd grown a second head. By the end of the trip, they'd made her promise to open an account so they could keep up with each other over the summer. The still lingering anti-social part of Krystal was struck by the fact she'd actually miss these people after the murals were complete.

Chapter 21

As desperately as she wished to stop, Krystal had relapsed twice. With all the stress, especially from school, she couldn't abstain and had given in.

After the second time, she was so guilt-ridden she'd thrown her glass heart into the concrete wall of her bathroom and vowed never to cut again. She wrote her vows in her notebook of prayers with a date and signature. She failed.

Unfortunately, the stress of trying to refrain from cutting had morphed into something else. Now haunted by anxiety that intensified so quickly at times, it left her nauseated. Krystal didn't understand the panic that welled up inside her chest. It attacked her very being. It spread into every cavity and expanded until she became so consumed it was as if she had to create the exit in order for it to vacate her body.

The attacks confounded her. In the past, her cutting was always provoked by her anger and emotions. But now, she would be sitting on her bed, doing homework and be blindsided by the invisible force, driving into her like a bullet, then fragmenting.

Em had randomly checked her arms as promised, but Krystal no longer cut on her arms at all. In fact, they were the most healed she'd ever seen them. Instead, she stuck to the tops of her thighs, her hips, her stomach…the result was crushing self-reproach, and she was more ashamed than ever. By consistently lying to her best friend and not telling Nick the whole story, she was a coward and a phony.

Deep down, she wanted to come clean. But she knew that if she did, Em and Nick would most certainly tell her mom. Em had said as much, and of course, Nick being an adult, he would want to get her help. She didn't want outside help. Convinced she could work this out on her own, she stayed busy and kept a smile on her face, which wasn't hard most of the time until she was alone.

In the midst of all the crazy, she still managed to write her prayers to God. Some nights it might only be a couple of sentences, but her goal was to write every single night. Her relationship with God was dysfunctional at best. Nonetheless, her prayer journal had become important to her. Although she didn't understand God, she knew her recent blessings had a lot, if not everything, to do with him. There was an apology for her failures in every entry. Krystal was sometimes terrified God wouldn't continue to bless her if she didn't get her act together.

Chapter 22

"I passed everything!" Krystal hooted from the top of the stairs in front of the school. Em was stunned into silence. Her best friend's pink bangs and long hair formed an interesting blur of a tornado. Krystal spun around, then held up a piece of paper in the air above her head before running down the stairs to breathlessly greet her.

Em put an arm around Krystal's shoulder. "Selfie!" Holding up her phone, she clicked the shutter button. It was the best picture of Krystal ever; she looked so truly happy. "What's next?" Em asked.

"Um, I don't know." Krystal laughed. "All I know is I don't have any homework for the next three months! I could totally cry right now."

Em couldn't bring herself to do one last random check on Krystal's arms. She wasn't about to ruin Krystal's mood. Besides, she was pretty certain Krystal wasn't cutting. Krystal had changed so much in the last couple months and her arms didn't look anything like that first day.

Em set the new picture as her background photo and slid her phone into her bag. Her eyes lit up with silent laughter as she saw Brandon sneaking up behind Krystal.

"So what should we do tonight?" Em asked to aid with a diversion.

Just as Krystal opened her mouth to answer, Brandon got right behind her ear and yelled BOO and grabbed her at the waist at the same time. Krystal startled so badly she threw her hands up, backhanding Brandon right in the nose.

"Oh, that went so bad!" Em said, standing with one hand on her forehead and her mouth agape.

Krystal, on the other hand, laughed hysterically.

"Ah, that hurts." Brandon moaned.

"That's what you get," Krystal said smartly.

Moving his hand from his face, he looked at Krystal. "You should kiss it and make it better."

Dutifully, Krystal gave him a light peck on his nose. "You'll live, I'm sure of it."

"Gosh, no sympathy from you." Changing the subject, he said, "We should all watch a movie at my place tonight. My mom won't care."

Em called her mom to see if she could spend time with Krystal and Brandon. Sometimes she felt like a third wheel, but Krystal was the only friend she spent any time with and she wasn't giving her up to a boy. Not even a cool one like Brandon.

She appreciated they'd never once made her feel unwanted or unwelcome. They were quite the trio, even though seeing K and B together made her wish she had a boyfriend of her own.

"Mom said she'd pick me up at eight," Em said. "I have twenty dollars, we should order a pizza."

"Sweet!" Krystal said. "I want jalapeños on my half."

"Your half? You mean your third?" Brandon corrected.

"Um, if I'm buying, I'm not dying. Jalapeños vetoed." Em snapped her fingers with attitude and then smiled.

In the end, Krystal and Brandon put in another ten dollars between them so they ended up with two pizzas and some breadsticks. Everyone was happy. Krystal got her jalapeños, and Brandon's brother even managed to snag a couple pieces before he ran back upstairs. Em didn't mind, she thought Brandon's older brother was cute. Too bad he was eighteen…and totally not interested in her…at all.

Em got a little drowsy after eating and the action-packed movie filled with grunts and multiple *Hiii-yahs* was totally not her thing. Putting her head back on the couch, she drifted off.

Opening her eyes, she knew it had to be close to eight. She heard a snicker and instead of turning her head, she moved only her eyes to the right. She could see Brandon leaning in toward Krystal.

"What are you doing?" she snapped, and they both jumped. If they'd been cats, she would have been peeling them both from the ceiling. "You don't think a first kiss in front of a snoozing best friend is a little awkward?"

"How do you know it would be our first?" Brandon retorted.

It was a lame attempt at regaining his composure, so Em didn't bother with a verbal answer. Instead, she cocked her head and raised a brow. "Where are your mom and brother anyway?" she asked.

"At the store," Krystal piped in, turning her head so Brandon couldn't see her face. She gave Em a big-eyed look that said, 'chill out!'

Chapter 23

y noon Saturday, the very last brushstroke graced the wall of the nursery; it was complete. The other two rooms had been finished too. Everyone stood in a reverent silence admiring all their hard work.

"Come closer, everyone," Nick said. Without any further instruction, everyone joined hands and bowed their heads as Nick said a prayer thanking God for the blessing of each individual who helped with the daycare in any capacity. At the end, they all said a collective "Amen!"

"Pizza party!" Nick announced. "It should be here any time now. I ordered it well over a half an hour ago. Krystal silently promised herself she'd do a sit up or jumping jack later as a way to compensate for all the pizza lately.

Ralph came through the door with a stack of pizza boxes as they were setting up tables and chairs in the main room. Walt came in behind him carrying a bag with a couple of two-liters and cups. Peety stood by his side, as usual.

"Hey!" Krystal exclaimed, with a big smile on her face as she took the soda from Walt.

"Well, I had to see how it all turned out." Walt smiled back. "Judging by this room, I'd say breathtaking." Krystal walked Walt through the other two rooms. As they stood in front of the Noah's Ark mural, Walt shook his head. "You have a way of creating a new perspective on even the oldest story around," he said softly.

"I'm glad you like it," Krystal said, smiling up at him. "I knew we'd already have a lot of ocean with the Jonah and the Whale mural, so I decided to go inside the ark."

Walt stared and Krystal watched him as he did.

"The only water you see in this mural is outside the windows, and it's mostly rain," Walt said with reverence in his voice. "The interior of the ark has a warm candlelight glow which gives it a perfect tone that is neither overly bright nor overly dark. Somehow you painted God's presence right into the scene."

Noah and his family were all with various animals, either playing with them or feeding them. Love was woven into the relationships between human and animal. Walt laughed, pointing at the scene of two brothers who were using an apple to play keep away with an elephant, their faces lit up with laughter. Birds were in the air, bugs on the wall…. Walt even found the spider web up high and a mouse at the very bottom. Krystal had never enjoyed a project as much as this one.

"I surmise it would take me more than a week to note every bit of detail you painted in, my little friend."

"Thanks, Walt," Krystal said. "Let's go eat and you can look at it later." The fact was that his compliments deeply affected her, but she didn't want to go getting all sappy on him. How she loved that old man, though.

Going back into the main room, Ralph was setting up a speaker for music. When Krystal saw him pull out an iPod, she couldn't stop her reaction. "Whoa! You know how to operate that thing?"

"Why do you all keep saying things like that?" His wounded expression was priceless. "You do know I'm an educated man, right? I got this."

When the music started playing, Ralph started dancing and the whole room fell into stitches. He was pretty good.

When Nick joined him and started doing some version of the funky chicken, they all lost it.

Krystal was thankful she had enough sense to grab her phone to get a video. She kept it rolling as everyone else joined in, including herself. Walt grabbed her hand and spun her.

Gosh, I love these people!

On the ride home, she and Nick stopped for ice cream.

"You know, Krystal, you're meant to be in an environment like the shelter. You have a quiet way with people that draws them to you and your art does all the talking for you."

"Thanks," Krystal said thoughtfully, pondering his words.

Nick laughed. "You still can't see in yourself what we see in you. That's okay—you'll grow into it. Are you still praying?" Looking at her out of the corner of his eye, he wanted to see her reaction. He was pleasantly surprised.

"Yep. I am."

"Do I feel a 'but' coming on?" He laughed.

"Not really. I have a prayer journal I write in every night. Sometimes I pray the regular way, too." Nick smiled. "Things have been a lot better for me. There are just still some things that aren't," Krystal admitted.

"Have you asked for helped with those things?"

"Not really."

"Well," Nick said, "I would if I were you, but God finds a way to help us even when we don't ask. So, just make sure you're not blocking help on your end," Nick finished with a wink.

Krystal stilled. The comment hit home.

"It's going to be very different on Saturdays without you here.

"You'll have to find me something else to do, but just not yet. We're going to begin going to my dad's on Saturdays starting today and coming home a bit earlier on Sunday for the next few weeks. I bet you can find me something else to paint," she winked and they both laughed.

"Thank you for everything, Nick." Krystal gave him an impulsive hug before she got out of the car. "That was the best experience ever."

"Ah, don't thank me," he said, grinning. You know whom to thank," he said, pointing his index finger upward.

"Believe it or not," she smiled back, "I do."

That night, Krystal decided that sometime during the summer she would tell Nick her whole story. She wanted to get a handle on things first. Maybe she would start by asking God to help instead of trying to do everything on her own.

Chapter 24

In a stampede, the kids rushed up Roberto's steps as Maria waved and drove away. "What are we doing tonight, Dad?" Rosie asked excitedly.

Although he already knew her answer, he looked down into his youngest daughter's eager eyes.

"What do you think we should do?"

"Play a game!" she retorted, and rose on her tiptoes, puckering her little lips. Roberto bent down to place a loud kiss on them.

Esme was bent down and scratching Lucky's ears. He purred, pushing his head into her palm.

"We should have brought Lucy with us," Esme said quietly.

"We'd have to see if they'd get along," Roberto said. "But that might stress your Lucy out, not being in the home she's used to."

"Yeah, you're probably right. I wouldn't want to upset him," Esme said gently.

"Him?" Roberto looked amused.

"Yeah, Lucy turned out to be a boy." Esme giggled. "But he'd already learned his name, so I wasn't going to change it.

Krystal noticed Esme withheld the fact it was the Man who'd been mistaken in Lucy's gender.

"Hey!" Jaime yelled, running into the house as the screen door slapped shut behind him.

"What's his deal?" Krystal asked, perplexed by her brother's behavior."

Peering in to see what Jaime saw, Rosie yelled "ALEX!" before sprinting into the house. However, the door didn't have a chance to slam again because Esme and Krystal were rushing in, too.

Roberto laughed and closed the door quietly after entering the room filled in pandemonium.

Krystal swept her cousin Alex up in a big hug before going to her Uncle Domingo next.

"How long have you been here?" she asked, still not believing they were standing there.

They tried to come every summer, traveling from Anahuac, Chihuahua, in Mexico. Their two-week stays always included updates on the family, many cookouts and lots of visitors coming by to say hi.

Part of her was sad she wouldn't see them every day while they were here. The old annoyance at her mom for the change in their family was pushing its way into her heart. But this time she pushed back; she didn't want to lose her joy. Smiling to herself for taking Nick's advice, she laughed when Rosie, Jaime, and Alex stormed back outside.

Looking at her dad, she noticed he wore a wounded expression. Without even thinking about it, she had spoken in Spanish to her uncle and cousin. Honestly, it had come out naturally, and what was she supposed to do? They barely spoke any English.

It turned out her siblings and her would spend most of the next two weeks at their dad's house. Roberto could only take a few days off because his crew was in the middle of a huge project, but since Domingo would be at his house during the days, the kids could stay. Em's parents picked her up and dropped her back off there, so she didn't miss her nights at the shelter. It all worked out perfectly.

As much as she missed seeing Brandon and Em, she seized the opportunity to ask her uncle a million questions about her family's history. She was pretty sure he enjoyed talking about them as much as she enjoyed listening. She'd asked so many questions he had to email some of his uncles to get more information. At the end of two weeks, she'd drawn her uncle and cousin numerous times and sent a few of the drawings home with them so they could keep one and give the others away.

A gloomy cloud sat over her at their Saturday departure. Their presence had brought back a sense of the old days of being at her dad's house. Even though her mom wasn't present, it had almost been…normal. They'd played games, talked, cooked, and even played little pranks on each other. One night while her Uncle Domingo had been napping in the recliner, they'd painted his nails with the pink polish Esme brought along. Of course, she took pictures. She'd even opened a new Facebook account, so she shared those along with the videos she took of Ralph, Nick, and of everyone dancing at the pizza party.

There had been a huge difference in her dad; he had been so happy to get home each day. Now he had to go back to coming home to an empty house every day after work again.

It will get better when I can drive.

She wondered if the silence would be deafening for him. Krystal put her hands over her eyes trying to hold back the tears. Tired of crying, she sighed heavily and exhaled. Her dad put his arm around her shoulders, pulling her in.

"Te amo, Papa," she said, putting her arm around his waist.

Chapter 25

June 13th. Nick scribbled the date on the container of applesauce, circled the M for Monday, and slid it into its rightful spot on the shelf in the huge walk-in refrigerator. Peeling off his gloves, he pushed the door closed with his elbow and tossed them in the trash. Lastly, he pulled his red apron over his head and hung it on the rusty hook in the back room.

"Have a good night, everyone! I've got a bit of paperwork to do and then I'm going home. Wasn't too bad for a Monday, huh?" He winked, then waved as everyone called back variations of 'goodnight,' 'have a nice evening,' and a good-natured yet sarcastic 'yeah right!' Nick chuckled.

Following the halls to the shared office space, Nick sat down at the desk. Within the glass-enclosed office he could see the common area, entryway, and check-in desk all at once. With the film-covered glass, seeing out was no problem, but you had to look much harder to be able to see into the office from the outside. It was a good way to keep an eye on the main entrance without everyone knowing you were doing it. Often the desk jockeys would entertain themselves during downtime by making crazy faces at whoever might be occupying the office…often Nick or

Ralph. It was usually pretty entertaining for both parties on either side of the glass.

This was the time of night when the majority of the guests were making their way through check-in to secure a bed for the night. Since this was the men's unit, it went quicker and smoother since it was rare there were children staying, and there were no families in this wing. Those already checked in were milling around getting ready for bed or making phone calls. Others played cards or chess. Lights-out was still a little more than two hours away so the common area was a hive of activity during this hour.

Nick busied himself finishing a small order for some staple items that would be needed for the kitchen soon. He leaned against the back of the chair and into a stretch when suddenly, the two volunteers at the desk, Mike and Nathan, synchronously backed up to the glass so fast it caused the windows to vibrate from the impact. Bodies stiff, they both were holding their hands up in front of them. People around the desk scattered like mice, some dropping to the floor, others backing against the wall. One of the chessboards was knocked from a table when the players took flight, all of the game pieces scattering. The men closest to the door backed right out the entrance and ran.

Not wanting to stand up and risk being noticed, Nick rolled his chair to the right and saw a man, small in stature, who was pointing a gun at Mike and Nathan. Looking at this man's face, he saw angry, wild eyes that were full of fear. With his training and years of experience, Nick quickly deduced the man was quite possibly under the influence of drugs. Probably heroin or steroids, and the man could be in the early stages of withdrawal. If so, it meant the man might be more than willing to use his weapon to get what he wanted. Whatever the case, he needed to defuse this situation and fast!

Reaching under the desk, he flicked the latch that popped open the hard gray cover to the panic button and depressed it. Hopefully the police were already on their way since some of the guests made it outside. Praying as he stood, he could see the man was now ushering the guests to the opposite side of the room. When an older gentleman didn't move fast enough, the man became so agitated he began twitching.

He held his gun in the air and fired once, then screeched. "I said MOVE!"

The crack of the gunshot was immediately followed by the smack of the bullet striking the ceiling. Residual noise from the shot fired echoed down the halls as debris fell from the ceiling where the bullet lodged. Only the sound of the man's labored breathing remained in the room.

Silently asking God to lead him, Nick put his hands up in front of him in plain view as he stepped out of the office.

"It's going to be okay," Nick spoke directly to the young, distraught man who was now sweating profusely. Startled, the man swung the gun violently to the right where Nick was and faced him. "My name is Nick; how about we let all these folks go and I can help you with anything you need."

"Why should I let them go? These two," he cried loudly, waving his gun towards Mike and Nathan, "they think this place is too good to let me stay here. They said I'd have to take a test first. None of the others had to take a test!" He spat on the floor. By the childlike tone of his voice, Nick half expected him to follow with—'It's not fair!'

"I'm so sorry about that," Nick said gently. "I'll be happy to make sure you have a bed for the night." He wasn't going to mention it would be in a jail cell at this point, but he wasn't lying to the man.

The man seemed to believe the note of sincerity in Nick's voice. Suddenly, he turned towards Mike and Nathan again, who visibly recoiled.

"You two are not nice!" he said in a whiny voice. While he had his back turned, Nick motioned to the guests who were near the back hall to go.

Very carefully, they eased down the hall, disappearing into dorm rooms a few at a time.

"How about we go into my office and talk, my friend?" Nick kept his movements miniscule, his tone gentle but unwavering; he was solid as a rock. "We really do love everyone here and I promise you I care about you and what happens to you. I know you're not having the greatest day, but God loves you and wants to take care of you. I truly want to help God do that."

As the man fixated on Nick's voice, the other guests were still soundlessly tiptoeing away.

"Come on in," Nick urged him, inclining his head toward the office. Although it was barely an inch, the damaged man began to lower his weapon. Looking at Nick, he took a small step forward as tears began to rain down his cheeks. All Nick could see was a very distraught child, hidden in a man's body.

"Hello," said a tinny-sounding voice from outside. Someone was speaking through a megaphone.

The man raised his trembling hand, sucking in air. He pointed the gun at Nick, who remained calm.

"My name is Officer Scarborough. We don't want anyone to get hurt. Please come out with your hands in the air," the tiny voice echoed.

"I'm not going out there!" he screamed. Frantically, he looked at Nick. "You said you'd help me. You lied!" Sobbing now, the man spun around, holding the gun straight out, and noticed that all but a few of the guests had exited.

Nick had a sorrowful look on his face that was completely heartfelt. Seeing how this man was hurting made him hurt too. Knowing this man had likely been through a life of pain and rejection, and who knew what else, he wished he could have been the one to help him see God.

"You lied. You tricked me." The man cried so softly it was just a whisper; then he pulled the trigger. Nick fell backwards, grabbing his chest with one hand and reaching for the wall with his other. His strength dissipated after leaning on the wall for only a moment. He slid down to the floor.

Guests screamed.

One of the men who had snuck down the hall with the others cried out. He called Nick's name as he sobbed. He tried to run to Nick, but several of the other men were holding him back, scared the shooter would fire again.

Putting his palm on his forehead, in a frenzied voice, the little man kept repeating himself. "I'm sorry. I'm sorry. I didn't mean to. I mean—I didn't want to." He moaned, completely defeated as he put the gun under his chin and closed his eyes.

All at once Mike leaped onto the counter and pushed himself off the edge. He launched his body onto the little man, knocking the gun from his hands and landing directly on top of him. Using his bodyweight to keep him pinned, he grabbed both of the man's wrists and spread them out to the sides like wings. The little man's thrashings weakened.

Having heard the gunshot, officers rushed in. Immediately they relieved Mike and cuffed the man. Medics, directed by Nathan, rushed to Nick.

The officers pulled the man to his feet. Guests started filtering back in various states of distress, some shaking their heads, some crying, and others were staring blankly with mouths agape—in shock. Police ushered them back out. It felt like hours, but the entire incident hadn't lasted much more than a few minutes.

Nick, whose breathing was shallow and labored, looked at the little man. "What's your name, my friend?" he struggled to ask.

"I'm Kenny," the man replied, sounding like a small child. He began weeping in a high-pitched tone. "And I'm sorry, I didn't mean to. I don't know why I did it." If it weren't for the officers holding Kenny up, he would have collapsed to the floor in a puddle.

"Kenny," Nick whispered weakly before closing his eyes. "I forgive you. Jesus loves you. Love him back. Okay?"

"Nooo! Don't go," Kenny cried out.

Nick took his last breath.

Chapter 26

"Where are they again?" Krystal called out in a crabby voice from outside the bathroom on the main floor of the house.

"At the very bottom," Josefina called back, "in the little pink basket."

"Since when did you start buying so much toothpaste and deodorant?" Krystal whined. On her knees, digging through the bottom of the linen closet cluttered with toiletries, she knew all this stuff hadn't been there just a couple months ago.

"I started couponing!" Josefina chirped, as she walked up behind her. "I only paid taxes on most of that stuff! Good, huh?"

"Yeah, but it will take us a whole year to use all of this," Krystal said dryly.

"Aye! Krystal, there are seven of us."

Krystal turned around to look up at her mom, and then immediately grimaced.

"Sorry, I found them," Josefina said, holding a handful of goggles. "Rosie never took them out of the bag like I asked her to the last time we went."

Krystal was thoroughly disgruntled as she started shoving tubes of toothpaste and bottles of shampoo back in the bottom of the closet. "Hurry and get changed so we can go."

"I really don't want to go swimming, Mom! Let me just stay here. I'd rather talk to Em and Brandon."

"You're not staying here alone while we are all gone, not with Brandon living right down there," Josefina replied, pointing her thumb in the direction of Brandon's house.

"It's not like that!" At her mother's words, Krystal needed to think fast. No way could she be seen in any type of swimsuit, and swimming in long sleeves would surely cause a scene.

"I know it's not like that, and it's staying that way," Josefina replied judiciously.

Rosie's voice carried from the front door. "C'mon!"

"We're coming," Josefina snapped back. "If you'd put things where I tell you, we'd be gone already. Get in the car!"

Rosie knew better than to say another word, as she quietly closed the door and did as her mother told her.

"You know I'm working at the shelter tonight; what if we're not back in time?"

"Krystal," Josefina was becoming agitated and her already thick accent was about to roll right into Spanish if Krystal kept pressing her. "It's only one o'clock. We'll be back in plenty of time before Emily's parents come for you. Besides, it's not going to hurt you to get some sun and exercise."

"What are you trying to say?" Krystal crossed her arms, offended.

Josefina threw her hands in the air, causing a pair of goggles to fly out of the beach bag. "Dios, ayudame porfavor," she petitioned God for help and took a deep breath, then exhaled. "Just that exercise is good. And nooo, I'm not saying you're fat. You know you're not. I'm glad you care more about your appearance than before, and I'm glad you got rid of that pink hair last night, but you have been inside more than out since school ended."

Running her hands through her hair, Krystal was tapping her foot. "Not true, I was outside a lot at dad's house. We all were. What if the chlorine makes the pink come back?" She knew it was a last ditch effort and not a very good one.

"Krystal, I'm done with this conversation. Get your stuff and be outside in three minutes." Josefina headed for the front door.

An unexpected sob escaped from Krystal.

Josefina stopped in her tracks and turned around, seeing Krystal standing there with her hands covering her eyes.

"What's really going on? Why are you so upset about swimming? Is it because of Eli?"

Krystal shook her head no at her mom's last question, but was unable to find words. How could she escape this situation? Her stress level was in the red, and she wasn't ready for the aftermath of her mom seeing her scars. When she finally opened her mouth to speak, the phone rang.

"Want me to get it?" she asked through sniffles. Any diversion would be welcome right now.

"I will." Josefina picked it up right after the third ring. "Bueno," she said into the receiver.

Krystal was trying to put her thoughts together when she saw her mom lean against the counter and place her hand on her forehead.

"No, I haven't. Oh no," she gasped softly and gulped audibly. "Oh no," she whispered. Josefina glanced at Krystal and then quickly away. She was silent for a bit before she said, "I'm so sorry. Of course…. No, I'll tell her."

"Mom," Krystal said questioningly. Panic rose from the pit of her stomach and crawled into her chest. "What is it? What's wrong?" Her mom held up a halting hand and Krystal saw her eyes shining with tears.

"Thank you for calling." She hung up the phone. "Wait here, Krystal."

Josefina went outside with the bag and came back just a minute later empty handed. Krystal could hear the sound of the car leaving. Ice crawled through her veins, and she broke out in a cold sweat. She knew what it was.

Em told Mom about my cutting or told her mom who told my mom. Why would she do that? Did she somehow know I haven't really stopped? Thoughts racing, her body went rigid and she wanted to throw up.

"Let's sit down, mija," Josefina said soothingly.

"I don't want to sit down. Just say what you need to," she gushed defensively. With a gurgling stomach and sweaty palms, she just wanted to get this over with so she could go to her room.

"Nick died last night. I'm so sorry," Josefina said, wrapping Krystal in her arms.

Krystal froze, and her mind went completely blank. "What?" Krystal said uncertainly. Squinting in confusion, she couldn't reconcile what her mom said with truth. "What?"

Josefina grabbed Krystal's hand and held it.

"No. No," Krystal whispered, pulling her hand away and putting it on her head. At the same time, she reached for the wall for support. A chill ran through her and she shuddered. As the impact of the news hit her, her strength instantly vanished and she swooned. Krystal spun toward the floor.

Josefina was unable to support her and they slid down to the floor together.

Krystal's lips trembled uncontrollably.

"Wh-what happened?" she stuttered.

Josefina took a deep breath and held Krystal tightly as she relayed what Ralph had told her. Krystal wept loudly at first and then silently.

It was nearly 2:30 p.m. when her mom helped her to her bedroom and told her to lie down. Vaguely aware her shoes were being pulled off, she felt the weight shift as her mom sat down on the edge of the bed and stroked her hair. Krystal's tears slipped into her pillow. Somehow she drifted off to sleep.

When Krystal awoke, the clock read 6:38. Unsure if it was morning or evening, she stood and her head spun. Reaching for the nightstand to steady herself, the loss of Nick slammed into her all over again.

A gasp erupted from her, nearly doubling her over. Guilt washed over her, knowing she'd missed her night at the shelter. Images of Walt, Ralph, Mel, and the other faces flooded her mind and she hurt for them too.

How could Nick be gone? How could anyone have hurt someone who loved everyone? Why would God allow that to happen? Him of all people? Seemed like God allowed an awful lot of bad things to happen these days. Fury piqued, working to flush out the sadness in her chest, but instead they pooled together into a toxic blend.

Retching, she covered her mouth and grabbed onto anything she could to keep herself upright as she tried to make it to the toilet. She didn't make it.

Afterward, she crawled the short distance to the cool concrete portion of the floor until she could rise to go to the sink.

Splashing water on her face, a familiar fear snaked up her spine causing all the fine hairs on her neck and arms to stand up. *No!* she told herself. *No!* Frozen where she stood, she clutched the front of her shirt, scared she might have a heart attack. In terror, she stumbled to the dresser. If she just cut, it would stop. She could stop it! She knew she could!

Fighting to catch her breath, she reached for the book, pulling it open by its cover. The glass fell out with a clang. She grabbed it with her right hand and without hesitation, in one fluid motion, sliced at her left arm, already closing her eyes in anticipation of relief.

Warm and familiar, she gasped once more and then was able to breathe. The horror that had gripped her was now seeping out of the fresh opening. Still holding the glass, she realized she was shivering. Putting her hands up to the dresser to steady herself, she felt something wet on her cheek. Opening her eyes, she saw all the blood. Lightly spurting like a small fountain out of her wrist, she covered her wrist with her other hand, trying to stem the flow.

There'd never been this much blood before. For a moment she just stared, then swayed, then thought, *I need to get a towel.* But she couldn't get a hold on the spinning. Despite the dizziness, she spotted the dark blue towel just steps away. Moving to get it, her foot slipped in a small pool of blood on the floor. Landing on her wounded hand, white-hot pain exploded in her body. Her soundless scream echoed in her head before everything went dark.

Chapter 27

Krystal's eyes fluttered. She fought to keep them open, but the brightness of the room prevailed and her lashes were drawn down as her head began to pound. Putting her hand on her head, she felt a lump.

How did that get there? She had no idea.

Dread filled her as she realized she was in the hospital. Sorrow fought for space and won when she remembered Nick was no longer here. He wasn't at the shelter serving a meal. He wasn't listening intently as someone spoke of his or her troubles. He wasn't teasing Ralph about his bald head. He would never wink at her again. His wink that told her she mattered; that she was part of the team. He was gone forever.

Hearing voices in the room, she tried to focus her mind. What grogginess remained was quickly evaporating. One of voices belonged to her mother, she was certain.

Peering from under her lashes, she tried to see who the other person was. Her blurred vision began to clear, but the pain in her head kept her from moving too much. It was her dad! Elation and then confusion were stirred into her melting pot of emotions.

Convinced she was dreaming, she shut her eyes again. She let the language that meant home drift to her as she eavesdropped on their imaginary conversation.

"I'm so sorry," Roberto looked at Josefina and hung his head. "You've never told the kids about the things I did in the past. You took all the blame. This is all my fault."

What did he mean? Krystal wondered. *What did he do?*

"This is not all your fault, Roberto. We both have been very selfish, and the kids have suffered for it, especially Krystal. I kept telling myself she would get past the anger. She seemed so much better recently. But I never knew she had been hurting herself. I promise I didn't know," Josefina's voice cracked. "I can't believe she wanted to die." Sobbing now, she covered her face as Roberto awkwardly patted her on the back.

Alarmed at her mom's words, Krystal's eyes opened and she squinted against the intrusion of light.

"Mom, I wasn't trying to kill myself," she whispered, her voice a little raspy.

"Mija, you're awake." Josefina and Roberto rushed over going to opposite sides of the bed. "How are you feeling? Are you hurting?" Josefina clutched Krystal's good hand and kissed the back of it.

Roberto leaned over and planted a kiss on her forehead. He looked a dozen years older than when she'd last seen him only days ago.

"Hi, baby," he said and rested his forehead against hers for a moment.

"I'm fine, I think. I'm sore and I have a terrible headache. What happened to my head?" Becoming aware there was something wrapped around her head, she reached up to feel it. That's when she became entirely conscious of her exposure. In jerky motions, she began arranging the blanket to cover her forearms.

Josefina could see the distress in Krystal's face and immediately began to soothe her. "Shhhh. Krystal, look at me." Josefina looked her directly in the eyes, still holding her hand. "We are going to get through this together. Okay?"

"Okay," Krystal whispered before taking a deep breath.

She sat in the bed as her parents looked at her. Her mind struggled to reconcile the fact that her parents now knew everything. They'd probably seen every cut she ever made. Attempting to wipe the relentless tears with her wounded hand and not pull on the IV was quite a task. She held up her hand, trying to figure out what must have happened. The bandage ran from the middle of her hand up past her wrist. It was obvious she'd cut herself way worse than ever before.

The door to her room swung open and a nurse came in. "Hi, Krystal. I'm Annie. Think you can eat something?" she asked cheerfully.

"I'm not too hungry, but I can try."

"That a girl! Chicken noodle sound okay?"

"I guess," she shrugged. She was ready to go home.

"I'll get it ordered for you as soon as we check your vitals."

The nurse was fluttering around: checking her eyes, taking her temperature, reading numbers on the machine, and making notes.

Reaching for a control, Annie pushed a button and the bed came up, leaving Krystal in a sitting position. When she finished, Annie smiled sweetly and exited.

"When can I go home?" Krystal asked her parents.

Josefina and Roberto glanced at each other uneasily.

"What?" Krystal asked. "Is it still Tuesday?"

"No, honey," her mom answered. "It's Wednesday, and it's nearly noon."

Dinner rolled in on a silver cart steered by someone who didn't look much older than Krystal. Not used to having her scars on display, Krystal crossed her arms while the girl unloaded her food.

"Enjoy your lunch," the girl said and hurriedly pushed the cart back out.

"That was fast," Krystal said. Even less hungry now that she was looking at the soup, her chest tightened. It only made her think of Nick and the shelter. "Can I have something else?"

"Of course. I'll order you a grilled cheese and some fries."

Krystal's unanswered questions were weighing heavy in the room, so she tried again. "What happened?"

To appease her parents, she worked on the lime green Jell-O that wiggled on her tray.

"That's what we need to know," Roberto said gently. "We didn't know things were this bad for you. Why didn't you tell us?" Krystal gave them a look that made them both sigh dolefully.

"Let her eat before we talk," Josefina insisted. "It's important for you to get something in your stomach. Finish your lunch; we'll talk about all of this, okay?"

It wasn't okay, but Krystal nodded nonetheless.

"I'll just go to the cafeteria and get it," he said and left.

"How am I supposed to go to the bathroom? What is all this stuff?"

"Let me call the nurse." Josefina said. She walked to the door and she peeked out, waving at whomever she spotted, motioning them to the room. A second later, Nurse Annie came back in to help.

Annie disconnected Krystal from everything except the IV, which had to be rolled on the stand next to her as she went.

Standing with Annie's help, her knees shook and her head swam. Josefina went to her other side for extra support.

"Why am I feeling like this?"

"You lost a lot of blood," Annie replied. "Once you get some food in you, that will help. It won't take any time for you to feel better."

Krystal knew better than that, but didn't comment. She grabbed the rail when they reached the restroom.

"I can get it from here."

"I'll stand in the doorway," Annie replied.

"I'm fine. You can close the door."

"I'm sorry, honey," Annie said, "but you're on suicide watch, and I can't leave you alone, not even for a short time.

"But I'm not suicidal!" Shaking even more now, she said, "I wasn't trying to kill myself."

"I'll stand there," Josefina said. "Calm down, Krystal. She's just doing her job." Josefina turned up the TV and turned the water on full blast. She stood in the doorway, holding onto the knob and putting her back to Krystal to give her as much privacy as possible.

Krystal didn't say another word until after she was back in bed and Annie was gone.

"I'm not suicidal!" Krystal slammed her head back against her pillow, instantly regretting it. "Ouch," she said, raising her good hand to her head.

Roberto walked back into the room with an arm-full of food. He gave Krystal a bag that had a grilled cheese and fries and then gave Josefina one with a small hamburger and onion rings.

"Thank you," she said. "I'm pretty hungry."

"Me too," he said as he opened his bag.

The door opened—a man in a white coat walked in with a clipboard.

"I'm Dr. Phillip." He smiled.

"When can I go home?" Krystal asked.

"Right to the point, you are. I understand." Pulling up a chair, he sat down and faced Krystal. "We will be releasing you from this wing in the morning. That is, as long as you are doing as well as we think you should be. I know you're probably feeling pretty weak and woozy, but that will pass pretty quickly, especially since you're eating and drinking." Krystal couldn't help but wonder if the word woozy was a medical term.

"You're a very lucky girl," he said, looking her in the eyes. "When you passed out, you landed on your wrist. Your bodyweight kept you from bleeding out. That saved your life."

Krystal's eyes grew wide. "I almost died?"

"It's a miracle you didn't. Thankfully, your mom found you in time."

Tears sprung into Krystal's eyes as she thought of her mom finding her like that and she turned to her. "Mom, I'm sorry. But I promise you, I wasn't trying to kill myself."

"Even if you weren't trying, you almost did," Dr. Phillip said matter-of-factly. "When you arrived, you were given a blood transfusion and we were able to stitch you up. After a cut like yours, most people would have at the very least lost their hand, and most others die. Must not have been your time to go."

Krystal stared blankly ahead unable to react to his words.

"You are on suicide watch," Dr Phillip continued with a softer voice. "Due to this incident, you won't be going home right away. After we release you from here, it is mandatory you spend at least the next seventy-two hours in our psychiatric ward for evaluation. It could be longer, but that's for the doctors there to decide."

"No!" Krystal cried. "I can't be away three days!" Looking at her mother with wide, pleading eyes, she begged her, "You know I need to see Walt and Ralph. What about Nick's funeral?" Her voice cracked. "I have to go. I want to be there. Don't make me miss it. I didn't try to kill myself, I swear it!"

Nurse Annie rushed in with a small syringe. "Hold still, dear," was all she said before dabbing her skin with a cotton ball. Krystal barely registered the prick in her arm.

Dr. Phillip waited for Annie to leave. "Krystal, even if you weren't trying to commit suicide, you have a pretty severe cutting problem. We're trying to help you, not punish you. Keep that in mind. You were lucky this time. Try to accept that and allow us help you."

Krystal's body was getting very heavy. She looked at Dr. Phillip, listening intently and forcing her mind to focus.

"Mija," Josefina said. "I will keep in contact with Ralph and see what I can do so that you can go to Nick's funeral. I know how important he was to you."

"Thanks, Mom," she said groggily. "Dad, I'm sorry I made you miss work. I know you never miss."

"You're my daughter. I'm sorry you feel like you have to apologize for that." Walking over, he sat on the edge of the bed and lightly touched the fingers on her hurt hand. "Now I know how much I have failed you. I'm sorry."

"You haven't failed, Dad."

Deep down she knew they'd all failed, but it didn't matter anymore. "Things will be easier now that you two aren't acting like you hate each other."

Josefina smiled sadly. Krystal could see guilt and regret on her mother's face, in her eyes.

"We don't, Krystal." Looking at Roberto, she said, "We will learn to be friends. God has been very good to us."

"I don't want to talk about God," Krystal interrupted, furrowing her brows.

"Krystal," Josefina's voice softly reprimanded.

"I don't. Not at all, not after what he let happen to Nick."

"Do you realize what he's done for you today…yesterday? For all of us?" Josefina countered. "I'm so thankful to God for not taking you. We could have lost you! I'm so sorry about Nick, but…." Her voice was shaking; she inhaled deeply to calm herself.

Krystal gulped hard, but turned her head and remained silent. She just wanted to sleep.

Josefina went home to shower and change. When she returned, it was Roberto's turn to go home for a bit.

Krystal was awake again.

"I'll see you later, okay?" Roberto said, hugging her and kissing her cheek.

"Okay."

Soon after the door closed behind Roberto, she asked her mom, "Do Em and Brandon know I'm here?"

Wearily, Josefina nodded.

Krystal sunk into her pillows.

"What all happened, Mom? Just tell me everything."

Josefina inched closer, tucking a loose strand of hair behind her ear.

"After you went to sleep, I called Emily's mom to tell her you wouldn't be going. Apparently, a local church group ended up taking last night's shifts to allow the regulars time to grieve."

Krystal's heart constricted in her chest, but she took a deep breath and waited for her mom to continue.

"We told the kids what had happened so they would understand why you would be so sad in the coming days. Rosie and Jaime decided to go make you cards."

Krystal smiled sadly.

"They didn't fight at all," Josefina said, as if she was still surprised. "Esme was in tears for you."

Krystal wished she could hug them all that very instant.

"She asked if she could go to your room to see you, but I told her no because you were resting. Then, Eli made arrangements so that he didn't have to work today, so I would be available to take you anywhere you needed to go."

"I know he's a good guy, Mom. It's been hard to deal with, but I know he is."

Josefina smiled and took Krystal's good hand, giving it a gentle squeeze. "Thank you for saying so, mija. That means a lot, and he really is." Sighing heavily, she continued. "You'd been sleeping so long I was getting more concerned, but I wasn't sure if I should wake you or not. I checked on you again sometime after six, and you were still asleep, I couldn't believe it. I decided I would go make you a plate of food and bring it to you.

"When I was in the kitchen making your plate, Sofia began crying. Eli had just gone out the door with a bag of garbage, so I went to go check on her."

Josefina began talking faster and Krystal heard the distress in her voice as she explained all the things she felt kept her from checking on her sooner.

"I made Jaime go take his bath and when Eli came back in, he took Sofia. Right when I was about to bring you the plate, there was a knock at the door. It was Brandon and his mom. He had been trying to call and text you, and he was worried when you didn't answer. He knew about Nick and wanted to see you. We all talked for a little while and they went back home. By the time I got back to your food, it was cold so I heated it again." Josefina rested her head in her hand—tears clung to Josefina's lashes.

"Mom, I'm fine. This isn't your fault," Krystal said, holding up her injured wrist. "Just calm down, okay?"

Josefina inhaled deeply. "Krystal, when I got down there and saw you lying on the floor like that, I thought you were dead. I screamed for Eli and he called the ambulance. When I found your pulse, I started thanking God. But I didn't move you since I couldn't find where the blood came from. I was so scared I would make it worse. All I could do was stay there and pray until the ambulance came." Grabbing tissues from the box on the bedside table, she blew her nose.

"Mom, I'm so sorry I put you and everyone else through that. It wasn't intentional, please believe me."

"I believe you." Josefina used a magazine off the shelf to fan her face. "The good thing is now we can help you the way you need."

Krystal smiled weakly.

"The ambulance came and fire trucks too. When the medics found your wrist, they wrapped it up right away and kept it in the air to keep you from losing any more blood. They had a hard time with the stretcher in the basement, and when they brought you up, the kids became hysterical when they saw you. You were covered in blood. Eli was trying to soothe them. I rode with you in the ambulance, and Eli called your father so he could meet us there."

Krystal's eyes snapped up in surprise. "Whoa," was all she said.

"Your dad was already here when we arrived. The whole block was outside when we left, and poor Brandon...."

"Does he know I'm okay?"

"Yes. He came here with his mom last night. Emily was here with her parents. They stayed until they knew you were going to be okay. The hospital told them it was better for them to go home because only your father and I could be in here. Emily was crying and saying it was all her fault…said she should have told somebody. She didn't think you were cutting anymore."

Closing her eyes, Krystal let the guilt crawl over her, seeping into her pores. She deserved it. She'd been a horrible friend to Em, to everyone.

"It wasn't her fault, Mom. I lied to her and made her think I wasn't cutting anymore." Krystal didn't know how she was going to face Em and Brandon ever again. Resting her head on the pillow, she sighed heavily as her throat thickened. Tired of crying, she swallowed hard.

"Let's focus on the now, Krystal. You will have a chance to work things out with Em. But it's time for you to get better."

Chapter 28

The pancakes and eggs she had for breakfast swirled in Krystal's stomach as she got dressed in the clothes her mom had brought from home. Thankful for the faithful covering of her long sleeves, she wondered how many days she'd have to be in the hospital. She knew three for sure, but her terror intensified with the prospect it could be even longer.

"Mom, I'm scared. I don't want to do this. Can't I just go home? I promise I won't cut anymore," Krystal said.

She meant it too; she never wanted to cut again. She felt like she was letting Nick down not being with everyone else. Then she began to wonder what Nick would have said when she told him about what she'd been doing to herself. Her throat thickened again. She'd never know because she'd been such a chicken about revealing herself to him.

"I know you feel that way and I want nothing more than for you to come home. But you need some help, and it's the kind of help that I don't know how to give you, Krystal. These people will help you learn how to cope with your feelings in other ways that don't involve hurting yourself."

Sighing deeply, Krystal left it alone. It was obvious the doctor had spoken with her mother since she sounded like she was reciting information from a brochure.

Josefina kneeled down next to the chair Krystal now sat in and put her arms around her. "Honey, this will go by faster than you think. Just do your best to let them help you. While you're in there, we will be learning how to help you better too."

Krystal was staring at the floor and Josefina gently took her chin, guiding Krystal's face toward her own. "I know this is my fault and I'm sorry. I was too selfish to see how it affected you. If you're going to be mad at somebody, be mad at me. Not God. God is not punishing you."

"How do you know?"

"Because God loves you and doesn't do things for the sole purpose of hurting you. God always has a plan, mija. It was Nick's time to go. None of us will stay here forever and we never know when our time is up."

"Why would it be Nick's time to go when he was spending his life helping people every day? I hope that man rots in prison," Krystal said between clenched teeth, speaking of the man who shot Nick.

Josefina sighed.

"Ralph told me that man was very sorry for what he did. He was broken. Try to forgive him, Krystal."

"Forgive him?" she asked incredulously. "Are you seri…." The word lodged in her throat. Not wanting to get emotional, she turned away. "Where's all this coming from, anyway? Why are you all the sudden taking God's side on everything?"

"Because for a long time, I've felt guilty about how I led my life. Your father and I never married, then when I left him for all the reasons I did, I was still unmarried. I felt too guilty to talk to God or even about God much. I felt I didn't have a right to. But God has shown our family mercy, Krystal. I will never stop thanking him for saving you and I will never leave Him again. Now I know He never left me."

Opening her mouth to speak, she was distracted by the sound of a herd of elephants nearby.

She couldn't stop the smile that erupted from the sight of Rosie and Jaime bursting into the room. Esme walked behind them, smiling too. Jaime almost made it to her first, but at the last second Rosie shoved him just hard enough that he slid and fell.

"Rosie!" Josefina reprimanded sharply and went to Jaime. Lifting him by his right arm as Roberto took his left, together they raised him from the floor and planted him on his feet.

Pretending to not hear the rebuke, Rosie landed in Krystal's arms with a thud. Trying not to wince at the pain in her wrist, she hugged her tight.

"Love you," Rosie said and puckered her lips, waiting for Krystal to plant a kiss on them.

"Muah!" Krystal added the sound effect, knowing it would make Rosie's smile bigger. "Love you, too."

Rosie touched her bandage. "Sorry you fell and got cut."

Relief and shame converged in her heart, but she was grateful for the obvious cover story they'd been told. She'd fallen. And she'd been cut. So it wasn't exactly a lie.

Esme hugged her next as Jaime stood back waiting, now subdued by his embarrassment from Rosie shoving him. Krystal reached her arm out, and he shyly walked into it.

"This was the only chance they'd have to see you until you came home," Roberto said. "They needed to see that you are perfectly okay."

"Of course," Krystal said. "Is Tia Maria here?" she asked, looking toward the door.

"No," replied Roberto.

"How'd they get here?"

"I picked them up."

Krystal's mouth opened, but nothing came out.

Jaime reached into his pocket and drew out a piece of crumpled construction paper. "Rosie made it more wrinkled when she pushed me," he said.

"That's okay. I'm sure it's fine," Krystal replied as she unfolded the picture of a boy on a skateboard. A big sun hung in the corner and a message reading GET BETTER at the bottom.

"It's me," he explained.

"I know that, silly. I love it like I love you."

Jaime smiled, and Krystal hugged him again.

"I saw Brandon today," Esme said. "He asked me to tell you he misses you." Krystal melted in relief. She'd considered the possibility Brandon might not want a girlfriend with issues like hers.

"Who's Brandon?" Roberto asked. "Was he the boy who was here last night?"

"Her boooyyyfriend," Rosie said, dragging out the word for what felt like ten years.

Roberto's groan sounded more like a growl. The only thing that saved Krystal from her father's wrath was her current circumstances. He handled the news of her having a boyfriend rather well. After his growl, he stayed red for a couple minutes and then silent for about five more. He must have told himself to not make a scene. Roberto's audible deep breaths made Krystal want to laugh. She held back, but her mother didn't.

"You know that's not the end of that," Josefina said after Roberto left to take the kids home.

"I know," Krystal said, shrugging her shoulders. "That's the least of my problems right now."

Being admitted to the psyche ward was quickly becoming the worst experience of Krystal's life. She'd been sitting at the same table at the Family Services & Wellness Center for nearly two hours now, answering redundant questions.

If I'm not crazy yet, I will be by the time these doctors are done with me.

Crossing her arms over her chest, she stretched her legs out in front of her, crossing them at the ankles. "Are we almost done?" she asked.

"Soon," said the lab coat clad woman, with glasses that came right out of the 1940's.

She needs to give those back.

Her voice was even more monotone than Krystal's. The voice was now incredibly annoying since she had been questioning her forever—asking the same stupid questions in ten different ways. She documented Krystal's answers and moved right along as if she was doing no more than a survey on…cheese!

"How often do you think about dying?"

Well, I'm thinking about it right now, because I'm bored to death!

"Sometimes," Krystal answered honestly. "But like I said, I'm not suicidal. I've never planned my death or anything."

"You described having panic attacks. How often do you have them and do you know what triggers them?"

"I've been having variations of them since my parents separated. But in the last couple of months, they have been worse than ever. I guess my feelings bring them on. I really don't know."

Aren't you supposed to figure that out for me? Gosh!

"Have you tried marijuana?"

"No! I told you, I've never used drugs at all. I don't drink alcohol either. Well, except when I was four, I grabbed my dad's beer can and took a drink. It was gross, and I've never tried it again."

Why did I tell her that? She doesn't care. Probably because I'm having to repeat all this a million freaking times.

"Do you ever see things that aren't there?"

How would I know it wasn't there if I could see it?

My butt hurts. She shifted in her seat. Obviously this question went along with the one about ghosts and such earlier. "No."

"Do you ever hear voices or other noises that aren't real?"

"No." It was technically true. The only time she felt God tell her something, it wasn't in a voice. *It was just a thought, a knowing; yeah…an unexplainable knowing.* But she hadn't heard from God like that since then.

He's probably mad I didn't quit cutting and now He's going to take everything back.

Just take it all! she thought angrily. But she knew she didn't mean it. She didn't want him to take anything else away. Taking Nick was more than enough.

"Why do you cut?" the lab coat asked dully, still looking at her notes.

Krystal just sat there. She'd already told this lady more than she had ever considered telling Em, but she seemed like she could care less. Taking a deep breath, Krystal reminded herself for the hundredth time, *I don't want to be here any longer than necessary. Just answer the question.*

Being honest from the beginning had been a smart move. After all the variations of questions, she doubted she would have kept her story straight had she lied. They might've locked her up for good. She shuddered at the thought.

"Because I can't handle my emotions." *Surely she's going to ask me to elaborate,* Krystal thought. *Sure enough….*

With the first hint of fluctuation in her voice, the lab coat looked up at Krystal. "Go deeper than that. Why did you start cutting? Then tell me why you continued."

Pulling her legs in, Krystal rested her elbows on her knees and looked down at the floor in thought. She let out a long whoosh of air, and without looking up, she tried to explain. "Because I felt helpless. Because I thought I should have been able to do something about my parents' separation. Because for a while, I didn't think my mom loved me anymore. Because it helped me. Because once I started, I didn't want to stop, and even when I did want to stop, I really didn't." Krystal's eyes were full and tired as she raised her head. "Because I'm addicted to it!"

"Thank you," the lab coat said with a gulp. After making her last note, she said, "Wait here, please." She left the room, leaving the door open.

Krystal stood and stretched, looking around the bland room wondering what was next. She didn't have to wait long for the answer.

Another lab coat walked in. This one had a bit more of a personality. "I know you're probably sick to death of all the questions, but it's a must. So if you will have a seat, we'll get started." She smiled sweetly.

Crying on the inside, Krystal lumbered back to her chair and slowly lowered herself down. Resting her elbows on the table, she waited.

The sweeter lab coat turned out to be the devil in disguise. It all started out okay. She had asked about her family and friends. Then came the 'do you have a boyfriend?' and 'do you have sex?' questions. The worst questions of all came after those. Questions no one had ever asked before and ones she felt no one had a right to ask. Questions she would never repeat to anyone else. She had never been so uncomfortable and embarrassed.

It was past lunchtime when it was over. It didn't matter, because Krystal didn't have an appetite. Resting her head in her hands, she heard the door click shut behind the sweet demon lab coat and then instantly open again. Looking up, she saw her mom standing there. Krystal stood up so fast she nearly knocked her chair over. Running around the table, she threw herself into her mother's arms and cried.

"Oh, my poor baby girl," Josefina said, squeezing her eyes shut so she didn't cry too. "I'm sorry. I know how hard this must be for you."

Josefina and Krystal had lunch together in the same drab little room.

"I have a little bit of good news," Josefina said in between bites. She ate as if famished while Krystal barely touched her food. Krystal sat building a potato house with her fries, lost in thought. Taking a quick sip of her soda, Josefina said, "I spoke with Ralph and they are not having the funeral until next week."

"So I should be able to go?" Krystal straightened to attention.

"Yes, it seems they are having difficulty connecting with Nick's family and need more time."

Slumping back down in her chair, Krystal tried to remember if Nick had ever said anything about his family. *No, he hadn't.* And she hadn't asked him either. As much as she loved listening to Nick talk, she never once asked him to tell his story. She'd heard countless other peoples' stories, but not his.

"Stop biting your nails, it's disgusting," Josefina said, pushing Krystal's hand down.

"Mom," Krystal said, rolling her eyes. Krystal twisted her legs around to face her mom. "What did Dad do that you kept a secret?"

"Aye, honey. First of all, your father should be the only one to give you that information. But let me tell you this. You can choose whether or not to ask him, but I advise against it. What purpose will it serve by you knowing?"

"None, I guess," Krystal replied, pushing her tray away and laying her head down on her arms. Her question came out muffled, "Do you have any idea about the kinds of questions they are asking me? It's horrible!"

"I do," Josefina said, grabbing Krystal's hand. "I hate you have to go through all this. I love you, Krystal, and I'm sorry I did this to you. I got too wrapped up in my own problems. I'm so sorry. Please forgive me." As hard as Josefina tried to be strong, she couldn't keep the tremor out of her lips. Pressing them tightly together, she hugged her daughter tightly.

"I love you too, Mom." Krystal spoke quietly into her mom's ear. "But please stop apologizing now. I'm the one who needs to be forgiven."

"There's nothing to forgive," Josefina said, leaning in until their foreheads touched.

Roberto walked in, and Krystal rose to go to him. Wrapping her arms around him, he too enveloped her in his arms. Feeling like his little girl again, she squeezed him tighter. Standing on her tiptoes, she kissed his cheek.

"How are things going?" he asked, looking down at her.

"It kind of sucks, to be honest. Really bad."

"I'm sorry," he said. "Your mom and I have been answering lots of questions, and I guess now it's time to answer some more, but this time it's all of us together."

"Ugh, I'm so tired of this." Krystal leaned into the crook of her dad's arm, letting him bear her weight. He draped his arm in front of her, resting his hand on her shoulder. Krystal recognized the moment for what it was.

While it wasn't under good circumstances, she was with both of her parents, and they weren't at each other's throats. There were no lingering questions on whether or not they loved her. She was sure of it, and she was sure she loved them in return.

A male lab coat with a salt and pepper beard walked through the door and asked them all to sit down. He asked many of the questions that the 1940's lab coat did and none of the ones the sweet demon lab coat had asked, thankfully. That would have been unbearable.

This lab coat's name was Dr. Ray, and unlike his two predecessors, he was compassionate. While he asked as many, if not more, questions than the others, it wasn't hard to endure. It seemed as if he cared about their answers. He truly seemed to listen, and even asked Krystal detailed questions about her art. It was more of a long conversation than a grilling by a robot or being taken off guard by a monster pretending to be all nice and sweet.

Leaning forward in his chair, Dr. Ray looked Krystal in the eyes. "I need you to understand something. I believe you weren't trying to kill yourself. Most of the time, people who cut aren't suicidal."

"Thank you," Krystal said, stunned to realize that her problem was classifiable.

"Here's the problem, though."

Krystal stiffened and a sense of foreboding gripped her.

"The way you cut your wrist makes it seem as if you were purposely trying to kill yourself."

Looking down at her bandaged wrist, it suddenly throbbed as if in response to the accusations.

"Therefore, I can't risk being wrong. You have to be admitted as a possible suicide risk. But I promise I will make extensive notes about my beliefs in your case so that your position is well documented. We are declaring 'suicide risk' as a precaution only."

Krystal laid her head on her good hand and sighed. "Okay."

Josefina and Roberto, who were each sitting on either side of her, reached out to comfort her.

"It's nice to see cases like this once in a while," Dr. Ray addressed them all. "Many of the families I see fight their way through the entire session. At times, there's so much animosity, I'm not sure if the necessary love is there to help the healing process. We aren't going to have that problem. I have great faith that you're going to be just fine, Krystal," he said, and winked before he left the room.

Warm little tingles raced up Krystal's arms, causing all the hairs to awaken. Sitting up straight, she squared her shoulders.

"Yes, I will be."

Her newfound strength was short-lived as she walked up the steps and read the long name on the glass of the front doors: Mental Health Hospital and Rehabilitation Facility of Kansas. Anxiety subdued by the medicine she'd been given now threatened her, and she halted abruptly.

Using the breathing techniques Dr. Ray had advised, she looked into her mother's eyes.

"It's okay, mija. You can do this," Josefina encouraged.

Krystal reached into her pocket and touched the construction paper Jaime had given her; it gave her comfort. She could see the concern in her father's eyes and resolved once again to be strong. One last deep breath and Krystal forced herself to walk through the doors.

After a brief meeting with various staff members, she sat in a room with her parents and waited for the therapist who'd been assigned to her. After a short time, a large, busty woman entered the room, closing the door behind her.

"Hello," she said, her voice sweet as honey. "I'm Dr. Tovina. I'm a clinical psychologist and will be working with Krystal during her stay."

After sitting at her desk, she read through Krystal's newly created file. Krystal watched as her eyebrows arched in response to whatever she had just read. "Well, I see we have a bit of a miracle case here," she said, glancing at Krystal's bandaged hand.

"Yes," Josefina said. "We are very blessed not to have lost her."

"I agree wholeheartedly." Dr. Tovina smiled, closing the file and putting her hands together in front of her.

It was obvious Dr. Tovina believed in God. Krystal could sense it in her personality, see it in her eyes, and hear it in how she spoke. She was pretty sure Dr. Ray was one of those people too.

She believed in God, but she wasn't one of those people. She had almost been one of them. Now, they reminded her of Nick, and it made her happy and sad at the same time. Happy that there were people like him, as well as Walt and Ralph, out there. Sad because it didn't always mean everything would be okay.

She sat quietly in the office while Dr. Tovina discussed treatment with her parents. Too tired to listen closely, her mind wandered. Though the pain was still fresh, Monday seemed to have happened ages ago. She thought of Brandon and how she already missed talking to him and holding his hand. They were supposed to go to the movies tomorrow night, she remembered. Would talking to him be awkward now, after everything she'd done?

Then there was Em, whom she owed the biggest apology to. Knowing her best friend as she did, she knew

Em had already forgiven her. There was a comfort in that, but also hurt. Krystal was certain Em felt responsible, as if what happened was in some way her fault.

She thought about her little brother and how she wouldn't be able to listen to him read for at least three days. Jaime would miss it just as much as she would. *Was Esme as easily fooled as the younger two?* she wondered. *Doubtful.* Krystal would have some explaining to do. The idea of discussing cutting with Esme turned her stomach.

Because she couldn't stop herself, she thought of Nick. He had so quickly become part of her life, and his loss now left a fresh, gaping wound. One that wasn't self inflicted.

Krystal envisioned going to the shelter right now, ringing the buzzer at the back door, and Nick swinging the door wide open with a big smile on his face. He'd bellow out a greeting and usher them all in. Nick was a big, happy presence and had become so important to her in just a couple of months.

She'd loved becoming a member of the Misfits. But that was all over now. The shelter would never be able to fill his shoes. He was irreplaceable. He brought something to her life that she couldn't even find words to describe. Her hands itched for a pencil to draw his face—

"Okay, Krystal?"

"What?" Krystal said, trying to clear her thoughts. She looked at Dr. Tovina. "I'm sorry. What did you say?"

"I'm going to give you a few minutes with your parents and then walk you over to check in."

"Okay."

Dr. Tovina left the room and her dad walked over to her first. Roberto wrapped her in a warm hug before planting a kiss on her forehead. "I'll come during the visiting hour every night," he told her.

"I love you, Dad. Don't worry about me," she said and gave his hand a squeeze.

"You're amazing," he said. "How is it you are trying to console me when I want to console you?"

"I just don't want you to worry."

"Ha," he said weakly. "That's not possible." He waved to Josefina and nodded. She too nodded and smiled.

As Roberto left the room, Josefina took ahold of Krystal's good hand.

"This is going to be the most difficult thing you've dealt with so far."

The old Krystal would have balked at this, but she knew what her mom meant and stayed quiet.

"When you feel weak, pray."

"Okay, Mom."

Chapter 29

Blinded by the flash of the camera, Krystal blinked to restore her vision.

"Turn to the right," commanded the rudest individual Krystal had encountered thus far in this entire experience.

After this lady had rifled through her belongs, cramming them back into the bag without even a hint of regard for her possessions, she made Krystal empty her pockets. All she had in them was the picture Jaime had drawn for her.

"You draw this?" the nurse had asked sarcastically, with a laugh before she shoved it into the bag with the clothes.

Stocky and gruff, this lady's face wore an invariable scowl. Her brows were permanently knit together from years of discontentment. When she laughed, only an explosion of sound came out, unaccompanied by the telling facial expression that would indicate humor. Had a deaf person been watching her, they would have had no idea that she'd just barked out a laugh. They'd probably have thought she had coughed instead.

Krystal was tempted to remind her she worked in a hospital and not a jail.

"Left."

Krystal turned the opposite direction and imagined drawing her with a great big head, warts on her face, a hairy body, and witchy hands holding a nightstick.

Not a bad idea, she thought, and was smiling when the flash went off.

"Oh, you think this is fun? We'll see how much fun you're having after we're done here."

Krystal made it a point to look at her nametag. It read Mattie. *I bet that stands for Matilda,* Krystal thought as she moved to the direction of the woman's curt head nod.

"We don't have all day. You want dinner, don't you?"

Every muscle in Krystal's forehead responded as her brows met and dipped. Her lips curled as if she smelled something foul. It took all her willpower not to retort. Instead, she inhaled deeply and sucked in her cheeks.

Mean Mattie gathered Krystal's paperwork and slid it into a manila folder that had Krystal's full name on it. Then she picked up Krystal's bag.

"Follow me." She led Krystal into a room that looked like a doctor's office. Two other staff women appeared.

"Krystal," one of the women said, "my name is Susan and I'm a nurse practitioner, and this is Katie, my assistant." She motioned to the very young lady who stood near the door with a clipboard in hand. Katie smiled as a greeting.

She doesn't look much older than me.

"I want to explain what we are getting ready to do and why." Despite the kind tone of this woman, Krystal stood as still as a statue. The fact they were in an examination room wasn't a good sign. "You can sit down if you like."

"I'm fine," she said.

"Due to the fact you're a suicide risk and have self-harmed, we have to do a body and cavity search. Do you know what that means?"

Krystal's eyes shot up. She knew exactly what it meant, and her stomach churned violently. Mattie stood there, and in spite of her scowl, she looked pleased, as if she was looking forward to this.

"I won't get undressed in front of her," Krystal said, looking at Mattie and then back at Katie. She didn't bother to explain she wasn't suicidal, knowing it would fall on deaf ears at this point. It didn't matter, anyway; she would do her days here and be done.

"Why not?" Susan asked, not sounding the least bit surprised.

"Because she's been rude to me from the moment I met her and I'm not comfortable around her," Krystal said as she straightened, looking Susan directly in the eyes. *And because she gives me the creeps.*

Susan's eyes brightened and she cleared her throat. "Well," she said, turning to Mattie, "the rules do state only two need to be present, so Katie and I can handle this."

Mattie turned various shades of red until she looked like a beet with eyeballs. Throwing back her shoulders, her bulging eyes were shooting daggers at Krystal. "You're just going to take her word for it? I should be allowed to do my job! This is my job."

"We don't have to," Susan said. "If you prefer, we can ask Krystal to fill out a complaint form. An investigation will be opened and—"

Before Susan could complete her sentence, Mattie stalked out of the room, slamming the door so hard it blew a small stack of papers off the table. Katie promptly gathered them up.

"Whoa," Krystal said.

"Please excuse me for a few minutes," Susan said, before she left the room and closed the door behind her.

"Mattie's in trouuubbble," Katie said, now wide-eyed and covering her mouth with her hand. "Oops. I didn't mean to say that out loud. Please don't tell Susan."

Krystal smiled. She liked Katie and would have liked to ask how old she was, but refrained.

"I won't. How does she even work here? She's horrible."

"Matilda the Hun?" Katie snorted. "No idea. But you aren't the first person who's complained. She must have thought you were weak. Guess she was wrong."

"I'm not exactly strong either."

"You're stronger than you think," Katie said. "That was pretty bold."

Susan came back in. "I'm sorry, Krystal. You're probably starving. Dinner is in another fifteen minutes and as soon as we're done, we will make sure you eat before we show you around, okay?"

Krystal nodded.

"All right," Susan said, "We are going to do this step by step. Let me know if you need a break at any point."

"Okay," Krystal said.

"Remain standing for now and remove your shirt. You don't need to take your bra off yet."

Quietly following Susan's instructions, she removed her top. Susan handed it to Katie who shook the fabric and felt it to make sure nothing Krystal could use to harm herself was hidden inside.

They covered every inch of her skin, counting every single cut, then marking them with a special type of ink that would last for a few days through showers. Arms were first, then her stomach, and lastly her thighs.

Now standing in only her bra and underwear, Krystal's hands were shaking and she was using her breathing techniques to fight the anxiety caused by the acute embarrassment of the experience. Never had she disrobed in front of anyone, not even Em, and though it hadn't been more than ten minutes, it seemed as if she'd been standing there for hours.

"How many total?" Susan asked Katie.

"One hundred and thirty-three."

Krystal blanched, but didn't speak.

"Krystal," Susan said, looking her in the eyes, "We have to check you every day for new cuts. If you self-harm while you're here, we will know. Do you understand?"

"Yes."

"Good. We are going to give you a hospital gown—it has an open back. You'll remove your bra and give it to Katie to check. We'll give you a bag to put your underwear in and then you can lay on the examination table."

Once the exam ended and Krystal was dressed, Katie led her to the dining area, which was just to the right of the door that led into the youth wing. She introduced her to a couple of the other staff members before departing, referring to them as 'counselors.'

About a dozen other kids of various ages sat around already eating enchiladas, rice, and beans, with chocolate chip cookies for dessert.

Go figure. Mexican food. Not like my mom's, I'm sure.

She started to sit down in an unoccupied section of one of the long, bench-style lunch tables when one of the counselors spoke to her. "Could you sit down here, please?"

Krystal did and found herself face to face with a little girl who was even younger than Rosie.

"Hi!" the little girl said.

"Hi."

"What's your name?"

"Krystal. What's yours?

"Taylor. How old are you?"

"Fourteen. How old are you?"

"Six!" she exclaimed, making her long, blonde curls dance over her shoulders. "Almost seven." Her grin showed all of her teeth. She reminded Krystal of a little piranha. "Why are you here?"

"Taylor," the counselor gently admonished.

"Sorry," Taylor said and then smiled again. "You're pretty."

"Thanks," Krystal said as she grinned back. "You are too. You remind me of my little sister," she said, thinking of Rosie. "She's not one bit shy either."

Krystal and Taylor talked for the next thirty minutes. She learned Taylor's favorite colors were pink and purple and that she loved panda bears and butterflies. Dancing was her number one hobby and singing came in second.

After dinner, Krystal went into the common area with Taylor where they huddled together on a couple of beanbags in the corner. Taylor brought some books over and asked Krystal to read with her. Krystal's heart tightened in her chest as she wondered what her siblings were doing that very moment.

After reading for a short time, Krystal mostly listened as Taylor's raspy little voice filled her in on some of the other residents. Until then, Krystal made it a point not to look around too much.

"See that boy over there?" Taylor whispered.

Krystal followed Taylor's eyes, "Yeah."

"He doesn't do anything but read. He doesn't have any friends. He says books are his friends. If you try to talk to him when he's reading, he gets mad."

"Interesting," Krystal said. "He must be lonely."

Taylor lifted her shoulders and put her hands up. "I don't know, but I don't think so, because he doesn't want us to talk to him. But see that girl over there?" Taylor pointed.

"Don't point, Taylor!" Krystal reached out, placing her hand over Taylor's.

"She can't see me," Taylor said, "she's blind."

"But everyone else can see you." Krystal lay back on her bag again and rested her hand on the wall. Taylor eyed her bandaged hand, but didn't say anything.

Krystal noticed the blind girl had been led into the common area shortly after dinner.

"People complained about her, so now she eats lunch in another room by herself," Taylor said.

"Well, that's mean." Krystal was amazed at how tuned in Taylor was to what went on in this place. She was young but sharp! Nothing got by her.

"It's because she eats with her hands and chews with her mouth open, like this," Taylor said, re-enacting the scenario. Krystal panicked at Taylor's display and started to sit up, but Taylor stopped. "It grossed everyone out, because she gets the food all over her and in her hair. But she won't let them help her eat." Taylor shrugged and put her hands up again. "I don't get it."

Krystal couldn't help but smile. That would explain why she came in with wet hair, she thought. She could imagine the scene; the girl had long, thick but wiry hair that nearly reached her waist.

"Does she always keep her eyes closed?" Krystal asked softly, looking over at her. The girl was sitting in a chair near the TV, rocking her upper body back and forth. Something was in her hands, but Krystal couldn't tell what it was.

"Yep, most of the time. I saw her open them one time, and it was scary. They were all white." As if reading Krystal's mind, Taylor continued, "She always has something in her hands. I don't know why, maybe so she isn't bored."

Taylor went on to tell her about one of the girls who wanted to eat all the time and another one who ate and threw up. There were several others who had drug-related problems. Krystal wondered if it was good for Taylor to know all these things.

"I know this is your first time here," Taylor said, out of the blue.

"How do you know?"

"Because you didn't know where you were going." Taylor giggled.

"How many times have you been here?"

"Nine times."

Krystal didn't know what to say, but she didn't have a chance to say anything.

Chaos erupted as several security officers rushed by, each holding the arm of someone who was screaming her head off. "This isn't over! You will hear from my lawyer!" It was Mattie.

One of the girls Taylor had mentioned stood up. Obviously suffering from anorexia, her upper arms were thinner than her forearms, and her elbow looked like a jutting rock between the two sections.

"Goodbye, Matilda the Hun!" she called and waved her emaciated arms sarcastically.

Mattie whipped her head around, looking over her shoulder.

"Shut up and go eat a cheeseburger!"

The girl only laughed which infuriated Mattie even more as they ushered her out the double doors. Krystal caught a glimpse of what she thought were police uniforms before the doors shut again.

"I think she needs to be in here more than we do," Taylor said.

Laughter burst out of Krystal, causing everyone in the room to look at her.

"Sorry," she said, covering her mouth, feeling foolish for drawing attention to herself. She needed to just fly under the radar here.

"Don't be," the anorexic girl said. "She's a witch. What's your name?" she asked from where she stood.

"Krystal. What's yours?"

"Eileen. Mattie got to you too, huh? It's obvious." She wasn't really asking, so Krystal didn't answer.

A counselor walked in the room.

"Group is in five minutes, everyone. Taylor, you'll show Krystal the way, won't you?"

"Yep!" Taylor smiled, nodding her little head emphatically, causing her locks to bounce. "I will."

Taylor led her down the south hall. Apparently, the north hall would lead them to their rooms. No one had come back to show her around, but she figured they'd been busy handling Mattie.

They walked into a largely unremarkable room, which was quite a contrast to the colorful common area. Chairs were arranged in a circle in the middle of the room. Taylor plopped down in one and patted the seat next to her. Krystal obeyed. Already she knew she'd miss Taylor when they parted ways. After just two hours, the little girl had grown on her and kept her occupied.

An older lady walked in carrying a manila folder and a bottle of water. She sat in one of the chairs and greeted everyone.

"Good evening, everyone. For those of you who haven't been in one of these before, my name is Sheryl. We will go around the room, and everyone can introduce themselves and talk about why we are here. Then we'll talk about ways that we can cope with our problems."

Oh great. She'd finally talked to her family and all the doctors about her 'problem,' and now she had to tell a bunch of strangers too? *How is this supposed to be helpful?*

She wiped her sweaty palms on her jeans. Fear gripped her and there was a sudden pressure in her head. She didn't realize she had closed her eyes until she felt a hand on her arm. It was Taylor's.

Looking down into Taylor's bright eyes, she saw an understanding that far surpassed Taylor's years. Taylor smiled and so did she. Her heartbeat slowed, and she was able to breathe freely. *Relax.* She rested her back against her chair.

The reader's name was Aidan and he'd brought his book with him. The therapist asked him to put it away. With shaking hands, he placed his bookmark into the crease and shut his book. It was obvious he didn't want to, but his face showed no emotion at all.

"Please put it under your chair," Sheryl asked in a soft, monotone voice.

Aidan sat, still holding the book. Despite the fact Aidan's face showed no emotion, Krystal knew there was an invisible struggle happening. He began tapping his foot and stared through a gap in the circle.

"Tell everyone your name," Sheryl coaxed.

"My name is Aidan."

"And why are you here?" asked the therapist.

"Because people don't like that I read."

"Do you think it's the reading they have a problem with or the fact that you only read? Do you spend time with your family?"

"My books are my family," he answered simply.

Krystal watched as Aidan's fingers twitched. They didn't know what to do without a page to turn. She'd heard of various addictions, but not one like this.

"Please put your book under your chair until after group, Aidan." After a moment, Aidan put the book under his chair and slid his feet back so that his heels touched the book at each end. Sheryl moved on to the next person.

Several of the kids who were there for drug-related reasons were sitting next to each other. One girl's addiction was cocaine and another's was taking some pills Krystal couldn't pronounce. The last person to speak set Krystal back because the boy's addiction was heroin. Her mom had mentioned that was the drug the man who killed Nick had been using. For a moment, she hated the boy as if he was the one who had shot Nick and sat still as a stone as she listened to him speak.

"At first, it seemed like a harmless drug. It didn't make me as weird as some of the other things I tried. It made me feel happy. For a while, I was getting all my schoolwork done, and working. My boss was giving me compliments on my work. Seemed liked everyone liked me better or something. I'm not sure if they did or if I felt that way because of the drug. It was so cheap, I didn't have any trouble paying for it from what I made working part-time. But after a couple months, I wasn't getting the same effect…the same high.

"It was like I had become immune to it, so I needed more to get the same feeling. One day, I was out of money, out of gas, and I was fired for being late too many times. My boss told me I was a good kid, but needed to get my act together. I asked him to pay me for the rest of my hours right then instead of on payday. When he refused, I tried to climb over the counter and take the money from the register. I'd never stolen anything—anything in my life— until that day. It was like it wasn't even me. I was given a choice of getting help or going to juvie. I chose help."

Krystal looked down at the floor as the boy continued to speak. She wanted nothing more than to be alone this very minute. For some reason she couldn't separate the boy from the man who shot Nick. But the boy seemed nice, and she didn't want him to seem nice, not at all.

The familiar urge crept up on her, tempted her to release her pain the way she had been for so long now. Mentally she shoved it all away. Not only did she not want to cut anymore, she couldn't. Despair began to overtake her and her mind started to just follow the pain along its path.

"Krystal, it's your turn. Tell us why you're here," said the therapist.

Krystal's head snapped up and her cloudy eyes cleared instantly. Quickly glancing at Taylor, she wished she could send her out of the room. But then she realized Taylor had probably already met someone like her, maybe lots of someones. She had to be who she was even if she was a disappointment.

"I'm here because I've been cutting." Krystal touched her bandaged wrist.

"Do you know why you cut?" the therapist asked.

"Because I was sad…and angry."

"Can you tell us why?"

Krystal didn't want to. She didn't want to disclose anything about her life to this group of strangers. *What if they call me uncooperative? I might have to stay longer.*

"My parents split and we had to move out of my dad's house."

The therapist looked at her expectantly. Taking a deep breath, she let the rest out in one long, fast stream of words. "My mom cheated on my dad and got pregnant. We all had to move into her boyfriend's house. I couldn't deal with all the changes and started cutting one day and didn't stop. Later, I wanted to stop and was even doing it way less, but something bad happened, and I cut too deep. Everyone thought I tried to commit suicide, but I didn't, and now I'm here." *And this is in no way helping me!*

The therapist pulled out a red sharpie and gave it to Krystal.

"As a way to help you cope, I brought you this red marker. Any time you get the urge to cut, I want you to use this on your skin instead."

What? This lady has to be joking. That is the stupidest thing I've ever heard.

Her thoughts must have registered on her face.

"I'm quite serious," Sheryl said.

"Okay," was all Krystal said as she took the marker.

The therapist moved to Taylor. *Thank God!* She wasn't sure if the lady would try to keep her talking.

Taylor introduced herself in her small, raspy voice.

"I'm here because I'm bipolar."

Krystal didn't know anything about what being bipolar meant, but Taylor seemed so normal…and happy. It was hard to believe she'd been here so many times.

"How have you been doing since our last visit?" the therapist asked Taylor.

"No episodes," Taylor said and gave the therapist a big smile.

"Good to hear, Miss Taylor. So you have been staying on your meds?"

"Yes." Taylor nodded like the little bobble-head puppy that sat on Krystal's Aunt Maria's dashboard.

The therapist smiled at Taylor and moved on around the circle. Eventually, time ran out, which was fine with Krystal.

It was 8:00 p.m. and the counselor announced that it was time for an art activity. Krystal's ears twitched. They were led a little further down the hall into another huge room. While it may have been impressive to some, it was a bit elementary to Krystal, but she supposed it was better than nothing.

Walking around the room, she checked out each station. One had sketchpads and colored pencils, and for a moment she thought she might stop there, but she kept looking. Coming to, then bypassing, the paint by numbers table, she arrived at a much larger area in the corner. Small plastic jars of paint sat huddled together in the middle of the table. There was a tall wooden shelf against the wall at the end of the table. It had three shelves on top and three on the bottom, with a middle section that had a door that opened outwardly. It was the kind that opened from the top when you pulled the handle.

Scanning the shelves, she saw dozens of paintbrushes, most in bad repair. On the third shelf down she spied a synthetic brush that appeared much newer. The bristles formed a point, which was good for detail. She knew there must be something to paint behind that door. She grabbed the handle and pulled the door down.

"Whoa!" She said for the second time that day. Inside were two more shelves lined with ceramic masks stacked three high. One of them appeared to be a delicate feminine face—one was a more rounded face that could be for a man or woman, depending on how you painted it. One was African, with a wider nose, fuller lips and high cheekbones. The last one she spotted was oblong with skinny features. She wanted to paint them all and was grateful she could do it with her good hand.

"Is this what you're going to do?" Taylor asked.

She'd forgotten Taylor was there.

"Oh, yeah," she replied, hoping Taylor would pick another station.

"Me too, then."

Krystal inwardly sighed, feeling a little guilty for wishing Taylor away, but smiled down at her new little friend.

"Which mask are you going to paint?"

"The girl one," Taylor answered. Obviously she already knew what all the masks looked like. Krystal grabbed two of them and handed one to Taylor. Looking around, she spotted cups, paper towels, and newspaper. She filled two cups with water and laid out the newspaper. Making sure she had a little distance between her seat and Taylor's, she sat down and lost herself for an hour. Amazingly, Taylor didn't speak again that whole time. She'd begun watching Krystal and never even started painting her mask.

The counselor came in to gather everyone up and make sure all the supplies were put away.

"Taylor, you didn't paint?" Hearing the counselor's voice brought Krystal out of her art-induced trance. She lifted her head and the cascade of hair that had served as a curtain concealing her work swooshed back to unveil it.

"You did that?" asked the counselor. "Well, of course you did, what a stupid question."

"It's okay," Krystal said.

"That is stunning. I've been working here for two years and have never seen anything like it." Blue and purple colors in feather patterns flowed over the face of the mask. Long painted black lashes and blue lips accented the design that traveled around the eyes and down the cheeks.

"Thanks," Krystal said, always awkward with compliments.

"Will you make me one?" Taylor asked. "Please?"

"Sure. You can have this one."

Taylor clasped her hands together and went up on her tippy toes. "Really?"

"Yep, really. But let's let it dry before we wrap it up in newspaper."

"You can let it dry on the shelf," the counselor said. "Gosh, if you're able, I'd love for you to paint one for me, too."

Chapter 30

Krystal stirred at the faint tap at the door. Groggy, she was unsure if she was dreaming or if the tap was real. But when the door opened, she shot up in her bed. Her heart pounded in her chest. A glance around reminded her of where she was and she started to calm down.

"Good morning," the nurse said in a near whisper. "Sorry to startle you. I'm here to get a blood sample; it'll only take a second."

Krystal stuck her arm out as requested and the nurse left. Krystal looked at the clock on the nightstand, shocked it read 5:57 a.m.

"Sheesh," she muttered and lay back down. Her head had barely touched her pillow when there was another tap at the door and a completely different nurse entered.

"I need to get a urine sample," she said, handing Krystal a cup.

"Seriously?" Krystal said, becoming disgruntled.

When Krystal returned to her bed, sleep evaded her and her thoughts raced. Unable to pick a topic to focus on, her emotions had to ride the waves of various images and thoughts about Nick, her family, Em, and Brandon. She even thought about Eliseo and Sofia without a hint of anger rising. It didn't escape her that she had thought of

Eliseo by name, but she didn't linger there—she moved on to the shelter.

At 6:30 a.m. another nurse came to her room carrying two tablets and a cup of water. After Krystal swallowed the pills, the nurse asked her to get dressed. Glad she hadn't fallen back to sleep to be awakened yet a third time, she got up, stretched and followed the nurse. By the time they were done counting her scars, she was ready to find sleep again, but it was time for breakfast.

"Krystal!"

She turned toward the little raspy voice bounding towards her and smiled.

"I'm going home today," Taylor beamed up at her with her head fully tilted back.

Krystal felt a small pang in her heart. "You are!" Krystal feigned enthusiasm, feeling a bit selfish for wanting Taylor to be there a bit longer to keep her company. She knelt down and gave Taylor a squeeze. "I can see you're excited. I'm happy for you."

"Yes, I miss my dad."

"I bet you do," Krystal said, as they walked to the cafeteria.

After breakfast, Taylor and Krystal sat in the corner playing UNO when a man walked in. He was so tall he had to duck down a bit to avoid hitting his head on the doorframe. He wore a bandana on his head, a black t-shirt covered by a leather vest, black jeans, and black boots that looked like they'd seen better days.

"Daddy!" Taylor cheered, leaping up, then running to him, launching herself at him. He caught her as if he'd done it a million times.

"How's my princess doing?"

"Fine!" She beamed and giggled. For the first time, Krystal thought, she seemed like a six-year-old little girl. Almost seven, she mentally corrected.

"Get your stuff and let's go home." He squeezed her before setting her back down on the floor.

"Okay!"

Taylor paused, turning back to Krystal. "I'll miss you more than any of the others," she stated matter-of-factly and gave Krystal a hug.

"I'll miss you, too. More than anyone else." She smiled at Taylor and then winked. She instantly realized what she'd done—it had come as natural as her smile had, but still caused an immense ache in her heart. Krystal was unable to keep her eyes from tearing up. Taylor thought it was because of her and gave her another hug, squeezing with all her might. Krystal hugged her back and said goodbye.

Strange as it may be, she didn't want to make friends with anyone else. Sadness settled over her as she realized too often recently she was making friends and then losing them. Though Em and Brandon hadn't left her, she didn't think things would ever be the same with them again.

She saw her little friend one more time as they headed out. Taylor turned and waved sweetly one more time and was off on what Krystal imagined was an excellent adventure with her father. She must have seen Taylor at her best, because the time she had spent with her gave no indication of what brought such a little girl to this place.

Time came to a screeching halt without Taylor there to keep her occupied. Krystal sat on one of the beanbags to look through a magazine. It didn't hold any interest for her and she dozed off.

A flutter of sound awakened Krystal and she looked over her shoulder. The blind girl had dropped the object she'd been holding in her hands to the floor. Making gasping noises, she fell to her knees. Wildly, she patted around trying to locate what Krystal saw was a small, red, plastic fish with big, googly eyes on each side.

"It's okay," Krystal said, picking it up and putting it into the girl's hand. "It's right here." Instantly calmed at having her little fish back, she felt her way backward and sat on the edge of the couch again. Rocking forward and backward, she began to sing a song that Krystal couldn't make out all the words to other than the word "fishy."

"Krystal, could you come with me?" One of the counselors had called to her from near the hall. She led Krystal to Dr. Tovina's office and closed the door behind her.

"How are you doing, Krystal?" Dr. Tovina smiled and greeted.

"Fine," Krystal said.

"Have a seat, please. Want anything to drink?"

"Water's fine."

Dr. Tovina pulled a small bottle of water out of a mini-fridge.

"Thanks," Krystal said and sat down.

She was a little surprised when Dr. Tovina came around the desk and took the seat next to her, turning it to face her. Out of politeness, Krystal adjusted her chair to face the doctor, who smiled in response.

"So, I've got good reports from all the counselors. No new cuts and all your tests checked out."

Krystal figured she was referring to the blood and urine samples that happened right past the vampire hours.

"As you know, I've spoken to your parents, but I wanted to take today and talk to you so that I can gain your perspective on things."

"Okay," Krystal said. She surprised herself. After answering so many questions in the last couple of days, she had zero anxiety about talking to Dr. Tovina.

"I want to start with the present and then work our way back," Dr. Tovina said, as she clicked her ballpoint pen and readied her tablet for notes. Looking Krystal in the eyes, she said, "You can trust me. I want to help you in any way I can and not just because it's my job."

Krystal believed her.

"Let's talk about Nick. How did you meet him?"

As Krystal began to tell the story, it was as if she was talking to a friend. Dr. Tovina seemed to know the right things to ask and she didn't say stupid things. Her questions didn't feel intrusive like when others asked. The conversation ebbed and flowed. Krystal found herself laughing at some of the things she remembered about Nick, like when he started dancing with Ralph. She talked about her prayer journal and some of the things Nick and she discussed and how she felt like she was letting him down now.

The hour went by so quickly Krystal was sorry when it was over.

"Let me tell you something, Krystal. I've met Nick. I didn't know him well, but we've had occasion to speak a few times. Some of the guests at the shelter were patients here at one time or another. I'm quite certain he's not disappointed in you. In fact, I'm sure of it. Sounds like he cared about you too."

"Not that I deserved it." Krystal looked down at her hands.

"He's the kind of person who loves like Jesus does. None of us deserve it, but it's freely given. And don't discount yourself. I happen to see a very compassionate young lady sitting in front of me. And even though I already know you'll come out on top of all this, I want to meet with you each week over the next few months, if that's all right with you. Unless you prefer another doctor, that is."

"No," Krystal's head shot up. "I'd rather meet with you."

"Glad to hear it. We'll sit down again tomorrow morning. I'm not sure what time you'll be going home, but it will probably be sometime in the afternoon."

"So I do get to go home tomorrow?" Krystal exhaled in relief. She had a sudden urge to leap in the air and do a fist pump, but she refrained. "Thank you! I'm so ready to go, and I don't want to miss Nick's funeral."

"I know you don't. Oh, I have something I'd like you to read. It's something that could help put things into perspective for you. You can read it during your down time. Sometimes, it gives people a little insight on how God works.

Krystal was surprised Dr. Tovina talked so openly about God and Jesus. This was a public hospital, but that didn't seem to faze her at all, and Krystal was glad. She was more at peace right now than she'd been since she'd found out about Nick. She was a little surprised at herself. She felt less angry at God. She took the paper Dr. Tovina held out to her and let the counselor lead her to lunch. Folding the paper and putting it in her back pocket, she decided to wait to read it until she could sit somewhere alone.

Every day in this place had a different schedule, with the exception of mealtimes. After lunch today, it was art time. Standing in front of the cabinet, she frowned when she saw the mask she'd painted the day before sitting where it'd been left to dry. Taylor had forgotten it. Deciding she'd keep that one, she sat down with the African mask this time. She painted an African queen with golden lips and small golden orbs that ran the length of her brows dipping slightly above the bridge of the nose. Fantastic bold colors on an espresso base had a beautiful air of power. It made her think of Dr. Tovina. A loving woman, with a power she only used for good, for God. She would gift this to her tomorrow before she left. She grabbed another mask and sat down to fulfill the request from the counselor the previous day.

Time began to move again, and after art, there was group, which consisted of more meaningless conversations that were useless. She wondered if this group helped anyone at all and stiffened when the lady asked if she'd used the marker.

"No," Krystal stated.

"Well, why not?" the lady asked, sticking her chin out.

"I didn't feel the need to," she stated plainly and left it at that.

With pursed lips and crossing her legs, the lady jabbed some notes down on her pad before moving to the next person, not looking Krystal's way again.

Great. It probably says something like 'she's a liar' or 'uncooperative'. She hoped this wasn't going to cause any problems with her being able to leave the next day. She was being honest.

In the cafeteria she gazed around as she got in line. Without Taylor there, she didn't know where she should sit, and now became more aware of all the others without the little ball of enthusiasm to keep her attention.

Tonight pizza, salad, and more cookies made dinner. It smelled surprisingly good, and since she couldn't just grab food whenever she got the urge, she was famished.

Spotting Eileen, she headed to her table. "Okay if I sit here?"

"Go right ahead." The spit-and-fire Eileen she'd seen when Mattie was hauled out was long gone. Instead, she had her head propped up on one hand, nibbling on her salad thoughtfully. Her very plain salad with no dressing, that is.

Krystal dug right in and looked up at Eileen curiously.

"Can I ask you a question? You don't have to answer if you don't want." Krystal had no idea where this newfound courage came from. She wasn't normally the one to strike up a conversation.

Eileen sat up and laid her fork down. "Ask anything you want. I'm an open book."

Krystal swallowed her food and laid her pizza back on her plate. "How long have you been here?"

"Two weeks. This time."

A repeat offender like Taylor, Krystal noted.

"Well, I'm kind of curious why you're in here. I mean, I get that anorexia is…."

"I know what you're thinking," Eileen said. "But I was in the hospital for awhile this last time. I had to gain a certain amount of weight before they let me come here."

Krystal focused on not letting her face register shock. *But geez, if that's what weight gain looks like, how much thinner could she have been?*

Eileen smiled, and her shoulders relaxed. "I know how I look to everyone else, logically, anyway," she said, placing her index finger to her head.

"But that's not what I see when I look in the mirror." Her eyes moved to her plate and she picked up her fork. "But I'm trying. For the first time, I want to get better. Not that this place is any major help."

"That's good. Well, the part about wanting to get better," Krystal said, and meant it before glancing at Eileen's plate. "That's the most important part, right?"

"Geez," Eileen said before picking up her fork. "They should just hire you here." Then she took a real bite of her salad.

"No, I didn't mean it like that! Obviously, I'm here too. I mean, if things hadn't gone the way they did with me, I probably would have never asked for help." The fact that it took a sequence of events that started with Nick's death wasn't lost on Krystal.

"Yeah, they check all kinds of stuff every day, including my weight. I have to eat at least 1200 calories, but they give me extra-small snacks throughout the day. I can't eat much in one sitting. What about you? Why are you here?" she asked and finally she took a bite of her pizza, though it was a small one.

"You already know," Krystal shrugged. "Cutting."

"Was what you said in group about your parents true? Or were you just giving her an answer?"

"No, it was true. But group is a joke. Why do they even make us go through all that?"

"I don't know. I think most of the stuff in here is just to monitor us and keep us occupied. Get our meds regulated. Keep us going from one thing to another. If they see you just sitting around not doing anything, then they will find more things to occupy you. But my therapist is great, so that's a plus, and they got rid of that witch." Krystal knew she was referring to Mattie.

"Do you have Dr. Tovina?" Krystal asked.

"Yes."

"I do too. How much longer are they keeping you here?"

"I'm not sure. To be honest, I don't mind it so much right now. Mattie was awful, but that was the first time I'd seen someone here who sucked like that. Most of them are okay. It's easier for me to do better while I'm here. Plus, my mom doesn't have to worry herself to death every second. What about you? When are you outta here?"

"Hopefully tomorrow. I'm worried now though because in group, that lady acted all offended because I don't want to draw on my arm with a red marker." Krystal blew out a breath. It was good to be able to vent to Eileen.

"Don't worry," Eileen said, holding up her fork with the tomato she'd just stabbed. "Dr. Tovina is the one who makes recommendations for release, not the group therapist. Trust me."

"Well, that's a relief. I know this is only my second day, but it feels like I've been here weeks."

"And that is precisely why I like it," Eileen said. Her salad was gone and now it was time for her to work on her pizza some more.

"It's really good," Krystal said, nodding at the pizza. "I expected the food to be horrible, but it's not."

Eileen ate about half the slice in small bites while they talked, before letting the pizza hit the plate.

"Can't do anymore. I am so full, and I have to be careful because when I feel overly full, it really makes me want to puke and then they might think I did it on purpose."

Heading back into the common area, Krystal broke out into a smile when she saw her parents sitting at one of the tables waiting. She would never take seeing them share the same space for granted and silently prayed for it never to stop. They just needed to be friends. However, she knew better than to wish for them to get back together. That wasn't a possibility, not with Sofia.

"Hi!" She greeted them both with hugs before taking a seat.

"How are you, mija?" Josefina asked.

"I'm okay, Mom."

"So, how is this place?" Roberto asked.

"Eh. It's different." Krystal shrugged and told her parents about Mattie and then Taylor. She asked about the kids, Em, and Brandon and if there was any new news about the shelter or Nick.

Josefina told her the kids asked about her incessantly and wanted to come see her. Em and Brandon had both contacted her. Em had called and Brandon had stopped by. Josefina told them all she was doing well and would hopefully be home on Saturday.

The visiting hour flew by, and before she knew it, it was time to say goodbye.

"We'll come pick you up as soon as they call," Josefina said.

"Krystal," Roberto said, "Promise me, once you are home, you will talk to us about how you're feeling. You'll let us help you."

She looked him in the eyes. "I promise."

"Things will be different now. For the better." He placed his hand on hers momentarily before standing and she knew what he meant. No more being in the middle. No more weird phone calls. No more rides from Aunt Maria.

After one last round of hugs, she watched her dad hold the door open for her mom to pass through before going through himself. She watched until the door closed and she could no longer see them.

After her parents had gone, Eileen asked her if she wanted to play cards. While they were playing, Hugh, the one who used heroin, asked if he could play too.

"I'm going to die of boredom if you say no," he said, smiling. Both of the people he'd made friends with had gone home that day, the girl who binged and the one who had used cocaine.

Eileen was thrilled he'd asked and welcomed him by dealing him in. Once the hand ended, Krystal excused herself, leaving Eileen with Hugh.

Krystal looked around. The boy who read a lot sat on a chair in the corner with his nose in a Stephen King book that looked to be about four inches thick. The blind girl sat on the couch with the same little, red fish in her hands. That was it, five of them.

Krystal looked at the blind girl, noticing her knuckles were white as she squeezed her fish with all her might. Then she began rocking bath and forth so abruptly, Krystal feared she might throw herself off the couch. It was just then she realized the fish she'd picked up for her earlier that day was the one from Dr. Seuss.

"One fish, two fish, red fish, blue fish," Krystal said without thinking about it. Visibly, the girl relaxed and began to repeat the words.

A counselor walked over to them. "Marsha," she said. "This is Krystal. Krystal, this is Marsha."

"Hi, Marsha. Nice to meet you," Krystal said, matching the tone the counselor used. Marsha's rocking slowed and she spoke quietly to herself. With a slight head nod, the counselor motioned for Krystal to follow. They moved a short distance away.

"Marsha has been through some very traumatic events and has become withdrawn as a result. Her dad died a few months ago and he'd always read Dr. Seuss to her when she was agitated. He was her rock. That was pretty perceptive of you," she said, before moving away.

"Krystal," a different counselor called out to her. Krystal looked and saw the counselor, whose name was Beth, motioning her over. "I want to introduce you to your new roommate. This is Sasha."

"Hi," Krystal said. Sasha stood there with puffy eyes and a swollen nose. Her arms crossed over her chest and she looked to the side, refusing to make eye contact. Krystal stood there awkwardly. "Nice to meet you," she tried again, but knew that the first moments in the place were the worst, and she wasn't going to hold it against her.

The counselor looked at Krystal apologetically before taking Sasha to her room. Looking around, she saw Marsha and Bryce in the same places as before. Eileen and Hugh were now playing checkers and getting along exceptionally well. Good for them. Admittedly, she hadn't paid a ton of attention, but she didn't remember Eileen spending time with anyone else before tonight.

Finally, it was bedtime. Krystal just wanted to go to sleep so she could wake up and it would finally be tomorrow.

After she'd showered and brushed her teeth, she gathered the clothes she'd worn that day and began to fold them up. She heard the sound of paper crumpling and remembered the paper Dr. Tovina had given her, damp now because she'd left her jeans on the floor near the shower.

Upon reading the first words, tears sprung to Krystal's eyes. She leaned against the counter and held the paper to her chest. It was the poem Nick had told her about. He'd asked her if she'd read it. When she'd said no, he'd explained it with flair. She began to read, not bothering to try and stop her tears.

She immediately found Nick in it, and Em, Brandon, her family, and God. She found God in it.

It went like this:

The Wind

People are like the wind
They come and they go

Sometimes a gentle breeze, quietly refreshing
They may teach you a lesson, encourage you, or be an answer
If only for a moment before drifting away

They can be a guide in the whirlwind confusion of life
Holding tight to the hand they are leading.
They weave in and out of the space around you
In their absence, you feel them still.

Some force their way in like a storm
Rushing and pushing until all balance and direction is lost
We stand in their wake, torn and tattered with scars that won't
completely fade.

Good or bad, right or wrong, we need the wind
To go with the flow of it or walk against it
To challenge the right to inhale it deeply and live.
A new journey awaits in the wind.

It was no accident Dr. Tovina had given it to her to read. Just like it wasn't an accident that Nick had told her about it. *There are no accidents*, she realized. A million tiny things and a thousand big things came full circle in her mind. *That man didn't take Nick's life. He didn't have the power to do that. It was Nick's time to go and God took him.* At that moment, the hate Krystal had been holding onto lifted.

She knew that the Man, Eliseo, wasn't responsible for breaking her parents up. He wasn't trying to replace her father or get in the way of her relationship with him. In fact, she recognized all of his efforts to bring harmony to the situation. And Sofia, her little baby sister…she was Sofia's big sister, and she was ready to act like it.

Krystal didn't have her notebook so she fell on her knees from where she stood.

"Thank you," she said over and over. "I understand." She understood the love. That's all she could feel in her and all around her. It was like God was giving her a hug. She stayed there a long time and only stood when she heard footsteps. Quickly, she rose and gathered her things, tucking the poem into the waistband of her sweats.

She couldn't stop smiling.

Temporarily forgetting she wasn't the only occupant in the room, she stopped short in the doorway when she saw Sasha. She was sitting there in her pajamas at the edge of the bed, arms still crossed over her chest, her eyes on the floor. Her inner turmoil was thick in the room, and Krystal could feel her sadness.

Walking to her bed, Krystal contemplated what she could say that might extract a response from her very short-term roommate. Sasha's hand came up and she held the Kleenex she'd been gripping to her nose and sniffled.

Krystal almost asked if she was okay before realizing that would be the worst question of all. It was pretty obvious she wasn't okay. The last thing she wanted to do was annoy her. Instead, Krystal pulled her bedcovers back and sat in the middle of the bed.

Give me words to say, she silently asked God.

"Wanna talk?" Krystal asked. Silence responded. "I'm going home tomorrow so if you decide you want to talk, I promise to keep it to myself." More silence. "Well, I'm here if you change your mind." Krystal turned the lamp beside her bed off. "I'll just be quiet now unless you decide you want to talk." Krystal slid her feet under the covers before lying down and thought she might have heard something that sounded like a short laugh.

Nearly an hour later, Krystal was still wide-awake. Having someone else in the room was awkward, especially since they didn't know each other. Krystal had a strong desire to help, but she wasn't exactly sure what to do, so she stayed quiet. She knew Sasha was still awake because she could hear her shifting positions every few minutes. Her breath hadn't once taken on the rhythmic breathing of a sleeping person.

If Sasha would go to sleep, then she'd probably be able to as well. But if she fell asleep first then she might snore or do something worse while she slept. That would be embarrassing. Maybe Sasha was thinking the same thing.

Krystal's hands itched for her sketchpad or even her notebook. Actually, she just wished she'd fall asleep so tomorrow could arrive. But she didn't even feel tired now. She started listing all the things she was thankful for in her mind.

"Are you asleep?" Sasha whispered.

"Nope. Are you?" Krystal asked, hoping to get a laugh.

It worked.

"Obviously not." Krystal could hear a smile in Sasha's voice. "So what are you in for?"

"Why are we whispering?" Krystal whispered.

Sasha laughed out loud. "I don't know," she said.

When Krystal had asked her if she wanted to talk, she'd meant for Sasha to talk about herself, not ask about her, though it was getting easier for her to be honest about what had brought her here. Maybe talking about herself would help Sasha somehow.

"Because of the problems I've been having, I was cutting." Krystal held up her bandaged hand. "Nobody really knew anything except for one friend, and the last time I did it, I cut too deep and ended up in the hospital. Everyone thought I tried to kill myself. But I didn't."

"So, do you like it here? I mean…." Sasha paused. "Has it helped?"

"Yes, in some ways," Krystal admitted. "I mean, some of it's just stupid. Like group, for instance. But I guess it's been nice to see that I'm not alone. And Dr. Tovina is awesome," she added.

"She's religious," Sasha stated dryly. Even though it was dark, Krystal would bet that Sasha had just rolled her eyes.

"Yeah, I guess you could say that." Krystal associated the word religious with rituals more than people like Dr. Tovina or Nick.

"Gets on my nerves." Sasha sighed.

"Give her a chance, Sasha. She cares. For real."

"People always say that. My dad said he cared about me every time he raped me. That's why I did try to kill myself. I just didn't do it right."

Krystal's heart stopped. Stunned silent, she kept asking God for words. *What do I say? What do I say?*

"Sasha, I can't even begin to say I know how you feel, but I can tell you God really does love you."

"You too?" Sasha said, her volume going several notches higher. "I just tell you my father raped me and your response is to tell me God loves me? I don't get you people."

"What do you mean, 'you people?'" Krystal asked. She was surprised at how calm she was.

"You religious people. It's like you have to tell yourself these things in order to make yourself feel better about being alive or something."

Krystal's heart broke over the pain Sasha was in. But she thought about the poem and knew she would be one of those people for Sasha right now. She wasn't quite sure if she was a guide or a force, but this was what God wanted her to be doing this very minute and she knew it without a doubt. She was right where she was supposed to be.

"Sasha, God gives people choices and some people choose to do bad things. Your father chose to do those horrible things. None of us are robots and God doesn't force us to do the right thing. When we do the wrong thing, we end up hurting other people too. But I promise you that if you give God a chance, you'll see it's more than just a need to believe in something to make ourselves feel better. Let what you've gone through make you stronger instead of weaker. I'm seriously just learning all this myself. Just tonight even!"

Sasha sighed heavily.

"Look, Krystal, I can tell you mean well. I can. But there's no room for fairytales. Those are for little girls."

Krystal wasn't offended. It was like God had downloaded some measure of maturity in her soul. She knew God was in control here and not her. There was no reason for her to get bent out of shape.

Krystal found herself telling Sasha her story. From beginning to end. All the ugly and beautiful details. They laughed and cried together. Krystal wasn't sure if it was more beneficial for herself or for Sasha. It didn't matter. She was supposed to do it and she knew it wouldn't be the last time she'd tell her story. It was the first of many.

"Take all the good you can get from this place, Sasha. Talk to Dr. Tovina and talk to other people here. You're meant to be here. You're meant to be alive right now. That's why your attempt failed, because you can't die if it's not your time. You're here for a reason—take time to find out what it is."

Krystal knew to stop at that moment. She could feel the end of the sentence and somehow knew even one more word could undo whatever Sasha might be thinking about.

She lied awake a long time after their conversation, thinking and praying. She'd felt God working within her and it was amazing. It wasn't a fairytale, but it was…magical. She smiled in the dark and asked God to send Nick a wink from her. This was God's magic.

Epilogue

Hi, everyone!

It's me, Krystal. I thought I should tell you the rest myself. Before I left the hospital the next day, I left the poem Dr. Tovina gave me on Sasha's bed with my phone number and a note telling her to call me if she ever wanted to talk. Eileen and I exchanged numbers too.

Then I had my exit meeting with Dr. Tovina before my mom picked me up.

When I got home, the house was dark, and when my mom turned the lights on, everyone was there! They were blowing on those noisy party favors that roll out and back in, and there were balloons galore. Oh, and when I say everyone, I mean everyone. Yes, my dad and Eliseo were in the same room with all my siblings, including Sofia. It was amazing. Not that they are going to be best friends or anything, but I think they respect each other. Dad knows Eliseo is going to be good to us, and Eliseo knows my dad is an awesome dad.

Sofia is actually a pretty cute baby now that I'm paying attention. Not that she cared I was there. I think she was more thrilled with all the excitement and balloons. She's a happy baby, and yeah, I kinda love her. I'm glad she's still little and won't hold my previous attitude against me.

Em and Brandon had helped Esme, Rosie, and Jaime make huge welcome home banners for me.

My mom even invited Ralph and Walt. Peety's tail started swishing when he saw me. Then he ran over to me and Walt told him to treat me like a lady. He did! Ralph gave me a card that was signed by all of the Tuesday night volunteers from the shelter. Mel wrote me a note that said, 'Your experiences make you. No regrets. Reach up and reach out. See you soon.' He drew a winking smiley by his name. He really wouldn't change anything he'd been through even if he could, and you know what? Me neither.

Nick's funeral was just the way it should have been. It was an upbeat celebration of the life he lived. I'm sure he would have approved. I don't know what God's rules are, but I hope he got to watch.

Ralph drove a bus, which is what Walt and Peety came in on, and Mel brought a van. Both bus and van were at full capacity. All of the guests who wanted to attend were able to. Story after story was told about Nick's kindness, compassion, and orneriness. I cried the hardest and smiled the biggest when I saw the picture I'd given him framed and on a table near where he lay surrounded by sunflowers. His daughter hugged me tight and thanked me for drawing it. I told her I'd photograph the others I'd drawn and send them to her. She looks a lot like her dad—without the wild eyebrows.

Since that day, I've gone back to my Tuesday nights at the shelter. That's where I belong and I love being a part of this big group of misfits.

Even though I didn't exactly want to, I let my parents throw me a party for my Quinceañera. Let me tell you, I'm so glad I did. Now, I don't do dresses, but the one we got was totally beautiful and I didn't really mind that Brandon got to see me in it. Yep, his eyes about popped out of his head. I also got my first kiss later that night after the party was over. We were standing on the sidewalk between my house and his. I knew it was coming, and it was the sweetest and best thing ever. However, I was completely nervous and had a gazillion butterflies in my stomach, and right after he kissed me, I got the hiccups. We both laughed, and he timed my hiccups so he could kiss me again.

I'm a lucky girl. Let me correct that. I'm a blessed girl. Totally and completely blessed. God loved me enough to see me through all my troubles and show me that He's really there. He gave me the most awesome family, best friend, boyfriend, and now I'm a part of the best gang ever. I love being a misfit. My heart is with the shelter and always will be. I use my art to make other people happy now. God always seems to show me who I should help, and I benefit from giving as much as they do from receiving. It's a two-way blessing.

One day, I sat down and wrote Kenny a letter and mailed it in one of the shelter's business envelopes Ralph gave me. I wanted to share with him what God taught me. He needed forgiveness for what he'd done, just like we all need forgiveness for our sins, but he also needed to know he doesn't have enough power to take a life. I told him God loved him and would forgive him if he wanted forgiveness. I told him to pray and suggested he write out his prayers if it would help. He wrote me back and thanked me for reaching out and said my letter made him cry. He said he gave his life to Jesus shortly after that night. He'd been so remorseful of his actions, and he planned to prove to God and everyone that he would never go back to that old life again. For months now, he's been leading a prayer group at the prison. He told me he's right where he's supposed to be right now, but of course he'll be happy when he gets out. That's still a long time away.

To this day, I write a nightly prayer, but I also talk to God silently and aloud with my art, with my horrible singing voice, and any other way that comes about. I get what praying without ceasing means now. It's not literally praying all the time; it's simply a knowing, an awareness that God is always with you all the time. Acknowledging He's there just like you do your friends or family.

Oh yeah. Sasha and Eileen both contacted me. Eileen is doing pretty well. She's gaining weight steadily and says she is determined to not go back. I've invited both of them to volunteer with me at the shelter.

Sasha connected with Em's mom who had a similar experience of her own when she was growing up. I never knew that before, but it helped that Sasha had someone who could relate. She comes with us every Tuesday now.

Eileen came once, but it wasn't her thing. Ralph, however, realized she is a math genius and converted her to a volunteer tutor for the older kids at the shelter. She now rides in with him every Saturday and gets to answer his crazy riddles.

Nowadays Rosie is still kind of mean to Jaime but it's pretty funny; he can hold his own. She has the craziest sense of humor and usually has us all cracking up when she isn't being annoying. Jaime is doing way better in school and has practiced his way into some pretty amazing skateboarding skills. I think he could be a natural pro! Eliseo is trying to find an indoor skate park for when winter gets here.

Esme is the same as always, which is awesome. Lucy is a huge tomcat now, but still likes to sit on Esme's shoulder like some fat bird. I guess it's pretty adorable. I don't think he finds his name confusing. If Esme ever changes her mind about being a firefighter, I'm sure she'll choose something equally amazing.

All in all, life is good. It's truly good, but it's not easy. I can't say I don't get anxious anymore. It still happens. Sometimes things are hard, and I still get upset. But now, instead of reaching for my glass heart, I reach for God. I still write God every day. One day, maybe I'll put all my letters in a book.

Just trust God. The more I trust, the less anxious I get. It's like, you just have to keep putting one foot in front of the other and know the hard stuff is part of the journey of making…well, you! So become the best you possible.

Remember, God loves you just the way you are. I know you can't see me, but I just winked at you.
—Krystal

Acknowledgments

Mom, I love you. Thank you for always having my back. I know you'd still knock someone out if they tried to mess with me! I'm pretty sure I got this writing bug from you, so thanks for that too. ♥

Starkies, God couldn't have given me a better person to share my life with. You're my heart. You make me laugh the hardest, love the most, and have the ability to make me angrier than anyone else on earth. I know that goes both ways. It keeps our hearts beating. Thank you for believing in me and helping me to believe in myself. Whatever happens, the book is written. That's all that matters. You helped me to accomplish my goal. On to the next twenty years with more music and more books. I love you infinity~~I win…again. ♥

Krystal, thank you for being a willing muse, for letting me draw from your experiences, and most of all, for being one of the best people I know. We're all family forever. I love you and the four younger monsters with all my heart. ♥

To the Signal Soldier who wishes to remain unnamed, I couldn't have written Walt without you. You gave me so much of your time and I'm forever grateful. Thank you for sharing your experiences. Shout out to the other soldiers with whom I spoke, including my Uncle Phil and friend Cobbs. ♥♥

Earl, thank you for your efforts and time in putting together my website. You're so very much appreciated! ♥

I've had this huge circle of support that has kept me motivated and inspired. My family, friends, beta readers (April McMullen, Peggy McAloon, Sandy Larsen, Shelly Wright, Jabu Casey), and people who supported, encouraged, and assisted me just because, thank you! Clean Indie Reads group on Facebook/(#CR4U–www.cleanindiereads.com) – you're all positive, kind, educational, and just freaking awesome. To everyone who has helped me or said a kind word, thank you. Stacie-thank you. You know why. Mark-your turn. I want to keep naming people, but I can't. There's so many more. ♥

Buddy and Inky, thank you for keeping me company and constantly interrupting me at the worst possible time. But mostly, for putting up with the silence and lack of attention when I'm working. ♥

Melissa Manes (sciptionis.com) and Alex McGilvery (celticfrogediting.com) – Two of the kindest people and the best editors that God could have given me. Thank you both for all you've done for me. You're both worth your weight in gold and thank God you don't charge your value. ♥

Dear God, nothing I can say or write would express enough love and gratitude. Please read my heart and fix it where's it's broken. Thank you endless supply of putty that fills in the new cracks every single day. Thank you for blessing me so. I love you, but not more than you love me. ♥♥♥♥♥♥♥

Dear Reader—

I can't thank you enough for giving this story a chance. I hope you've come to love the characters in this story as much as I do. If you did, I would sincerely appreciate if you would stop by and leave a review on Amazon, Barnes & Noble, iTunes, Goodreads, or your blog. Reviews help other buyers find authors. So your time would be greatly appreciated. Hopefully, the next book will be out in the beginning of 2016. Please check back.

About the Author

C.L. Wells is a JANE-OF-ALL-TRADES, with a passion for writing and animals. She lives in Kansas with her family, which includes a fat doggie who is not named Toto and a cat who moonlights as an escape artist. Feel free to ask her about the 'escape artist.' She plans to write about it someday. She would love hearing from you.

If you would like to connect with her, there are multiple ways to do so.

f **Author.CLWELLS**

twitter.com/clwellsauthor

www.theclwells.com/

clwells.author@gmail.com ♥

www.ingramcontent.com/pod-product-compliance
Lightning Source LLC
Chambersburg PA
CBHW060952120726
47910CB00002B/610